Fishing for a Killer

Also by Glenn Ickler

A Carnival of Killing

Murder on the St. Croix

A Killing Fair

Fishing for a Killer

Glenn Ickler

North Star Press of St. Cloud, Inc.
St. Cloud, Minnesota

ISBN: 978-0-87839-793-8

First edition: May 2015

This is a work of fiction. Names, charactes, places, and incidents are the products of the author's imagination or are used fictitiously. Any resemblance to actual events or persons, living or dead, is entirely coincidental.

Printed in the United States of America

Published by
North Star Press of St. Cloud, Inc.
P.O. Box 451
St. Cloud, MN 56302

northstarpress.com

Dedication:

To the memory of my father and my Uncle Fritz, who took me on dozens of fishing trips with them when I was a little kid.

Chapter One

Wednesday Afternoon

MY MOTHER WASN'T SURE she'd heard me right.

"Did you say you're going up north fishing on Mother's Day?" she asked, raising her voice to a level that caused me to move the phone an inch farther from my ear.

"It's the Governor's Fishing Opener," I said. "It's a very big deal. Al and I have been assigned to cover it." Al is *St. Paul Daily Dispatch* staff photographer Alan Jeffrey, who has been my best friend since our freshman year at the University of Minnesota, and I'm staff writer Warren "Mitch" Mitchell.

"But you always come to visit your grandmother and me on Mother's Day," my mother said. She and her mother, both widowed, lived on a farm near the small city of Harmony, about 100 miles south of St. Paul.

"I'm sorry, but I can't do that this year," I said. "This is my job; I have to go where my editor sends me. And you and Grandma Goodie will be seeing us at the wedding the next weekend." By "us," I meant my gorgeous Cape Verdean lover, Martha Todd, and me. We were scheduled to tie the marriage knot the following Saturday afternoon.

"Well, I think your editor should know better than to send people away from their family on Mother's Day," my mother said.

"Somebody has to cover the governor's fishing opener every year, Mom. This year it's Al's and my turn." The assignment, not always the plum it would seem to be, was rotated annually among the staff reporters and photographers.

"Darn foolishness, if you ask me," Mom said. "I'll let you tell your grandmother the wonderful news." I groaned as I heard her pass the phone to Grandma Goodie, whose full last name is Goodrich.

"Warnie Baby, what's going on?" Grandma Goodie asked. I've been Warnie Baby to her since the day I was born, forty-two years and ten months ago.

I explained that Al and I had been assigned to cover the Governor's Fishing Opener, which, as it almost always does, coincided with the Mother's Day weekend. "This is the opening of the walleye season and it's a very big deal for Minnesota fishermen and the whole tourist industry," I said. "Martha and I will see you the following weekend at our wedding."

"Never heard of the governor's fishing opener," she said. "Is this something new?"

"No, it's older than I am. It was started back in 1958 by a governor named Rolvaag. I can't believe you've never heard of it."

"Sounds like a lot of nonsense to me. And so what if we'll see you at the wedding? Mother's Day is special."

"I know it is, but so is my job."

"I certainly hope they'll give you time off from fishing to go to church on Sunday."

"I'm sure they will," I said. I was also sure that I'd use that time for something more palatable, like sleeping-in. The last time I'd been inside a church was when she and Mom persuaded me to visit their tiny Methodist congregation the previous fall after a religious hiatus of many years. It had not been a comfortable experience.

"Well, see that you do get yourself to church, Warnie Baby," she said. "The salvation of your soul comes before any silly old fishing trip." Grandma Goodie worries constantly about the status of my soul, which saves me the trouble.

"I'll do my best. I'll talk to you next week before you come up for the wedding. Bye now." I put down the phone and sighed.

"Sounds like you got the reaction you expected," said Martha Todd, who was sitting next to me in the living room of our rented half of a Lincoln Avenue duplex. We had moved there from a cramped one-bedroom apartment in anticipation of our wedding. The ceremony would be the culmination of seven years of hemming and hawing, during which both of us were struggling to dump baggage from previous traumatic marriages and shattered romances.

Our landlady, a widow named Zhoumaya Jones, occupies the other half. She is a middle-aged, high-energy native of Nigeria who lives in a motorized wheelchair because of a motorcycle accident that killed her husband and left her paralyzed from the waist down.

"Exactly," I said. "The fact that they'll be with us the following weekend for the wedding means nothing. Mother's Day is bigger than Christmas to those two."

"Well, Warnie Baby, you're all they've got for male next of kin." That was true. I'm an only child and my mother has two sisters but no brothers.

"Lucky them," I said. "I almost said we'd see them next Mother's Day, but I remembered how Grandma Goodie always says she might not be here next year and starts running down her list of medical problems. I sure didn't want to get into that."

"No way. Do you think we'll be like that when we're in our eighties?"

"Probably," I said. "It's an easy way to manipulate people who love you."

* * *

THE DAY AFTER my conversation with Mom and Grandma Goodie, Al was driving and I was riding shotgun in a blue Ford Focus with a *Daily Dispatch* logo. We have teamed up on so many stories that our city editor, Don O'Rourke, calls us the Siamese twins, even though we look nothing alike. I am six-foot-two and slender, with light brown hair and a matching moustache, while Al is five-ten and stocky, with a dark brown beard and hair. Don says we are joined at the funny bone, which in our case he identifies as the skull.

On this assignment we were headed north on Highway 169, a colorless flat road flanked by long stretches of tall skinny pines on both sides. Our destination was Madrigal's Lodge on Gull Lake near the city of Brainerd, about 140 miles north of St. Paul. It was Thursday, the ninth of May, but the car windows were up and the heater was on. The dashboard thermometer was showing the outside air temperature at thirty-nine degrees as we came in view of the southern end of Mille Lacs, one of the largest of the state's much ballyhooed 10,000 lakes. The winter had been longer and colder than normal and the early spring warm-up hadn't been able to force its way in. We'd heard there was still ice on portions of the lake where we'd be fishing.

As I'd told Mom and Grandma Goodie, the Governor's Fishing Opener, officially written with uppercase letters, is a very big deal in Minnesota. It marks the start of the summer's pursuit of the wily walleye, which is the official state fish and the species most prized for its gustatory quality. As a fighting fish in the water, the sluggish walleye ranks below everything but its much smaller cousin, the yellow perch. As a broiled or batter-fried fish on the dinner plate, the scrumptious walleye stands fins and gills above anything else pulled from the state's lakes and rivers.

The opening weekend was first labeled the Governor's Fishing Party by its founder, Governor Karl Rolvaag. This governor had been a man who thoroughly enjoyed his liquor, according to more senior *Daily Dispatch* staff members who'd known him. Many of Rolvaag's guests shared his passion for alcohol and the governor's party quickly acquired an image of heavy drinking and rowdy behavior. In the mid-1960s, Al Quie, a soft-spoken, conservative governor, renamed the event, substituting the word "opener" for "party," and instigated a more dignified atmosphere, although the booze continued to flow.

"You know what's wrong with the sport of fishing?" I asked, breaking a thirty-mile silence.

"I can think of several things," Al said. "What do you have in mind?"

"It starts too damn early in the morning," I said. I was looking at the weekend schedule of events. "You should see this schedule for tomorrow. Live radio broadcasts start at 5:00 a.m. Breakfast starts at 5:30."

"Two more reasons to be glad you're not a radio announcer or a fisherman."

"Or a fish. Imagine getting hooked before six o'clock in the morning."

"Depends on the hooker," Al said.

"Surely you don't expect to encounter any practitioners of that historic trade this weekend."

"Oh, of course not. Who could imagine finding scarlet women at a large gathering of men loaded with booze and testosterone?"

"I've heard stories about hustlers knocking on the doors of fishermen's shacks during the ice fishing season. Do you suppose they'll be knocking on cabin doors this weekend?"

"Don't worry, old buddy," Al said. "If there's a knock on our door, I'll keep you safe and pure for your lovely bride-to-be. You won't see any knockers in our cabin."

"Martha would be pleased to know that you're guarding my virtue with such diligence," I said.

The wedding was set for Saturday, May 18, only nine days away—long after I'd be home from the Governor's Fishing Opener on Gull Lake. Although neither of us could be classified as religious, Martha and I had yielded to family pressure (most heavily applied by Grandma Goodie) and contracted with a church—Unitarian-Universalist, no less—as a venue for the ceremony.

Al and I drove on between two never-ending walls of tall, straight pines, with only an occasional billboard to break the monotony. My eyes were glazing over and the world had become a blur when Al said, "Hey, there's a place to stop." He was pointing at a billboard advertising a roadside nightclub. Beneath the establishment's name, in large letters, it said: "Dancers and Booze! What more can we say?"

That challenging question brought me back to consciousness for a few miles and I tried to think of an answer. What more could be said to entice men who'd left their women behind in order to spend a chilly weekend sitting in a boat on a windswept lake? Having found no answer by the time we passed the Grand Casino, where Mille Lacs-area Native Americans collect recompense for the white man's wrongful treatment of their ancestors, I tilted my seat back and closed my eyes. I thought about a relaxing weekend at a beautiful resort, with nothing to report on but happy people having a wonderful time. I pictured myself far from the city, in a northern paradise of lakes and pine trees where there would be nothing unpleasant to write about, no crimes to solve, no killers to pursue. Ignorance truly is bliss.

Chapter Two

Friday Morning

THE GRUMBLING FROM THE CROWD in the main lodge of Madrigal's Resort was getting louder. We—the flock (or is it garble?) of newspaper and TV crews from all over Minnesota covering the Governor's Fishing Opener on Gull Lake—had been summoned to a 6:00 a.m. news conference by Alex Gordon, the governor's press secretary. It was now 6:10 and Alex Gordon had yet to appear. Murmurings of discontent about being called to a meeting barely fifteen minutes after sunrise were morphing into loud bitching about Gordon being a no-show.

We were milling about the lounge, a room designed for comfort and serenity with circles of overstuffed chairs and sofas facing a central stone fireplace with openings on both sides. At the moment, nobody in the room was comfortable and the only feeling of serenity emanated from the stuffed head of an eight-point buck above the fireplace.

"We only waited for ten minutes for our college professors before we bailed out of their classrooms," said Barry Ziebart, a reporter for Channel Five in the Twin Cities. "How much longer should we give a political flack?"

"Hey, Alex went to Hahv'd," somebody at the back of the high-ceiling room yelled. "He's special; an Ivy League flack."

Gordon's assistant, Ann Rogers, walked toward the fireplace carrying a portable microphone and soon her contralto voice boomed out from under the deer's head. "People, people, please give Alex a few more minutes. I just sent a messenger to his room to get him. He's probably sleeping off last night's party."

"He had plenty to sleep off," said a voice behind me. "When I left at midnight the crowd had downed enough booze to float every boat on Gull Lake." I'd already observed that many of our media compatriots were displaying the hollow eyes and pallor that accompany a hangover. Fortunately, Al and I had not joined in this massive effort to exhaust the resort's supply of alcohol. As a recovering alcoholic I can't touch the stuff, and Al is smart enough to quit after two beers even when an unlimited flow is available.

We had been in bed by 11:00 p.m. Thursday and thus were bright-eyed and bushy-tailed when we joined the media mob at 6:00 a.m. on Friday. Well, maybe not entirely bright-eyed.

The din was momentarily reduced to a dull roar as Ann Rogers stood waiting under the antlered head. She was beginning to shift her weight from one foot to another by the time a young man wearing a dark blue Madrigal's Lodge shirt walked briskly up to her and said something in a low voice. His message caused Ann to shake her head and look alarmed.

Ann put the mike to her lips. "Ladies and gentlemen, give me your attention please," she said. She repeated the request and when the room was quiet except for a few whispers, she said, "Alex isn't in his room. I'm afraid we don't know where he is. You can either stay here and wait while we hunt for him or go have breakfast in the dining room and we'll call you."

"Oh, miss," shouted another young man in a Madrigal's shirt. He stood in a wide doorway that opened onto a narrow strip of grass between the lodge and the beach, waving his hands above his head. Miss," he yelled again.

"It's *Mizz* Rogers," Ann said in a voice that would have frozen a kettle of boiling water. "And what's on your mind?"

"There's a boat with its motor running going around in circles out in the bay," he said. "And we can't see nobody in it."

He had to jump out of the doorway the second he finished the last sentence. Stampeding buffalo would have been flung backward and crushed in the rush of reporters and photographers that erupted through the door and flowed like a mass of molten lava across the lawn toward the lake. None of the passing wordsmiths took the time to correct the man's grammar as they scrambled to reach the beach and the boat dock.

The beach was roped off by a waist-high white cord strung through a row of slotted white posts. A four-foot-wide blacktop path led to the marina, which was about 300 yards south of the lodge. The spreading flow of bodies had to be funneled through this narrow passageway, except for a few who risked spraining an ankle by running along the grass between the path and the beach. Elbows flew, and so did curse words as the media troopers fought their way to the boat dock.

The moving mass of media flowed onto the long, T-shaped dock, where the leaders stopped one step short of the end. Any further forward movement by those in the rear echelon would have created a domino effect resulting in a cold water bath for four men almost teetering at the top of the T. Because Al and I had been near the front inside the meeting room, we were now in a position of safety near the tail end of the crowd on the dock, even though we had passed some of the slower runners.

Immediately on our tail was Trish Valentine, a short, well-endowed reporter for TV Channel Four, who had been in the front row, as she always was at any media event. She muttered a string of expletives and wedged her way between Al and me before being blocked from further progress by her own wide-bodied cameraman.

"Slow down, Trish," I said. "If you keep going you'll knock somebody off the end of the dock."

"Think what a great shot we'd have if Channel Five's crew went into the drink," she said. "Trish Valentine, reporting live on the action at Gull Lake."

"I know you want to make a splash," Al said. "But think of the poor bastard who'd get wet. What if it was somebody who couldn't swim?"

"Even a greater shot as somebody dives in to rescue him," Trish said. "Where's your sense of breaking news?"

"You have no heart, Ms. Valentine," I said.

She giggled at the pun and took a cell phone out of her bag. "Time to alert the newsroom that we'll be having breaking news," she said.

While we were talking, two men had clambered aboard one of the resort's motor boats, cast off and started toward the circling craft, which was a small silhouette about two hundred yards away. The man who'd reported seeing it empty must have checked it out with binoculars because the naked eye could not discern for certain whether or not it was occupied.

Taking a cue from Trish, I punched my cell phone keys for our newsroom and for Don O'Rourke's extension. Al had already begun shooting pictures of the crowd on the dock and the departing boat.

"What the hell are you doing up at this hour?" asked Don, who started his shift at 5:30 a.m. every Monday through Friday.

"Watching a boat go 'round in circles," I said.

"For that you got up at sunrise?"

"It looks like there's nobody in the boat. And the governor's press secretary seems to be missing this morning."

"Is there a connection?"

"That's what the entire Minnesota press corps is waiting by the water to find out."

"Keep us posted. We can update our website as soon as you know something worth posting."

"Al's shooting pix of the rescue boat and the mob scene on the dock," I said. "He'll send you a couple in a few minutes."

"I'll be watching for them," Don said. "Oh, hey, what's the missing man's name?"

"Alex Gordon. There's background on him in the files."

"Isn't he the smartass with the Boston accent who bragged about going to some big shot college when the governor hired him?"

"That's the one. Alex went to Hahv'd and he's not shy about telling that to people."

"Did Hahv'd teach him to swim?"

"Maybe we're going to find out this morning," I said.

Don broke the connection and I turned my attention back to the action on the water. The two-man rescue crew brought their boat alongside the seemingly empty, circling boat. As one of the rescuers held his hand up to his face, Trish's cameraman, peering through a long telephoto lens, said, "He's talking on his cell. Must be calling somebody back here to say if there's anybody laying in the bottom of the boat."

"Who's he calling, I wonder?" Trish said.

"Don't know," I said as I turned and looked around behind us. I saw Martin Johansen, manager of the resort, standing on the front steps talking on a cell phone. I began trotting toward him, and my action caused another mass movement as the herd that was now behind me started to follow.

I reached Johansen as he was ending the call. "What's the word?" I asked.

"Nobody in the boat," he said. "Now we have to find out who checked it out."

"Could it have been Alex Gordon?"

"Could have been the Easter Bunny for all I know," Johansen said. He turned and headed for the boat checkout desk with the crowd in hot pursuit. Al and I, and of course Trish Valentine, were in the lead again.

"Think the Easter Bunny really stays here?" Trish asked.

"Too expensive," I said. "He holes up in a briar patch down the beach a ways."

"He'd be hopping mad if he ever fell out of a boat," Al said.

When we caught up to Johansen, he was holding a clipboard. Trish, who had sprinted past me, yelled, "Was it Alex?"

Johansen nodded and pulled out his cell phone again. "I'm calling the sheriff for a dive team," he said.

Chapter Three

The Search Begins

THE SMELL OF CIGAR SMOKE heralded the arrival of Lieutenant Governor Aaron Ross. He was a tall, gangly man who had played forward on the University of Minnesota basketball team twenty-five years in the past. Now he was constantly puffing on a cigar and I was sure that running the length of a basketball court would send him into cardiac arrest.

Ross was wearing a black-and-red plaid bathrobe that concealed the incongruous pot belly he'd developed through plush living as a corporate lawyer and a tax-slashing Republican politician. He was in the final year of his second term as lieutenant governor, and looked like a shoo-in to be his party's gubernatorial candidate in the November election because Governor Anders A. (for Andrew) Anderson would not be running again.

Ross scuffled toward the front of the crowd in leather bedroom slippers, moving with all the authority and purpose of a man walking in his sleep. No doubt he'd been one of the last to leave the Thursday night booze bout.

Smoke curled upward from the ever-present cigar, which was dangling from Ross's lips at an angle that reminded me of a partially-expended erection. He walked up to Martin Johansen and removed the drooping stogie long enough to ask, "What the hell's going on out here?"

"Man overboard," Al yelled, leading a chorus of replies that meshed into an indiscernible jumble of sound.

"Will all of you shut up and let Marty talk?" Ross yelled. He drew in a long drag of cigar smoke while waiting for the yammering to cease.

"One of our men spotted an empty boat going in circles out in the bay," Johansen said. "It was signed out by the governor's press secretary."

"Good god, is Alex okay?" This was the deep bass voice of Governor Anderson, who was a couple of steps behind Ross. The governor had taken time to put on khaki cargo pants, a dark blue wool shirt and white, fresh-out-of-the-box boat shoes, but he was dragging his feet as wearily as Aaron Ross.

"I'm afraid Alex is missing, Governor," Johansen said. "He went out in the boat sometime before sunrise and one of our men saw it going around in circles with nobody in it when it got light at a little after six. No telling when he went into the water. The sheriff's dive team is coming to look for him."

"You're sure he went into the water?" Anderson asked.

"I don't know where else he could have gone," Johansen said.

"Maybe an eagle swooped down and carried him off," Al whispered.

"I've often thought he was for the birds," I said.

"Couldn't he have swum to shore somewhere?" the governor asked.

"I suppose that's possible if he was real strong swimmer," Johansen said. "But the water is awful cold to survive in for very long and the boat was a good two hundred yards out when our guys spotted it."

"Shouldn't we start searching the shoreline in case he made it?" Ross said through teeth clenched around the cigar.

"Ah, that's showing the kind of leadership that will make him our next governor," I whispered.

"Oh, don't say that," Trish Valentine said. "He's the biggest jerk I've ever dealt with. Always trying to cop a feel when he thinks nobody's looking. And he always stinks like the worst kind of cigar smoke."

Johansen told the governor that he would put together two groups of resort employees to search the shoreline in both directions from the dock. He hustled off to round up a crew, the governor and lieutenant governor retreated toward the lodge and the rest of us got busy calling our respective news desks as we straggled along behind.

Minutes later the Crow Wing County Sheriff's Jeep Cherokee arrived with lights flashing and skidded to a stop in the parking lot in front of the lodge. The sheriff, a rugged-looking man of about sixty, got out, slapped a Smokey Bear hat on his bald head, scanned the multitude carrying notebooks, cameras and microphones, and said, "Who's in charge here?"

Since I was closest to the sheriff, I answered. "The manager, Mr. Johansen, is inside rounding up a crew to search the beach. The boat's out there." I pointed to the empty boat. Motor off, it had been secured to the rescue vessel and they were holding a position near the spot of interception, which I assumed was by orders from Johansen.

Two minutes later the Crow Wing County dive team rolled into the parking lot nearest the marina towing a boat full of underwater swimming gear. It was now a few minutes after 7:00 a.m., which meant that unless Alex Gordon had miraculously reached shore, he had been in the near-freezing water for at least an hour, possibly two. This definitely would be a search assignment, not a rescue mission.

The three dive team members crawled into their insulated black rubber suits, launched their boat and headed toward their target. While watching the boat's progress, several of us tried to question the sheriff. All we got out of him was his name, Val Holmberg, and the fact that he had been sheriff for eighteen years. Martin Johansen soon rejoined the group, followed first by Governor Anderson and then by the lieutenant governor, who had replaced his bathrobe with a green-and-black plaid wool shirt and faded blue jeans. However, he was still wearing the slippers and gnawing on the two-inch remains of the smoldering cigar. The trio surrounded the sheriff and they all drifted away from the reporters and the cameras, leaving a trail of cigar smoke in their wake.

I turned and looked out at the lake, where the dive team boat had joined the other two. Standing still, with no adrenalin pumping, it occurred to me that I was cold. The sheriff was wearing a leather jacket and everyone else seemed to be in long sleeves of some sort, but I had been late for the six o'clock meeting so I'd just pulled on a pair of khaki pants and a beige T-shirt with KEEP CALM AND CATCH WALLEYES in red block letters across the front.

"Why don't we go back to our cabin where it's warm and file our stuff?" I said. "There's nothing to see out here until they find the body. I assume the morning's schedule of fun and games is pretty much down the toilet." That schedule included a daylong golf tournament beginning at 8:00 a.m. and a kids' fishing event for those who had brought their families, set to run from 9:00 a.m. to 2:30 p.m.

Al agreed and we returned to our cabin, which stood on a hill facing the main lodge with a tree-blocked view of the lake in the distance. Apparently the *Daily Dispatch* had rented the resort's equivalent of affordable housing. As we passed a large circular thermometer attached to a tree beside the cabin I noted that the red needle was pointing at forty-two. Fortunately it was cozy inside as Al e-mailed his pix and I tapped out a brief account of the morning's events and sent it to Don O'Rourke.

"Keep us posted," was Don's reply. So what else was I going to do?

We'd been surprised to find that our cabin had two bedrooms, separated by a small living room and a kitchenette with a coffee maker and a microwave oven. When we'd seen this layout upon arrival Thursday afternoon, we'd talked about calling home and inviting Martha Todd and Al's wife, Carol, to join us on Saturday for the latter part of the weekend fun. The accommodations wouldn't cost any more if they joined us, and anyway the *Daily Dispatch* was paying the tab. Because Martha is a lawyer in a very busy firm and Carol is a teacher in a public school, they could not have come for the Friday program. Now it appeared that the Saturday festivities would be much less festive, if they continued at all. We decided not to make the call.

"What do you think the six o'clock meeting was supposed to be about?" Al asked. He was sitting in one overstuffed chair and I was occupying the other.

"I've got no idea," I said. "All Alex said last night was that he wanted everybody in the room at six."

"Think Annie would know?"

"She might. Should I call her?"

"Why not?

"Why do you answer everything with a question?"

"Do I really?"

I gave up, went over to my bed and punched "0" on the phone on the bedside table. The desk clerk answered on the second buzz. He rang Ann Rogers's room at my request and reported that there was no answer. I said I would try again later and hung up.

"Nobody home?" Al asked.

"No. Probably out watching the dive team," I said.

"Should we be out watching the dive team?"

Desperate to break Al's string of questions, I said, "Give me one reason for us to go out there in the cold."

"Aren't we supposed to be covering the news?" he said.

Again I gave up. "You can go out and cover the news if you want to, but I'm going to stay in here and take a nap," I said.

"Are you really that tired?"

"Aren't you?"

"Should I be?"

"Shut up," I said. "I'm going to lie down."

"Should I wake you for lunch?" Al asked.

I threw a spare pillow at him and stretched out on the bed. Soon I was dreaming of Martha Todd—her silky coffee-with-cream Cape Verde complexion, her dazzling smile, her out-of-this-world, perfectly sculpted ass. We were in a boat, circling in a broad expanse of water, when we heard alarm bells. The bells persisted until I opened my eyes and realized that the phone on the nightstand was ringing. As I reached for the receiver, I noticed that the digital alarm clock beside the phone was registering 11:43.

"Who could that be?" Al asked from the chair in which he'd been dozing. The pillow I'd thrown at him was tucked behind his head.

"Wouldn't you like to know?" I picked up the phone and said, "*Daily Dispatch* headquarters, all the news that fits in print, Mitch Mitchell at your service."

"This is Ann Rogers. Please come to the boat docks ASAP." She was gone before I could say "okay," "no" or "what the hell's going on."

I put down the phone and said, "Sounds like we might be covering some news."

"What do you know about that?" Al said.

Chapter Four

Quick Work

AL GRABBED HIS CAMERA, I picked up my notebook and mini tape recorder, and we joined a stream of people flowing to the marina. The media mob had grown, as additional news services had sent reporters and photographers when they learned of the search going on for Alex Gordon's body. Al left my side and sprinted for the dock so he would be up front where the action was.

We were halted ten yards from the foot of the dock by a strip of yellow plastic police tape and a row of sheriff's deputies and local police officers. While Al and I had been sleeping, the authorities had been taking charge of the accident scene. The only people on the dock side of the tape were Sheriff Val Holmberg, Governor Anders A. Anderson and Lieutenant Governor Aaron Ross, the latter equipped with a fresh cigar. Ann Rogers stood in front of the tape, helping the officers stop the charge of the media brigade.

"Please wait here," Ann was saying over and over again. "Please be patient. You'll all have a chance to get the story." Ann was always coiffed and made up like an actress walking onstage, but now her seemingly molded light brown curls were straggling like a pitchfork full of hay, a black line of dripping mascara was smudging her right cheek and the ruby red lipstick she'd been wearing at six o'clock was gone.

The dive team boat and the original rescue boat with the empty boat in tow were in a line approaching the dock where the governor, lieutenant governor and sheriff stood waiting. The dive team was about ten yards out when my cell phone rang. It was Martha Todd.

"What the heck is going on up there?" she said. "Are you guys okay? The TV is on in the break room and Trish Valentine is reporting live about bringing in a drowning victim." *Good old Trish.*

"It's the governor's press secretary," I said. "Apparently he went out fishing before dawn and fell out of the boat into water cold enough to form icicles on your butt. They're bringing him in to the dock as we speak."

"What kind of nut goes out fishing before dawn?" Martha said.

"I'm told that it's not unusual for this particular nut," I said. "Except in this case, he'd called us all to a meeting at six o'clock and went fishing a little after five. Doesn't seem like he'd have much time to fish."

"Maybe he wanted to bring in a walleye so he could show the press what they look like."

"I think most Minnesotans know that. I've got to go. Looks like the governor is about to say something."

"Keep me posted."

"I'm keeping Don O'Rourke posted. Look on the *Daily Dispatch* website."

"I'll just keep watching Trish Valentine reporting live," Martha said. That was a below-the-belt shot at my ego. She knows I hate being one-upped on a story by anyone reporting live on TV.

The sheriff spoke before the governor had a chance to talk. He asked us to move out of the way so the ambulance crew that had just arrived could make its way to the dock. The multitude parted like the Red Sea at the command of Moses and a couple of deputies lowered the yellow plastic tape as the ambulance beeped its way backwards across the lawn and stopped ten feet from the dock. Two men in blue EMT jackets opened the rear doors, dragged out a gurney, and carried it over the ten-foot strip of grass and sand to the dock.

Once on the dock, the men raised the gurney to waist level and wheeled it out to the end where the boats were tied up. The EMTs lowered the gurney to its lowest level and we all watched in silence as the dive team members hauled a loaded black body bag out of their boat and placed it on the waiting platform. Shutters snapped and TV cameras rolled as the gurney was raised, wheeled back to the beach, carried across the strip of sand and grass to the ambulance and loaded aboard. The babble of voices resumed, but at a lower decibel level, as the ambulance doors clanged shut.

I looked around for Al and saw that he had slipped through the opening in the yellow tape and was out at the end of the dock shooting pictures of the boats. He was leaning over the dead man's empty boat and taking some shots of the interior when a deputy clamped a hand on his shoulder and invited him to leave the dock. Al did not resist—he had collected all the photos he needed.

"You're lucky that deputy didn't try to take away your camera," I said when Al caught up to me.

"I can't picture him doing that," Al said.

"I shutter to think of it."

"At least with digital cameras, they can't open it up and grab the film and expose it like some of the smartass cops used to do."

"Exposing the film always had negative results," I said. "With your digital they could pull out the memory card and stomp on it."

"Forget about stomping the memory card," he said.

Ann Rogers was shouting in an effort to get the attention of the buzzing crowd, but her commanding voice had grown raspy and she was having no success. She was rescued by a booming bass voice that rose above the rumble. "Everybody shut the fuck up," Anders Anderson yelled. Unaccustomed to hearing an f-bomb blast forth from the mouth of our church-going Lutheran governor, everybody did shut the fuck up.

Anderson gestured toward Rogers, and she cupped her hands around her mouth to form a megaphone and said as loud as she could, "The governor will hold a press conference in the main meeting room at one o'clock. Thank you all for your cooperation."

"Hope the governor is more on time than his press secretary," said Channel Five's Barry Ziebart.

"He probably will be if he doesn't decide to go fishing in the meantime," Al said.

* * *

AL E-MAILED A HALF-DOZEN of his best shots and I e-mailed a fresh story during the half-hour we had free before the governor walked into the meeting room and picked up the portable microphone. The lieutenant governor trailed along behind him and stood slightly off to the right. His mouth held the customary cigar, but this time it wasn't lit. Still, I inhaled a dose of second-hand stogy smoke from his clothing when he walked past me on the way to his position. A couple more breaths like that and I'd be in serious danger of lung cancer.

Traffic at Brainerd's little airport must have been swarming like bees that morning because TV crews from ABC News, CBS News and NBC News had been added to the throng, along with a representative of Rupert Murdoch's publications. Never had a Governor's Fishing Opener been so thoroughly covered by the media. The air in the room was heavy with the odor of bodies that hadn't been bathed recently as dozens of us were crammed into close quarters with our fellow stinkers.

Governor Anderson flipped on the microphone and blew into it three times to make sure it was live. Technicians hate this method of testing because it sprays saliva into the instrument, but the trio of amplified whooshing sounds served also to quiet the audience. "Let me begin by saying that I'm deeply saddened by the tragic loss of my good friend and colleague, Alex Gordon," he began. "I have also phoned his lovely wife, Mari, and offered my condolences to her and the rest of Alex's splendid family. This is a sad, sad day for us all.

"Alex will be greatly missed by everyone who worked with him in the governor's office, and I dare say he will be missed by you folks—the press corps—as well. He always kept himself fully informed and up to the minute so that he'd have the answer to any question you folks might ask. He was a true professional in every sense of the word."

"Actually, he was a self-important little prick," Barry Ziebart whispered behind me. I nodded in agreement. Alex had always made it seem as if he were doing an inferior being a great favor by answering a question, and a reporter always had to drag the details of any complex situation out of him by asking question after question. I for one would not miss his attitude and his frequent references to his superior education at 'Hahv'd.'

"I have just appointed Alex's wonderful assistant, Ms. Ann Rogers, as acting press secretary," the governor said. "I will turn this meeting over to her now and let her answer any questions you might have."

With her hair whipped into a compliant shape by comb and brush, and armor plated with a fresh coat of lacquer, and her lipstick and eye makeup restored to radiant perfection, Ann stepped forward and took the microphone. As usual, the first question came from Trish Valentine. "Why would Alex go out fishing at five o'clock when he was scheduled to meet with us at six?"

"Alex was an avid fisherman," Ann said. "Those of you who covered the fishing opener in recent years might recall that Alex went out by himself before dawn every morning and returned in time to meet with the press."

"What was the purpose of the morning meeting?" I asked.

"I don't know all the details but I assume it was to brief you on the day's activities," Ann said. "That's pretty much what he did every year."

"So he didn't have any special message—just a general briefing?" asked a woman standing behind me.

"I don't know of anything special," Ann said. "But as I said before, he hadn't discussed the details with me."

"How'd they find the body so quick?" asked a man at my right. "Usually it takes forever to find a drowning victim."

"The divers said the water was so crystal clear that they could see for a long way under the surface," Ann said. "It wasn't like diving in murky or muddy water."

"Will there be an autopsy conducted?" asked the man from NBC News. Ah, at last we were getting down to the nitty-gritty.

"I believe an autopsy is standard for an accidental death or an unattended death," Ann said. "So, yes, I assume there will be an autopsy."

"How long before the medical examiner will issue a report?" asked the woman from CBS News. I'd been wondering about that. Would the cause of death be announced soon enough to warrant our staying in Brainerd beyond Sunday to wait for the report?

"I suppose the family will want Alex's body for the funeral as soon as possible," Ann said. "So I assume the ME will finish his work as soon as it's physically possible."

"So maybe by Sunday afternoon or evening?" asked a voice from the back.

"I really can't say for sure," Ann said. "Why don't I talk to the ME and get back to you people later on that?"

"Some of us have flights to schedule," said another voice.

"I understand that," Ann said. "But as I say, the timing is up to the ME."

Ann fielded a couple more questions before calling a halt. She concluded the session by telling us that the governor wished to salvage at least part of the day's schedule, which is what Alex would want him to do. This included a picnic on the lawn at 4:30 p.m. and an introduction to the guides who would accompany the governor and the lieutenant governor on their Saturday fishing expeditions. "You'll have a chance to meet the guides at seven thirty and ask them questions," she said. "They both have interesting stories to tell."

We left the meeting room and went to the circular, glassed-in dining room for a lunch of fish and chips. After a ten-minute wait, we were crammed into a table in the middle, surrounded by tables occupied by other reporters and photographers. "Do you suppose this is walleye that was caught out of season?" Al asked after swallowing the first crunchy, batter-fried mouthful. "Wouldn't that be a great story for you?"

"I can see the headline," I said. "Diners find something fishy about walleye."

"Subhead: Chef agrees to scale back 'til season opens."

"Hate to ruin your story, guys; but it's from Canada," said a man at the nearest table to my right.

"Of course. I should have recognized the accent," I replied.

After lunch we walked back to our cabin. As we passed the thermometer beside our door, Al pointed and said, "Oh, do you see that? Won't it be fun to have a picnic on the lawn in this lovely spring weather?" The arrow was pointing at forty-eight.

"Be of good cheer; the temperature has nowhere to go but down," I said. "Hope you packed your long johns."

"I'll be packing them with a little something extra to keep my package warm."

"More information than I need," I said, covering my ears with my hands. "Go back to asking questions every time you speak."

Chapter Five

Chilling Out

I called Martha at her office and brought her up to date. Devil that she is, she said she'd already heard all the details from Trish Valentine reporting live.

"They even showed the poor guy being dragged out of the boat in a body bag," Martha said. "And I thought I saw Al shooting pictures out on the dock. How'd he get away with that?"

"It's called chutzpah," I said. "Al just keeps zooming in with his camera until someone zooms him out, which someone eventually did, by the way."

"So what's going to happen with the rest of the big opening day hoopty-do? Are they calling off everything?"

"No, the governor is trying to salvage as much of the program as he can. Says Alex would want it that way. Personally, I don't think Alex would give a damn. Anyhow, we're having a picnic in forty-degree weather late this afternoon and then we get to meet the guides who will accompany our great leaders on the lake tomorrow."

"What time do you have to get up?"

"The fishing officially starts at 6:00 a.m. Should be some real bleary-eyed walleye chasers out there if people booze it up like they did last night," I said.

"Six o'clock on a Saturday?" Martha said. "I'll say a prayer for you when I roll over and go back to sleep at nine."

"You are insensitive and unkind, and you have no redeeming social value," I said.

"Is that why you love me?"

"That's as good a reason as any."

"Well, take care of yourself tomorrow and don't fall out of the boat. I don't have anyone else lined up to take your place at the wedding."

"Don't worry about me," I said. "The only danger I'm in is possibly being trampled by the herd the next time the governor calls a press conference."

We made kissy sounds at each other and hung up.

Ah, yes, the wedding. It was not going to be a major production because we'd both already gone through that kind of show. This was the second time around for both of us, and we both wanted to play it low-key. My first wife had been killed, along with our baby, when a jack-knifing semi-trailer crushed her little Toyota. Martha's first husband had disappeared to avoid prosecution after beating her up for the second time. In his absence, she had divorced him, claiming both physical and mental cruelty in addition to desertion.

But big or not, the ceremony would be a moment of triumph for both of us after years of frustration and struggling with our fears of another commitment. Al and Carol were scheduled to be our attendants, and the brief guest list included a few friends from the newsroom, a handful of Martha's friends, Martha's parents and grandmother, and my mom and Grandma Goodie, whose persistent nagging had persuaded us to abandon our original plan to hold the ceremony in a municipal judge's chambers.

A young Unitarian-Universalist minister had agreed to do the honors after subjecting Martha and me to a lengthy interview about our backgrounds and beliefs. Apparently she decided that our characters were diverse and unorthodox enough to be comfortable getting married in a U-U church.

* * *

I'VE RARELY BUNDLED UP as warmly for a day of downhill skiing as I did for the governor's picnic that afternoon. Clouds had moved in, the wind velocity had increased and the temperature had dropped to forty-three by the time the picnic began. I wore a T-shirt, a cotton turtleneck, a wool sweater, my regular undershorts, long johns, sweatpants, regular socks, wool socks and lined boots, topped off by a winter jacket and a knitted wool ski cap. When it comes to layering I can laminate clothing with the best of them. I also carried gloves in my jacket pockets in case my fingers got cold holding the plate.

Al was similarly weighted down with protective garments as we approached the array of eight-person picnic tables lined up across the lawn between the lodge and the beach. This time we had no problem finding a seat. Apparently many of our media cohorts had not brought appropriate clothing for springtime on Gull Lake.

We went through the food line, which contained the usual run of outdoor comestibles, including the traditional Minnesota salad made of canned fruit cocktail embedded in orange Jell-O topped with miniature marshmallows. I skipped this universal favorite in favor of a less colorful potato salad, to which I added some coleslaw and a chunk of smoked whitefish. I finished filling my plate with a cheeseburger that was almost shivering sitting on the grill.

We chose not to join a group of TV types talking shop at the closest table and took an unoccupied one nearer the beach where we could sit side by side facing the lake. A thin man with a red nose and a blue Madrigal's jacket approached and asked if we'd like something to drink. We both asked for coffee, thinking it would warm our hands and innards. This proved to be overly optimistic, as the dark liquid had cooled to lukewarm by the time the man set the cups on the table.

We gobbled our hamburgers as fast as we could in an effort to swallow them before the fat congealed in the cold. I was just stuffing in the last bite when Ann Rogers approached. "How are the happy picnickers doing?" she asked.

"Just like the Fourth of July, only there's no mosquitoes," Al said. "When do the fireworks start?"

"I think we had enough fireworks this morning," Ann said. She is what's known as a full-figured woman and is sexy in her own carefully put together way, but the wide-brimmed hat, puffy ski jacket and baggy jeans she was wearing as cold weather attire made her look like an overstuffed snowperson. All she needed was a carrot for a nose.

"Sit down and take a load off," I said. "You must be dead on your feet."

She plopped onto the bench across from us with a sigh. "Not as dead as poor Alex," she said.

"Were you two good friends as well as co-conspiring spinners of the news?" Al asked.

Ann frowned. "We never put a spin on the news about the governor. Well, almost never. But to answer your question, no, we weren't particularly good friends. Alex was too standoffish for anyone to really get close to him."

"The Hahv'd snob?" I said.

"The East Coast rich kid," Ann said. "He came from a big bucks, high society Boston family and never let you forget it."

"How'd he wind up in Minnesota, of all places?" Al asked.

"He followed a woman, a Harvard classmate who was from Minnetonka and came back to work for a Minneapolis law firm headed by none other than Anders A. Anderson."

"Gee, I wonder how he happened to get a job as the governor's press secretary," I said.

"It was a perfect fit," Ann said. "Nepotism aside, Alex was quick on his feet and had a Harvard political science degree. What else does a guy need for dealing with the press?"

"A personality would be nice," I said.

"How about you?" Al asked. "Will you be taking over the job permanently?"

"There's not much 'permanently' left," she said. "The election is in November and Governor Anderson isn't running for a third term. So, yeah, I'll probably finish it out."

"Who's running?" I asked. "On the Republican side, that is."

"Lieutenant Governor Ross," Ann said. I groaned and she smiled. "Actually, I think Alex would have liked to have run but he never could have beaten Aaron Ross, the good old native son, in a primary."

"Ross would have eaten him alive," I said. "Bluster and cigar smoke against an elite carpetbagger. Smog and bullshit win every time."

"I suppose you're right," Ann said. "Anyway, I should go schmooze some of the network reporters. Have a great picnic, guys; it's been fun talking to you." She rose and walked to a table where two fresh-faced young network reporters, one male and one female, were sitting close enough together to keep them both extremely warm.

"I'm sure she'll be appreciated over there," I said.

"Maybe her visit will encourage them to adjourn to one of their cabins," Al said.

"Speaking of, I'm about ready to adjourn to ours. There is a phenomenon known as heat in there."

"An excellent idea. We could grab a couple of desserts off the table and go make some hot coffee with the pot in the cabin."

I had stacked my cup on my plate and was wadding up my napkin so I could stuff it into the cup when we were joined by two more visitors.

"You guys look like you could use a little warming up," said one. "I'm Roxie." She was in her early twenties, with curly dark hair, a cute round face, a snub nose that was pink from the cold and sparkly brown eyes.

"And I'm Angie," said the other.

"Hi. I'm Alsie and he's Mitchie," Al said.

"Mind if we sit down?" Angie said. She was also in her early twenties, with straight blonde hair, an angular face, a straight Nordic nose and bright blue eyes. Both wore heavier eye makeup, darker rouge and brighter lipstick than was either appropriate for the occasion or necessary for the enhancement of their features.

"Sit ahead," I said.

"Sit on your head?" said Roxie. She giggled.

"Ooh, kinky," said Angie. Another giggle.

"Maybe later," said Roxie. She sat between me and the end of the bench, pressing her body and leg tight against me in order to get all of her butt on the seat. Said butt was nicely rounded and encased in jeans so tight they could have been painted on. Above the waist she wore a thin red jacket that flowed around the substantial curves of her upper body.

"Ya never know," said Angie. Her generously rounded lower body was similarly packaged in skin-hugging jeans and she wore an unzipped pink jacket that revealed a well-filled light green sweater. She snuggled up against Al and said, "Isn't this better?"

"Much warmer," Al said. I could see that at least his face was getting warmer as the color turned from wind-chilled pink to flustered medium red.

"Cozy," I said. I could feel my face getting warmer as the blood rose to my cheeks and forehead. My left leg was also warming because of the body heat flowing from the jeans pressed against my thigh. Those jeans were so tight I could have detected a mole if she'd had one anywhere on her leg. I've always marveled at the tightness of some women's jeans and tried to imagine how they put them on. Roxie seemed to be the kind of woman that one could ask about that process.

So I did. "How can you get into those jeans?" I said.

Roxie put her hand high up on my thigh, looked into my eyes and smiled. "Well, you could start by buying a girl a drink."

Chapter Six

Girls and Guides

THAT WAS THE DIRECTION I was expecting the conversation to take, only not quite so quickly. These two young women were not representatives of the media, nor were they fisherpersons staying at the resort in hopes of having a good time. Roxie and Angie were at the Governor's Fishing Opener in hopes of providing a good time for any unattached fisherman with an open wallet.

As much fun as it would be to continue talking naughty for awhile, I knew the end of the discussion would be disappointing to Roxie and Angie. There was no way either of us was going to spend time and money with either of them.

The question was whether to keep on building up the women's expectations or to be upfront and send them quickly on their way in search of more profitable male companionship. I opted for immediate honesty.

"I'm sorry, ladies, but we won't be buying drinks, and we also won't be buying any of what you're selling," I said. "We're old married men—at least, he is and I'm about to be."

Roxie sat up ramrod straight with her chin held high. "Whatever made you think that we might have anything for sale," she said, sounding like Queen Elizabeth. Then she giggled.

"You could still buy us a drink," Angie said. "Inside at the bar where it's warm."

"Yeah," Roxie said. "It's colder than a walleye's ass out here."

"You should dress warmer," Al said. "Either that or limit your advertising campaign to inside the lodge."

"A girl's gotta do what a girl's gotta do," Roxie said. "Come on, old married stiffs, buy us a drink in the bar and tell us about your wedding while I thaw out my boobs."

"Not much to tell," I said. I removed her hand from my thigh and got to my feet. "But I'll buy a round of drinks. How about you, Al?"

"I'm game," he said. "Just keep your eyes open for cell phone cameras. I don't want anybody seeing me with these two lovely young ladies on YouTube."

"Especially Carol?" I said.

"Especially Carol."

"What's the matter, Alsie? Doesn't your wife trust you?" Angie asked.

"I think she does but I'd rather not test her," he said.

"What about you, Mitchie?" said Roxie. "Does your bride-to-be trust you?"

"Of course she does," I said. "But I don't want to raise any doubts in her unsuspicious mind." I immediately wished I hadn't said that. It could easily put thoughts of blackmail into Roxie's mercenary mind.

I looked around to see who might be watching as we escorted Roxie and Angie back to the lodge. Most of the picnickers had eaten quickly and left, and the few remaining were concentrating on downing their picnic dinner at a pace that gave the term "fast food" a whole new meaning. I was glad that Ann Rogers was nowhere in sight.

The bar was another story. It was packed almost to capacity with our media colleagues and the noise level from competing conversations was nearing the 100-decibel mark. We found a small table with two chairs against a wall and the women sat down. Al went on a chair hunt while I took drink orders. Angie wanted white zinfandel and Roxie ordered scotch with a splash of water on the rocks. I knew Al would have a beer.

When I returned from the bar, Al was seated and there was an empty chair beside Roxie. I put down the tray and passed around the drinks. Roxie asked, "What's that you're drinking?"

"Ginger ale," I said. "I can't have booze."

"Jeez, you mean I can't even get you drunk and steal your money?" she said.

"Not a chance."

"Well, I guess we'll have to work on Alsie."

"I'm watching out for him," I said. "I'm palsy-walsy with Alsie."

"You're no fun at allsie," Roxie said. Another giggle.

But the next hour was fun. With no prospect of a sale, Roxie and Angie relaxed and seemed to enjoy the break in their search for paying customers. We learned that Angie's full name was Angelina and that Roxie was not Roxelina, but had been baptized Roxanne. They had graduated the previous spring from Bemidji State College, where, according to Roxie, they were "big bosom buddies." When they found that the northern Minnesota job market had no openings for tasks requiring the use of their brains they decided to support themselves by opening their bodies for business. The winter trade had been slow but they were looking forward to a profit boom with the onset of fishing season.

"Last summer we were waiting on tables in Bemidji and the guys kept grabbing our asses," Roxie said. "So we decided to start charging them for the pleasure."

"And now you're expanding your territory?" Al asked.

"Nothing happening in Bemidji yet; there's still ice on the lake," she said "But right now there's lots of action here with the governor's party and all."

"We took on a couple of high rollers last night," Angie said. "Paid big bucks up front but they were both so drunk they couldn't do anything."

"That was the best part," Roxie said. "If all our customers were like that we'd still be virgins."

"Speak for yourself, girl," said Angie.

"Oh, yeah, I forgot about Jimmy," Roxie said. "She was screwing like a bunny with a guy named Jimmy for two years at BSU."

"Whoa!" I said. "That's more than we need to know."

"Anyway, he went off to grad school in California," Angie said. "I really miss him."

Roxie observed that the early morning drowning accident hadn't dampened the party mood in the bar.

"It's actually made the party louder," I said. "The accident brought in more reporters to cover it. And nobody in the press who knows him feels like mourning the guy who drowned."

"Did the press all hate him?" Angie asked.

"Nobody hated him," I said. "But nobody liked him either."

After finishing her second scotch and water, delivered courtesy of Al, Roxie said it was time to start looking for some evening clients. "Fun talking to you guys," she said. "Been a long time since I spent a whole hour with a guy without taking off my clothes."

"Yeah," Angie said. "Me, too."

"Any time," I said. "It's been fun for us, too."

Roxie stood and leaned over me. Her left breast pressed against my shoulder and her lips and warm breath caressed my ear as she whispered, "You can get into these jeans any time, Mitchie, and it won't cost you a dime."

"What did she say?" Al asked as we watched Roxie and Angie walk away.

"She made me an offer that's hard to refuse," I said. "Please don't leave me alone with her. Martha may trust me but I'm not sure I can trust myself."

"Never fear, your pallie-wallie Allie will keep you in your pants and out of Roxie's."

A few minutes later, Ann Rogers walked into the bar carrying a portable microphone, quieted the crowd on the fourth or fifth bellow and announced that it was time for the fishing host/guest pairing meeting. We would have the opportunity to meet and question the guides paired with the governor and lieutenant governor for the next day's fishing expedition. After that, those of us who had signed up to go fishing would be introduced to our guides.

Like lemmings, we followed Ann to the conference room, where Governor Anders A. Anderson and Lieutenant Governor Aaron Ross, the latter with an unlit cigar clamped in his teeth, were seated between two men dressed in red plaid woolen shirts, faded blue jeans and scuffed brown leather boots. The one beside the governor had a weather-beaten face and a scruffy gray beard and wore a red cap with earlaps, which were folded up and tied in a bow at the top of his head. The other, a Native-American with long black braids, had a beat-up wide-brimmed black hat pulled down almost to his bushy eyebrows.

Ann Rogers started the session with a moment of silence for Alex Gordon, who she said was "taken from us in a terrible boating accident this morning." She followed the silence with the announcement that the medical examiner had said he would try to have autopsy results by noon on Sunday. "I'll inform you of the exact time when he's ready to make an announcement," she said. Normally everyone went home right after Sunday breakfast. Now it looked like we'd be hanging around for a few hours waiting for the ME's report.

"Now for the introductions," Rogers said. "First we have the guide who will accompany Lieutenant Governor Ross. His name is Leonard Tallchief, and he has been guiding fishermen on Gull Lake for over thirty years. During the winter Leonard lives on the White Earth Reservation and during the summer he stays here at this resort. Please feel free to ask him any question that comes to mind." She gestured toward the Indian, who rose, tipped his hat and took the microphone from Rogers.

"Good evening," Tallchief said. "I am very much honored to have this opportunity to guide the lieutenant governor to the best fishing spots on Gull Lake. I very much look forward to opening day tomorrow. I will be very proud if our lieutenant governor brings back the biggest walleye at the end of the day tomorrow." His unwavering tone made it obvious that he was reciting a memorized speech.

There was a second moment of silence as we waited for Tallchief to continue. When it became apparent he had nothing more to say, a TV reporter behind us asked, "Is Ms. Rogers correct? Do you live on the White Earth Reservation in the off-season?" The White Earth Reservation is about a hundred miles northwest, sort of halfway between Brainerd and Fargo, North Dakota.

"Ms. Rogers is correct," Tallchief said.

"What tribe do you belong to?" asked another man.

"Ojibway," was the answer.

"When did you first start fishing?"

"When I could hold a pole."

"How long have you been a guide?"

"Maybe thirty years."

"What do you do out there on the reservation all winter?"

"Not much," Tallchief said. "Guide hunters. Mostly watch crap on TV."

"Chatty soul, isn't he?" Al whispered.

"Can't shut him up," I replied.

Reporters kept trying. "Got any piece of the casino action?" asked another.

Tallchief's somber face relaxed almost into a smile. "If I had a piece of the casino, no way I'd be working here."

That response turned out to be the highlight of the interview, which ended a couple of minutes later after a series of one-word answers.

"Did you get every golden word?" I asked Trish Valentine, who was standing in front of me as usual.

"Got it all on digital," she said. "Were you able to take notes fast enough to keep up?"

"I may have missed a syllable or two when I was yawning," I said.

Next up was the governor's guide, who was introduced as "longtime Gull Lake veteran, Zachary Leroux, better known to his hundreds of fisherman friends as Frenchy."

"Frenchy has worked on this lake for over thirty years," Ann Rogers said. "He has guided three different governors in fishing openers held at this resort and he knows every rock and sandbar where the fish hang out." She held the mike out to Frenchy, who took it, grinned at the audience and said, "Hello, all you good looking people. We gonna have some fun this weekend or what?"

This brought a cheer from the crowd, followed by a question that brought forth a torrent of information. Frenchy had been born in the tiny town of Cuyuna, "just up Highway 210 a ways," and had started fishing with both of his grandfathers before he was old enough to go to school. He moved to the big city (Brainerd) as soon as he was old enough to leave his parents. He had worked as a lumberjack, a carpenter and a roofer before hooking on as a guide at Madrigal's. He'd been showing people where to catch fish for thirty-two years and knew the name and address of every walleye in the lake.

Frenchy had entered numerous fishing contests with his friends and had been among the top prize winners almost every time. He ran a children's fishing contest every spring and visited area classrooms during the school year to talk about fishing. When it came to talking about himself, Frenchy was everything that Tallchief was not.

"This job is hell of a lot better than putting shingles on roofs," Frenchy said. "Not as far to fall and water is a lot softer to land in. Also the tips are better, especially from governors." Frenchy actually drew a round of applause when his interview ended and he kept on chatting with some TV people after the session was officially complete.

Next on the schedule was an introduction to the man who would be our guide in the morning. Rogers picked us up and said she'd take us to meet him.

"I hope our guide is more talkative than the lieutenant governor's," I said.

"That was the biggest put-on I've ever seen," she said. "Leonard Tallchief has a master's degree in education and teaches fifth and sixth grades on the reservation. He also writes a weekly outdoors column for the Brainerd paper. I was falling off my chair laughing while he was playing stupid tonight."

Rogers led us to a middle-aged man who also was wearing a red-and-black plaid wool shirt and blue jeans. Apparently it was the uniform of the day. "I'd like you gentlemen to meet your guide for tomorrow, Henry Halvorsen, who spells his name with an 's-e-n,'" she said

I wrote that in my notepad before shaking hands and saying, "Good to meet you, Mr. Halvorsen." The skin on the hand was like coarse sandpaper and the power of the grip was a challenge to match.

"Evenin'," Halvorsen said. "Nice meetin' you. And you can call me Henry; the last name's too big a mouthful."

"Is it Finnish?" I asked.

"Yah, dat's all dere is," he said. Another joker in the pack.

"I meant is the nationality Finnish. Were your ancestors from Finland?"

"Oh, yah, dat too," he said.

Al had already taken a couple of photos when he lowered the camera and shook Henry's hand. Henry was shorter than either of us—about five-six—but his shoulders were broad and square, and his scaly hands were those of a much bigger man. His hair was black speckled with gray, and it was pulled back in a foot-long pony tail. The large brush of a moustache beneath his bulbous nose was also salted with gray. He smiled when he shook Al's hand, revealing teeth stained yellowish brown, probably from a lifetime of chewing tobacco.

Henry told us he'd been guiding fishermen on Gull Lake since he was a teenager, and that he lived in nearby Nisswa "Still livin' in the house I was born in," he said.

"So you've lived there your entire life?" I asked.

"Not yet," he said.

"Good point," I said. "I'll be careful how I word that when I write the story."

We discussed what time and where to meet and what to bring. We had our own fishing tackle, water bottles and snacks, so all we had to do was sign out a boat.

"You got your own lifejackets?" Henry asked.

"Oh, no," I said. "That we don't have."

"You gotta check out some lifejackets," he said. "Can't go in a boat without 'em."

"The guy who drowned this morning managed to get away without one," Al said.

"Dat's been puzzlin' me," Henry said. "Dat fella come up here from the Cities a day early and he went out fishin' two times yesterday, mornin' and evenin', with a lifejacket on. Had his own, in fact. Expensive lookin' one. Why wasn't he wearin' it today?"

"Seems like he picked the wrong day to leave it off," Al said.

"Seems like," said Henry. "Can't imagine why."

When I thought about it, neither could I.

Chapter Seven

Trolling

ALTHOUGH HENRY HAD TRIED to persuade us to go out at sunrise, we had insisted on a more civilized hour. Thus we joined a couple dozen other early birds at breakfast and met Henry on the dock at 6:30 Saturday morning, which was still too early as far as I was concerned. I wasn't sure I could cope with a fish that was awake enough to attack a baited hook before seven on a Saturday morning, but the governor and lieutenant governor were already in their boats and cruising out into the bay to begin what was billed as The Fishing Challenge. Since our job was to cover the action with words and pictures, we had no choice but to follow.

Henry had a boat, a bucket of large silver shiner minnows and the required life jackets waiting for us. Al and I struggled into the life jackets, squeezing them on over the heavy jackets we'd worn at the picnic the day before.

"Maybe this is why Alex didn't have his life jacket on," I said between grunts. "He couldn't get it on over his winter coat."

"Whatever," said Henry. "Still goddamn stupid."

"What's the temperature now?" Al asked.

"You don't wanna know," Henry said.

"I need to know," I said. "Part of the story."

"Would you believe t'irty-six?" Henry said.

"I'd believe twenty-six," I said. "I'm surprised there's not ice on the lake."

"There still is some ice on the big lakes nort' of us," he said. "Goddamn coldest walleye opener in twenty years."

"And lucky us, we get to cover it," Al said. "I've had warmer days shooting the ice sculptures at the Winter Carnival."

We joined a small armada of boats tagging after Governor Anders A. Anderson, whose guide was steering off to the left. The boat containing Lieutenant Governor Aaron Ross was heading directly toward an island about a quarter of a mile out in the bay. We could see blue cigar smoke streaming from his boat in the misty morning air.

"Frenchy's takin' the governor to a sandbar over dere," Henry said. "Usually good for a couple of fish."

"Where's the lieutenant governor going?" I asked.

"Dere's some rocks about fifty feet off dat island," Henry said. "Walleyes feed dere pretty much all day long. But dey don't generally run as big as on the sand bar."

"Is the contest between the gov and the lieutenant for the biggest fish or the most fish?"

"I t'ink dey got prizes for both," Henry said. "Dey're set up in teams—though the governor is short one team member because of the guy dat drowned."

From thirty feet away, Al shot pix of Frenchy putting a minnow on the governor's hook, casting it out into the water and handing the rod to the governor. I took note of the time and left a blank space to record the time and size of the governor's first catch.

"You gents ready to fish?" Henry asked. He had slowed the boat to trolling speed to shadow the governor. I nodded and picked up my rod.

"I can bait my own hook," I said. I dipped a silver shiner out of the icy water in the bucket, slid the hook through its upper and lower lips, cast it out and played out some line. Al stopped shooting pictures and did the same, keeping an eye on the governor with the camera hanging at the ready around his neck.

Back and forth we went for what seemed like days, trolling across the sandbar without so much as a nibble. The blank space

I'd left to record the governor's first catch remained blank. There were five other media-bearing boats in our group and nobody in any of them pulled in a fish. Frenchy broke the monotony by leading the flotilla to another spot where we all trolled with similar results. Ditto in a third spot.

Lunch was scheduled for 11:30 a.m. and shortly before 11:00, Frenchy shouted that the fishermen in the governor's boat were pulling in their lines and returning to the lodge. This was the best news I'd heard all day. My butt was sore, my legs were cramped and my bladder was filled to capacity.

Al put my worst problem into words: "Hurry up and get to shore. My back teeth are floating."

As we were reeling in our lines, we heard a shriek from the governor's boat. Ann Rogers had hooked a walleye.

"Get in close," Al yelled as he forgot about his bladder distress and swung his camera into action. Henry turned up the motor and steered toward the governor's boat. Five other guides did the same thing with their boats. The six of us were on course to meet at the governor's boat and all eyes were on Frenchy as he scooped Ann's fish from the water with his net and hoisted it head high to celebrate the day's first catch.

Anders A. Anderson raised his arms in triumph and looked around for an audience. What he saw was the bows of six boats closing in on his stationary vessel at flank speed. "Get the hell away from us," he yelled, waving his arms like a manic traffic cop in a fast forward film.

Six guides cut their engines and swung their rudders to avoid a six-point collision with the governor. Two of the boats turned toward each other and slammed together. A television cameraman who was standing in the bow of one of them was flung forward onto his knees. His fur hat flew off and miraculously landed in the governor's boat. Al got a photo of the two guides flipping each other the bird as they backed their boats away from the spot of the crash. He also got a shot of Anders A. Anderson laughing as Frenchy Leroux placed the unfortunate photographer's fur hat on the gubernatorial head. "Guaranteed page one," Al said.

* * *

LIEUTENANT GOVERNOR AARON ROSS had been more fortunate. He and his crew had reeled in a total of four walleyes, which they displayed with gusto on the dock. Ross made sure we all had plenty of photo ops showing him holding up the two biggest fish, one on each side of his smoldering cigar.

"Your caption can say 'Minnesota's next governor shows how it's done,'" Ross said.

"Is that the official announcement of your candidacy?" I asked.

"You can call it a preliminary announcement. The formal campaign kick-off won't come until June first, but you should all follow me on the lake this afternoon for some real fishing action."

The lunch had been advertised as an outdoor event, but manager Martin Johansen mercifully moved it into the dining room. Those of us who had spent the morning on the lake grasping fishing rods in numb hands gave him a standing ovation when he greeted us inside.

"You gents goin' out again?" Henry asked as we warmed our hands around cups full of hot coffee.

"That's what we're here for," Al said. "I need to get some shots of the next governor of Minnesota catching fish and fouling the clear northern Minnesota air with cigar smoke this afternoon."

"I can see the cut line now," I said. "'Aaron Ross, far right, is shown angling for governor.'"

"How about, 'Aaron Ross shows how he'll hook the nomination,'" Al said.

"That's a reel good line."

"I knew you'd take the bait."

Henry shook his head. "I'll see you gents at the boat," he said as he rose from his chair.

"Was it something I said?" Al asked as we watched our guide walk to another table.

"These outdoor types don't appreciate high-class humor," I said.

"Or maybe they do."

On the lake again an hour later, we followed the boat carrying Aaron Ross and his party as Leonard Tallchief took them back to the rocky ledge near the island. Henry, following our instructions to stay upwind out of the cloud of Ross's cigar smoke, kept us close but not too close.

The next governor of Minnesota's team caught four more walleyes, including one by the great man himself. I chose to keep my hands warm in my coat pockets rather than fish, and Al quit after losing a hook in the rocks. "My fingers are too stiff to tie on another one," he said.

The challenge officially ended at 4:00 p.m. and we returned to the dock a few minutes before the hour. The governor and the media fleet following his boat were already tied up when we arrived. Posing for pictures on the dock with the biggest walleye of the day was a familiar figure. "Trish Valentine reporting live," yelled the five-foot-tall blond bombshell as she hoisted a seven-pounder for the cameras. Its tail was almost dragging on the ground.

* * *

"Why aren't you on the evening news holding up a big fish?" Martha Todd asked. Al and I had decided to skip the Celebration Reception (more booze) and call home from our cabin as soon as our hands were supple enough to press the correct cell phone keys.

"Blame it on the weather," I said.

"Too cold for the fish?"

"Too cold for me to hold a rod and reel all day."

"Not too cold for Trish Valentine," Martha said. "It looks like she's having fun."

"Why don't you watch some other channel?" I said.

"You're just jealous because she's reporting live."

"Better she should be reporting dead."

"You don't mean that."

"You're right," I said. "I like Trish but I'm getting tired of her stealing the show up here."

"So go catch a big fish," Martha said. "And maybe Trish will show it live on Channel 4."

"Enough about Trish already. How are you doing on the wedding plans?"

"Everything is in place except the groom." Of course it would be. Martha always has everything that she can control under control well ahead of time.

"The groom is doing his best," I said. "If the ME issues his autopsy report tomorrow as promised, the groom will be on the road for home faster than a walleye can grab Trish Valentine's boo, uh . . . bait."

We chatted for another ten minutes, during which I learned that Sherlock Holmes, the homeless cat I had adopted several years ago, was asking where I was. "He goes around the bedroom meowing and he's sleeping on your pillow every night," Martha said. "And most of the day, too."

"Oh, great," I said. "I'll come home to a pillowcase full of cat hair."

"I'll change it tomorrow so it won't get in your nose."

"Thanks. That's nothing to sneeze at."

"There is one little problem that came up here yesterday," Martha said. "Grandma Mendes got a surprise phone call from the immigration authorities about her status. They want her to come to their office to, quote, 'discuss the situation,' unquote. She's been in this country for fifty-eight years without any questions asked but now all of a sudden the government is telling her that their records show she's not a legal immigrant. The problem is that she never applied for any kind of work permit or for U.S. citizenship because she never worked outside the home."

"My god, are they going to deport her?"

"Not if I can help it. I'm glad I've got the wedding pretty much under control because Grandma will be my top priority for next week."

Grandma Mendes had come to Minnesota from Cape Verde with her husband when both were twenty-five years old. They became the parents of two daughters, one of whom married Arthur Todd and gave birth to a beautiful baby girl named Martha. Grandpa Mendes worked at the Ford plant in St. Paul, retired at the age of sixty-five and died at seventy-one. Grandma Mendes, now eighty-three, has lived with Martha's parents ever since.

"How did they find her after all these years?" I said.

"She took a bus downtown to go shopping Thursday afternoon and slipped and fell getting off," Martha said. "Her ankle was sprained and the cops who answered the bus driver's call took her to the emergency room at Regions Hospital. Of course the first things they ask for are your driver's license and your insurance card and of course she didn't have either one. Things went downhill from there and Grandma called me from the hospital."

"Did they treat her ankle?"

"After I showed up they did."

"Well, good luck dealing with Immigration," I said. She thanked me and we made kissy sounds and signed off.

"What's going on at home?" Al asked.

"Sherlock's sleeping on my pillow twenty-three hours a day," I said.

"Pretty soft."

"And Immigration wants to deport Grandma Mendes to Cape Verde."

"Far out."

I filled Al in on the details of Grandma Mendes's misfortune while we walked to the lodge for the official Celebration Dinner. We agreed that she was lucky to have a sharp lawyer like Martha for a granddaughter.

The circular dining room was filling rapidly, the decibel level was rising and the smell of alcohol was in the air as we looked around for a place to sit. We saw two pairs of hands waving near the outer ring of tables and recognized the faces below them. One of the hands pointed to two empty chairs. It was an offer we couldn't refuse.

"Hi, Allie Wallie," said Angie.

"Hi, Allie Wallie's pally," said Roxie.

We returned the greetings and sat down. "Aren't you working tonight?" I asked.

"Jeez, a girl's gotta eat," said Roxie.

"Can't turn a trick on an empty stomach," said Angie.

"They say an army travels on its stomach," Al said. "I suppose that's also true of a gaggle of goodtime girls."

"You'd be surprised what we can do on our stomachs," Roxie said.

"That's more information than we need," I said. "Let's talk about something else. Did you catch any fish today?"

"Caught a couple of suckers this afternoon," Roxie said. "But I suppose that's more information than you need."

"Dumb question, Mitchie," Al said. "What sort of catch do you expect from hookers?"

"Let's talk about the weather," I said. Facing a third consecutive night away from Martha, I didn't want to hear even double entendres about sex.

When we'd finished the meal, the women got up to "mingle with the crowd." Again Roxie put her soft warm lips against my ear and whispered, "Remember, Mitchie, into these pants any time, free of charge." As I watched the movement of her ass retreating in the skintight jeans, I was forced to remind myself that I'd be embracing Martha in less than twenty-four hours.

Another moment of silence was held for Alex Gordon before the grand finale began. Speeches were given, prizes were awarded and somebody won the raffle for a boat and motor. Lieutenant Governor Aaron Ross, dead cigar stub protruding from mouth, accepted the Governor's Trophy for the biggest walleye (Trish Valentine's wasn't allowed in the competition) and for the most fish caught. His acceptance speech sounded like the kickoff of his gubernatorial campaign.

"What a windbag," Al said. "Please don't let him get elected."

"It'll be close," I said. "The voting public is split almost dead even between Democrats and Republicans."

As the program ended and the drinking resumed, I saw Roxie leave the room holding hands with a middle-aged, sagging-bellied member of the governor's staff. I felt a twang of envy and again reminded myself that Martha's open arms would be waiting for me on the morrow.

Chapter Eight

Waiting for Bordeaux

WE SLEPT UNTIL EIGHT O'CLOCK Sunday morning and barely made it to the dining room, where they stopped serving breakfast at nine. Normally the media crowd would be clearing out and heading for home, but on this day we were milling about in the lounge like chickens in a pen, waiting to hear from Doctor Louis Bordeaux, the Crow Wing County medical examiner.

I caught up with Ann Rogers as she bustled about the room talking to reporters and asked, "What time do you expect the autopsy report?"

"Haven't heard from Doctor Bordeaux yet this morning," Ann said. "I'll make an announcement as soon as I do."

"So we've probably got time to go to our cabin and pack?"

"If you pack quick," she said as she turned and hurried away.

"Quickly," I said, but only Al heard me.

"Quickly what?" he asked.

"I was correcting Ann. She said we should pack quick but the correct word is quickly."

"Oh, god, are you into the picky grammar thing again?"

"Can't help it," I said. "It's a knee-jerk reaction. I almost had to stuff my hat into my mouth listening to Henry in the boat yesterday."

"Henry's job is to find fish, not teach them to speak proper English," Al said.

"So what is taught in a school of fish?"

"Big fish teach little fish to keep their mouths shut. That's why we didn't catch any yesterday."

We packed quickly and returned to the lodge to wait impatiently for Doctor Bordeaux, who we hoped would be arriving shortly. The weather was improving and we were eager to get on the road.

While packing my fishing gear I remembered our guide's puzzlement about Alex Gordon's missing lifejacket. The mystery of its whereabouts was still bugging me when we returned to the lodge. I beckoned Al to follow me and we intercepted Ann Rogers, who was touring the lounge trying to keep everybody calm. I asked her if anyone had gone through Gordon's personal effects in his cabin. Ann replied that she and a member of Madrigal's security staff had searched the room and packed everything they found for transport home.

"Was there a lifejacket in his room?" I asked.

"No," she said. "Why are you asking about a lifejacket?"

"Because our guide said he saw Alex wearing his own personal lifejacket Thursday morning, but he wasn't wearing one Friday morning when he fell out of the boat. If he wasn't wearing it and it wasn't in his room, where is it?"

Ann thought about it for a moment and said, "I can't imagine. Maybe he dropped it somewhere while he was getting his fishing gear into the boat."

"Hard to imagine him being that careless with his personal lifejacket."

She shook her head. "I don't know what to tell you."

"What all was in the boat?" I asked.

"A rod for trolling and his tackle box, I guess," Ann said.

"Minnow bucket?" Al asked.

"I suppose so. Look, guys, I really don't know for sure what all was in the boat. You'd have to ask the sheriff. He took custody of everything that came out of it. Said it was evidence from an accident scene."

"I think I will ask the sheriff," I said. "You got his phone number?"

"No," she said. "But I'm sure you can get it at the desk here in the lodge."

This was something I could do while we were waiting for Doctor Bordeaux. I went to the desk and got the sheriff's number. I added it to the numbers stored in my cell phone for possible future use and then called it. A woman answered and identified herself as Shirley. I asked for the sheriff and she informed me that Sheriff Holmberg did not come in on Sundays. I should have expected that.

"Can I help you with something?" Shirley asked.

"My name is Warren Mitchell and I'm a reporter for the *St. Paul Daily Dispatch*," I said. "And I'm looking for the list of evidence removed from the boat involved in the drowning at Madrigal's Friday morning. Can you help me with that?"

"Oh, I'm afraid not," Shirley said. "You'd definitely have to talk to Sheriff Holmberg about anything to do with evidence."

"Could you give me his home number?"

"Not if I want to keep my job. Sorry, but Sheriff Holmberg is very particular about getting calls at home unless it's an emergency."

I had expected that but figured it was worth a try. "When will the sheriff be in?" I asked.

"He's always here by seven o'clock on Monday morning," she said. "Did you want to leave a message?"

I gave her my cell number and the number at my desk in St. Paul, thanked her and said, "Goodbye, Shirley."

"Have a good day, Mr. Warren," Shirley said.

We found Trish Valentine curled up in an overstuffed arm chair and she agreed to share it, with me perched on the left arm and Al on the right. This took the load off my feet and gave me a vantage point for looking down Trish's partially unbuttoned blouse. After all, it's a reporter's duty to observe everything within observable range. In this case I observed two partially uncovered, perfectly formed mammaries that must have been propped up from below by a sturdy support bra. Mitch Mitchell reporting live.

Trish asked what we'd been talking to Ann Rogers about and I said nothing in particular, just chitchat about the weekend. Trish's expression indicated that she did not believe me, but before she could follow up Ann Rogers shouted, "Attention, please. Please give me your attention." She was holding her cell phone in her right hand.

When the room grew quiet, Ann said, "I'm afraid I have bad news for you. Doctor Bordeaux has been in an accident and was taken to the hospital in Brainerd in an ambulance. I'm calling the hospital now to see if I can find out more about his injuries."

"Oh, my god," Al said. "What if they keep him in the hospital?"

"Maybe we go to the hospital," I said.

"Good idea," Trish said. "Trish Valentine reporting live from the bedside of Doctor Louis Bordeaux, Crow Wing County medical examiner." She uncurled her body and legs and rose from the chair.

"It's too early to crash the hospital," I said. "What if he's in critical condition? For the moment I think we just sit and wait for more word from Ann."

Trish plopped back down. "I suppose you're right," she said. "They'd probably throw our asses out if thirty people all went traipsing up to the hospital now."

"I was thinking more of two people slipping out of here quietly while the rest of the mob wasn't looking," I said.

Trish rose from the chair again. "How about four people? I'm off to have a quiet talk with my cameraman. Bye, boys, maybe see you at the hospital."

"Why did I mention going to the hospital out loud?" I said after she'd gone.

"Because you love to hear her say 'Trish Valentine reporting live,'" Al said.

We slid our butts off the chair arms and sat back to back sharing the seat, with our legs hanging over the arms. The rumble of voices filled the air around us and I was half asleep when Ann Rogers again called for our attention. She positioned herself in front of the exit before delivering the news.

"Doctor Bordeaux has a head injury and is being kept in the hospital overnight for observation," Ann said. This brought a chorus of groans.

"And in case any of you have ideas about going to the hospital, they're not letting any media in," she said. More groans.

"If all goes well, Doctor Bordeaux will be released in the morning and will come here to give his autopsy report." A third round of groans.

"What time?" somebody asked.

"That hasn't been determined," Ann said. "I'll let you know as soon as I find out." She turned and ducked out the door.

"Now what?" Al said, hauling himself out of the chair.

"Now we call the desk," I said getting to my feet. "I'm betting we have another night together in our cabin by the lake."

"Somehow I had a better roommate in mind for tonight."

"Likewise, I'm sure."

"That's kind of the shits, ain't it guys?" said a female voice behind me. I turned and found myself looking into Roxie's upturned face.

"That's a fair assessment of the situation," I said.

"Huh?" Roxie said.

"That means I agree with you; it is the shits."

"Gives you girls another night's work," Al said.

"That's a fact," Angie said. "Maybe we can even slip in an extra John this afternoon."

"If somebody nice bought us a drink we could watch the traffic in the bar," Roxie said. She stepped forward and pressed her soft warm body tight against mine. "Or Mitchie could come to my place for a freebie," she whispered.

I put my hands on her shoulders and pushed myself away. "Not going to happen," I said. "And the bar isn't open until lunch time. This is Sunday in Minnesota, remember?"

"You're no fun," Roxie said. "Come on, Angie, let's go mingle with some of those hot guys over by the fireplace." And away they went to talk to a couple of young TV reporters with perfectly blow-combed hair.

"Let's us go where it's quiet and call the desk," I said. I led the way through the outside door with Al a step behind. I called Gordon Holmquist, the Sunday city editor, gave him the bad news and asked if we should stay for the next day's meeting with Doctor Bordeaux. Gordon said he'd call Don O'Rourke at his home and ask for instructions. "Sit tight. I'll get back to you right away," he said.

Five minutes after that conversation, my cell phone rang. "Must be Gordon," I said. Instead it was Don O'Rourke.

"What the hell's going on up there?" Don asked.

I filled him in on the postponement of the autopsy report and asked if we should stay another night. The fingers of my empty hand were crossed, hoping he'd say no.

"Is everybody else staying?" he said.

I had to tell the truth. "It looks like it. There hasn't been a rush for the parking lot."

"The guy accidentally fell out of a boat and drowned, right?"

"That's what it looks like, but there's one little hitch. The guy normally wore a lifejacket that he brought along with him, but for some reason he wasn't wearing it when he fell out of the boat and the jacket wasn't found in his room. I don't know if anybody but us is aware of the missing jacket."

"Wasn't it in the boat?" Don asked.

"Don't know," I said. "The sheriff has custody of everything that was in the boat and he's not taking calls until Monday morning."

After a moment of silence, Don said, "Oh, what the hell, stay for the autopsy report and talk to the sheriff. But don't put any fancy dinners or high-buck bottles of wine on your expense accounts."

"You don't have to worry about me with wine but Al drinks only the finest French imports," I said.

"Tell him the paper will pay for one glass of house red," Don said. "And get your butts on the road as soon as the press conference is over tomorrow."

"Aye, aye, sir," I said, but Don had already hung up.

"From the look on your face I assume we're staying," Al said.

"We're waiting for Bordeaux. I shouldn't have mentioned the missing lifejacket."

"Too late to divest yourself of that. So what do we do the rest of the day?"

"Well, there's always lunch to be eaten. And after that—the sun is out and the temperature is rising. We could go fishing."

"Can we find the walleyes without our trusty fishing guide?"

"According to local piscatorial experts, the walleyes are in the water, and the water is right there," I said, pointing toward the lake.

"Very professional. You could be a reporter," Al said.

"Thanks. Right now I'm going to report our new schedule to Martha, and I suggest you do the same with Carol." He agreed, and we separated to make our calls.

As I expected, Martha was not happy with my report. "Couldn't you come home today and get the autopsy results by phone or e-mail or carrier pigeon tomorrow?" she asked.

"It's a matter of showing the flag," I said. "Remember, we're competing with everybody from Trish Valentine down to the bloggers on the Web, and they're all staying another night. The hand that feeds us wants us to stay here with them."

"Well, the arms that love you want you to be here with them."

"Believe me, I'd much rather be with those arms but the command to stay with the troops has been given. I promise I'll be in your arms tomorrow."

"The arms will be open and waiting. So what are you doing with the rest of today?"

"We're going fishing without the TV cameras this afternoon. I might even catch a walleye to bring home for dinner after I show it live to Trish Valentine."

"Better make it a big one. You're going to need plenty of nourishment after I get done with you."

"Sounds like I'd better fortify myself before I get there," I said.

"Don't waste a lot of time sitting in a restaurant," Martha said. "Get something at the drive through window." This from a vegetarian who wouldn't stop at the Golden Arches if she'd been without food for a week.

Our conversation continued for a few minutes and as we were starting our goodbye ritual Martha said, "Don't forget to call your mother."

"Oh, my god, that's right, it's Mother's Day," I said. "Thank you for reminding me. Mom and Grandma Goodie would give me holy hell if I forgot to call today."

"Just call me your little holy reminder angel."

"I'll call you a lot of other good things as well."

"Just don't call me with any more news about staying another day."

"Can't happen," I said. As I noted earlier, ignorance really is bliss.

After Martha and I had signed off with our customary kissy sounds, I punched in my mother's number. After seven rings I got her voicemail instructing me to leave a message. I should have known that she and Grandma Goodie would be in church at that hour. I left a happy Mother's Day greeting and said I'd call back later in the day.

Al returned and we exchanged what little we'd heard beyond complaints about the schedule change. Al had also called his mother and left a message. "She doesn't go to church that regular any more," he said. "She's probably gone to my sister's for Mother's Day."

I clamped my teeth together to keep from saying "regularly" and we went back to our cabin to read the online edition of the Sunday paper until lunch. In the local section I found a list of things to do with your mother on Mother's Day. I cursed the woman who wrote that piece because I could imagine Mom spotting it in the print edition and reading it aloud to a son who went on goofy fishing expeditions on this of all weekends.

Chapter Nine

Island Bound

I WAS STUFFING THE LAST french fry into my mouth when Roxie pulled up a chair and sat down at our lunch table. "Hi, Mitchie; hi, Allie," she said. She was wearing those incredible jeans and a too-small T-shirt with a picture of a sea turtle on the front. The word ENDANGERED was stretched to the limit across her boobs.

We both greeted her and I asked what was endangered, the turtle on the shirt or the body parts inside the shirt. She giggled and said, "All three."

"So where's your bosom buddy?" Al asked.

"She's got herself an all-day John," Roxie said. "One of the creeps from the governor's office is paying her big bucks to go fishing with him this afternoon, have dinner with him at some fancy place in Brainerd and play games with him in his bedroom all night. Wish I could hook a sucker like that."

"Sounds like Angie really hit the jackpot," Al said. "How are you doing?"

"I struck out this morning. I suppose you two choir boys are still saving yourselves for your ladies back home."

"That's right," we said in unison.

"We're going to be good boys and go fishing this afternoon," Al said.

"Want company?" Roxie said.

"That's one thing we can't put on the expense account," I said.

"No charge. I got nothing else to do," she said.

"You could be trolling the lodge for that sucker," Al said.

"Business will be better after supper," Roxie said. "If you take me along you might catch something. After all, I *am* a hooker."

Al looked at me and I looked at him. We both shrugged. "Okay," I said. "Meet us on the dock in half an hour. We'll check out a boat and some lifejackets. Do you want us to get you a rod and reel?"

"Never mind," she said. "You won't let me play with the only rod I really want."

* * *

ROXIE WAS ALREADY on the dock when we arrived carrying our rods, tackle boxes, a landing net, three lifejackets and a bucket containing a dozen silver shiner minnows that were almost big enough to filet. She was dressed in a white sleeveless blouse, baggy tan shorts that went down to mid-thigh and white canvas sneakers. The blouse was unbuttoned and hung open revealing a seriously yellow bikini top underneath.

We found our boat and loaded our gear. I sat in the stern seat and took charge of the outboard motor. Roxie grabbed the bow seat and sat facing me, leaving Al the seat in the middle. After detaching the lines that held us to the dock, he dropped in and sat facing the bow so he could look at Roxie—a good choice in my book. The motor started on the first pull and I turned and headed into the bay.

The temperature had risen almost to seventy and the sun was shining in a cloudless sky as I steered the boat toward the underwater rock pile near the island. This seemed like the best place to start our excursion since it was there that most of the fish had been caught the previous day. Three other fishing parties with the same idea were already trolling the area so I joined the parade at a respectful distance from the nearest boat. Al and I put our trolling lines out and we started the routine of cruising back and forth about thirty yards out from the island, which was about half a mile long. The island was heavily wooded with pines and budding deciduous trees behind an uninviting rockbound shoreline. It was not a place you'd go ashore to have a picnic.

Roxie put on her sunglasses. "Time to catch some rays," she said. She peeled off the blouse, pulled off the shorts and stretched out facing Al and me, an eye-catching vision in her electric yellow bikini. I was silently debating whether or not the entire bikini would yield enough fabric to make a man's handkerchief when Roxie reached behind her back and tugged on the knot that secured the top. The knot came untied and the bikini top dropped into her lap. Her breasts, perky with the firmness of youth, popped out and hung suspended, looking like two orbiting globes complete with pinkish-brown polar regions at the tips.

"Hey," Al said. "That's a little too much exposure."

"What's your problem?" Roxie said. "Are you some kind of prude or what?" She bent over and pulled off her sneakers.

"I have no problem looking at your bare tits but there are people in the other boats who might," Al said.

"Fuck 'em," Roxie said. "I gotta get an even tan."

"Then slide down on the seat and keep a low profile," I said. "Or as low as you can with that mountain range sticking up."

"How about I take off the bottom for an all-over tan?"

"No," we both said, again in unison.

"You guys really are old sticks in the mud. Real men pay money to see what I've got."

"Well, these real men don't want you flashing what you've got on a public lake with three other boats sharing the view," I said. "Keep that scanty panty on or I'll take you back to the dock and kick your little bare ass out of the boat."

"What about you, Alsie," Roxie said. "Are you afraid to see what's in my panties?"

"Save it for your clients tonight," Al said. "You'll have guys diving out of the other boats and swimming over here if you take off any more."

"God, what a couple of grumpy old farts you guys are," she said. "You sound like my grandmother." But she slid down as far as she could, stretching out her legs and putting her bare feet against Al's sneakers as she did. I noticed that he didn't pull his feet away. I also noticed that two guys in the nearest neighboring boat were in danger of falling over the side as they leaned our way to ogle Roxie. To prevent another accident, I shut down our motor and drifted for a few minutes to widen the gap between us.

When we resumed trolling, I found it difficult to watch the other boats and tend to my drifting fishing line while my eyes kept drifting back to view the scenic Roxie mountain range. Ah, if Don O'Rourke only knew what his dynamic reporter/photographer duo was doing on company time. God help us if he ever found out. And not even God could help us if Martha and Carol found out.

I missed a strike and lost my minnow to a walleye because of this distraction. I was chasing a replacement minnow around the bucket when Al said, "I hate to say this but I had too much coffee at lunch. It's hitting bottom and I need to get rid of it."

"Well, you can't do it over the side," I said.

"Wouldn't bother me," Roxie said.

"I'm not worried about you," I said. "It's the other boats." One of them had given up and departed, but two were still close enough to require discretion, especially the one that carried a woman and a little girl.

"There's a point sticking out on the south end of the island," Al said. "How about we putz around behind that to where those boats can't see us? Maybe there'll even be a place we can land and I can go pee in the woods."

"Okay. Reel in your line," I said.

"Can I sit up now?" Roxie asked.

"Not until we get around the point and out of sight," I said. "You'll have the boat with two guys following us if you flash those titties."

"Maybe I can line up some business for tonight."

"Not while I'm running the boat. Keep those hooters down."

Al reeled his line in and I opened the throttle gradually so the roar of the motor wouldn't attract attention to our new course. We eventually reached cruising speed and I took us around the point and turned to run parallel with the shore on that side of the island. There were no boats in sight so I told Roxie to turn around and watch ahead of us for obstacles or shallow water. She knelt on the bow seat facing forward with her bare breasts sticking out, like the figurehead on the prow of an old-time sailing ship.

The shoreline of the island looked too rocky to risk a landing. Al was asking me to slow down so he could pee over the side when I spotted a small patch of open sand. "Keep your fly zipped," I said, pointing toward the miniature beach. "It looks like we could slip in there."

"Hurry up and do it or my fly is going to get wet," Al said.

I swung the bow toward the strip of sand. "Here we go, just like D-Day, except nobody is shooting at us."

"Yeah, only this is P-Day and the danger is from within."

"You guys are just plain nuts," Roxie said.

"Don't worry about us. Just keep your eyes open for rocks and stuff," I said.

"I'm watching," she said. And then she screamed, "Turn right. Quick."

Ignoring the grammatical malfunction, I turned right quickly, and we skimmed past the tip of a rock six inches below the surface on the left side. "Good call," I said.

"I told you I'm watching," Roxie said.

We reached the beach without any further emergencies. I cut the motor and lifted the propeller out of the water about ten feet before the bow hit sand and we slid to a stop. We were actually still moving when Roxie leaped out over the bow and dropped her bikini bottom onto the sand. "Me first," she yelled, running naked into the trees. "I gotta pee worse than you do."

Al clambered out and trotted to a different part of the woods. I took my time getting out of the boat and dragging it a couple of feet further onto the sand. Although I could feel nature's beckoning, the call wasn't urgent enough to require leaving the beach before Roxie came back to get her bikini bottom.

Soon she appeared, dodging rocks and fallen sticks on tiptoe like a barefoot naked nymph. She picked up the swatch of yellow and waved it at me. "On or off?" she asked. Before I could reply the cell phone in my pocket played its tune. I pulled it out and checked the caller ID. It was Mom. I punched the button to answer.

"Leave it off for all I care," I said to Roxie.

"Leave what off?" said my mother.

"That wasn't for you," I said. "There is another, um . . . there are other people here."

"What are they leaving off?" she asked. In full frontal nudity, Roxie was walking toward me swaying her hips from side to side. She was displaying a complete bikini wax job with a gleaming silver stud decorating the denuded area.

"Uh, the radio," I said to Mom. "One of them asked about playing the portable radio."

"Where are you?"

"Al and I are fishing," I said. A more detailed and accurate response would have included the words "dangerously close to a naked female." Roxie was almost upon me, waving the bikini bottom above her head and rotating her physical bottom in a manner that inspired my manhood to respond and beads of sweat to emerge all across my forehead.

"Your message said you'd call me again but I haven't heard from you," Mom said.

"Look, Mom, I can't talk right now," I said. "I'm trying to hold a fishing rod and steer the boat and I'll drop something into the lake, probably my phone. I'll call you back in a little while, okay?" Roxie pressed her naked tits against my shoulder, giggled and kissed my unoccupied ear.

"Was that a woman laughing?" Mom asked.

"It was the radio. Al turned it on. Say hi to Grandma." I shut off the phone and tried to push Roxie away. She clamped her teeth onto my earlobe and pulled the bikini bottom over the top of my head and down over my eyes. I shut my eyes and I was trying to peel the bikini off when I heard Al's voice. "Having fun, you two?"

"Get her off me," I said. The bikini slid up and off, and when I opened my eyes I saw that Al had both hands clamped around Roxie's waist, trying to pull her away from me. Luckily, she released the dental grip my earlobe before he gave a yank that sent them both sprawling onto the sand, Al on his butt and Roxie in his lap. The thought of taking a picture with the cell phone in my hand flashed briefly through my mind but I decided that provoking my rescuer could be counterproductive.

Al pushed Roxie off and she rolled in the sand, still clutching the bikini. They both sat up and looked at each other. Roxie was laughing but Al said, "Quit playing games and put your clothes on. I found something in the woods that we need to look at."

Chapter Ten

Excavating

"What are we going to look at?" I asked as Al started toward the trees.

"You'll see when we get there," he said.

"Wait for me," Roxie said. "I gotta get my shoes." She had put on the bikini bottom and was running on tiptoes across the sand toward the boat.

Al and I waited at the edge of the woods and watched her slip on the sneakers and snuggle her boobs into the bikini top. When she caught up to us Al continued leading the way through the trees and underbrush. About thirty feet in from the beach he stopped and pointed to a small patch of ground that had recently been disturbed.

"Something or somebody was digging here," Al said. "I almost started to piss on it."

"It looks like somebody might have buried something," I said.

"What would anybody bury here?" Roxie said.

"No idea," Al said.

"Maybe somebody caught too many fish and buried what was over the limit," I said.

"If that's what it is, the fishing must have been a hell of a lot better on this side of the island than it was on ours," Al said.

"One way to find out," I said. I dropped to my knees and began removing hands full of sandy soil from the burial spot. Al got down beside me and started to dig while Roxie stood over us watching the excavation project.

I looked up at Roxie. "You could help, too," I said. "Busy hands are happy hands."

"No way I'm getting down on my bare knees on that rough ground," she said. "I'll be your rooting section."

"That's good because I just hit a root," Al said. He scraped away another inch of sand. "No, wait. It isn't a root. It's something bigger."

He had uncovered a patch of khaki canvas fabric. We both continued to scrape and dig and the object grew in size until we realized what it was.

"It's a lifejacket," we said, speaking in unison for the third time that day.

"Looks like an expensive one, like you'd get from a place like L.L. Bean," Al said.

We resumed scraping, our hands moving so fast that we created a sandstorm until the entire jacket, which was folded double, was uncovered. A small REI logo was showing above a breast pocket. And on the pocket flap were three letters printed with a black magic marker.

"Are those somebody's initials?" Roxie said. Bare knees or not, she was on the ground beside me. "What are they?"

"A.R.G.," Al said. "'ARG,' like all the pirates say."

"Or could they stand for Alex R. Gordon?" I said.

"They could," he said. "If his middle name started with 'R.'"

"The guy that drowned?" Roxie said.

"That's the one," I said.

"Jeez! What's his lifejacket doing here?" she asked.

"A very good question with no very good answer," Al said. He grabbed a corner of the lifejacket and started to pull it out of its resting place.

"Don't move it," I said. "Leave it just the way we found it and don't put any more of your fingerprints on it. We need to get hold of the sheriff."

"It's Sunday," Al said. "You can't get him, remember?"

"If I tell Shirley what we've found, I bet we can talk to the sheriff. I'm glad I plugged his office number into my phone this morning. Why don't you shoot some pix with your cell phone while I make the call?"

"I can do a lot better than cell phone pix," Al said. He stood up, pulled a small, flat digital camera out of a pants pocket and started shooting.

"Lucky you brought that camera," Roxie said.

"It's not luck. It's called being prepared. I'm like a Boy Scout. I never go anywhere without this little guy."

"Sheriff's office, Shirley speaking," said the voice on my cell phone. "How can I help you?"

"Hi, Shirley, it's reporter Warren Mitchell again," I said. "This time my problem is a little more urgent." I told her what we'd found and she agreed that I should talk to the sheriff. But she still wouldn't give me his home number. She said she would call him and have him call me. I gave her my number and ended the call. Less than three minutes later I was talking to Sheriff Val Holmberg.

The sheriff listened to my story without interrupting. When I'd finished, he said, "That's pretty damn weird. You say the initials are the same as the guy who drowned?"

"The first and last are right; I don't know about the middle one," I said. "And yesterday our guide told us that he'd seen Alex wearing a lifejacket that didn't come from the resort on Thursday, the day before he died. The guide was wondering why he wasn't wearing it when he fell out of the boat Friday morning."

"At first I was wondering why the victim wasn't wearing a lifevest myself," Holmberg said. "Then I figured he was one of those smartass government guys who don't think the laws are meant for them. But what the hell is his vest doing buried out there?"

"I don't know, but I'm pretty sure Alex didn't put it here," I said.

"Then who the hell did?"

"Looks like your accident investigation just became a little more complicated."

"Well, now wait a minute. We don't know for sure that it's his jacket."

"I'd say the odds are pretty good that it is. Are you coming out to look at it?"

"I guess I got no choice," he said, sounding less than enthusiastic. "Don't you guys move anything or touch anything. I'll round up a couple of deputies and we'll see you as soon as we can get there."

"How long will it be?" I asked.

"By the time we get to the lake, get the boat in the water and get out to the island, it'll be at least an hour."

"Good. That means I have time to call my mother."

"What? Call your mother?" He sounded like that was the craziest idea he'd ever heard.

"Don't you know it's Mother's Day?" I said.

"Oh, yeah, that's right. I sent my mother flowers a couple of days ago."

Now why hadn't I thought of that?

* * *

WE WENT BACK TO THE BEACH and sat on the warm sand to wait for the sheriff. Roxie took off the bikini and stretched out naked on her belly with her shorts rolled up for padding under her chin. Al called Carol to tell her about our new discovery. I got on the phone to my mother and grandmother. The former made me feel guilty for not calling earlier and the latter gave me holy hell for not seeking heaven by going to church.

"Maybe I did go to church," I said. "How can you be so sure that I didn't?"

"Because you called here and left a message during the time that all normal churches have services," Grandma Goodie said. No sense trying to fool the old girl. "You need to start thinking seriously about saving your soul, Warnie Baby."

"I'm counting on your prayers to do that," I said.

"Well, I won't be around forever, Warnie Baby. It's time you thought about that."

I didn't want to think about that. I told her I loved her and ended the call. Al was still talking to Carol, so I called Martha Todd and told her what we'd dug up.

"I hope that doesn't mean you'll have to stay up there even longer," Martha said.

I hadn't thought about that. "Me, too," I said. "Maybe we'll find out that it isn't Alex's lifejacket. Or maybe there will be an explanation that doesn't lead to a homicide investigation."

"Do you really think either of those maybes is a real possibility?"

"Not really. But maybe I can cover the story from the office by phone."

"I certainly hope so. We're getting married in six days, remember? Plus I've got to deal with Grandma Mendes's legal problem this week. I need you here for moral support."

"Is that all you need me for?"

"You know darn well what I need you for. And Sherlock misses you, too."

"Is he still snoozing on my pillow?"

"Twenty-three hours a day," Martha said. "I'll never get all the cat hair off that pillowcase."

When our conversation ended, it occurred to me how surreal it had been to talk to Martha while staring steadily at the soft pink mounds of Roxie's bare ass. Next it occurred to me that as much as I enjoyed the view, it wouldn't be appropriate to share it with company.

"Hey, Roxie, it's time to put your shirt and shorts on," I said. "The sheriff could be here any time now."

"Would you be embarrassed if I was still tanning my tush and titties?"

"Yes, and you would be, too. I don't think you're a total idiot."

"Wow. You sure know how to flatter a girl."

"You know what I mean," I said.

Roxie rose and, with a series of grand flourishes, brushed the sand off various parts of her body and put on both bits of the bikini. "The sun's getting low anyway," she said as she shook the sand out of her shorts. She stepped into them and walked back to the boat to get her shirt.

"Carol says hi," Al said as he put his phone away.

"Is that all she says?" I asked.

"She also says we better not get stuck up here covering a murder investigation."

"That's funny, Martha said basically the same thing."

"So what are you thinking?"

"I'm thinking that I wish you'd never had to take that piss."

"Me, too, but that's water over the dam."

"Really? I thought it was water under the trees."

The sound of a distant boat motor turned our attention toward the lake. The Crow Wing County sheriff's boat carrying three men was rounding the point. We walked to the water's edge to wave them toward our narrow wedge of beach. For the first time, we saw the V-shaped mark of another boat's bow carved into the sand next to ours.

Chapter Eleven

Hush Money

THE AVAILABLE SPACE FOR LANDING on the beach was wider to the left of our boat than the opening on the right, so the left side was where the sheriff's driver wanted to land. Unfortunately that was also the side bearing the mark of a previous landing. With much yelling, waving and pointing, we persuaded the new arrivals to take the spot on the right, which forced the driver to squeeze into a tight space between our boat and a large, jagged rock that jutted out from the beach. He made it with inches to spare on both sides.

With his boat safely on the sand, the sheriff's first question was obvious. "Why in hell are so determined to run us onto that rock?"

"We're trying to preserve evidence," I said. "Come and look." Sheriff Val Holmberg climbed over the bow of his boat onto the beach and followed me. I pointed to the groove in the sand, which Al was photographing. "That mark was probably made by the person who buried the lifejacket."

Holmberg walked slowly along the beach, studying the mark and the area around it. "That footprint one of yours?" he asked, pointing to an almost indiscernible disturbance in the sand.

"No, I don't think so," I said. "We all jumped out on the other side of our boat and never even looked over here until we came back to the water to wave at you."

"Not much to go on. I'll have my forensics guy photograph the boat mark and the footprint but I don't think they'll tell us a whole hell of a lot. The footprint is weak and boat bottoms are pretty much all alike. Now, where's this buried lifevest?"

"Follow me," I said. I led him into the woods and as he and his two deputies followed me through the trees he said, "I see you boys brought along a little playmate for the afternoon."

"She invited herself along."

"I'll bet she did. What's she charging? Is she giving you a special two-for-one rate?"

"It's not what it looks like," I said. "We're not buying and she's not selling."

"What do you means she's not selling?" Holmberg said. "I hear that she and her partner have been peddling their little asses all over the place this weekend."

"What I meant was Al and I are not buying what she's been selling. She came along for the ride when she heard we were going fishing."

"I suppose you've got a bridge you want to sell me too."

"Believe what you want to believe—but the fact is that we haven't been doing anything but talk to her and look at her in a bikini."

"So are both you guys gay or what?"

"I'm married and he's getting married Saturday," Al said. He'd finished shooting pictures of the marks in the sand and had caught up with us in time to hear the sheriff's comments. "We've been tasked with keeping each other on the straight and narrow."

"That can't be easy," Holmberg said. "Those two are a lot cuter than most of the whores we get up here."

We'd reached the burial site and I pointed out the lifejacket. Holmberg stopped, put his hands on his hips and looked at our excavation. "I suppose you trampled all over the ground around where you dug so there's no hope of finding footprints," he said.

"I'm sorry that we weren't more careful," I said. "We never imagined we'd find anything like this."

"Well, we'll tape it off and process the scene. It'll take a while so you boys might as well go back to Madrigal's."

"Are you calling it a crime scene?" I asked.

"I ain't calling it anything right now," Holmberg said. "We don't know for sure who the vest belongs to and if it was stolen or what. Those are the things we need to investigate."

I had to ask the big question. "Do you think whoever buried this might have murdered the owner?"

Holmberg stared at me for a moment before he answered. "There's probably a lot simpler explanation than that. This ain't the big city where people go around killing each other over every little thing."

"Maybe it was a big thing," Al said.

"Big or little, we got no reason to believe that anybody connected to this vest was murdered. I can see that you're looking to blow this way out proportion the way the media always likes to do. But before you boys get all hot and bothered about this, why don't you go on back to the lodge, tell everybody what you found and have a nice relaxing drink. After that take your little hooker out to your cottage and take turns screwing her. You know, if you both do it you won't be able to rat on each other. But what ever you do, don't go away from Madrigal's until you give me your statements tomorrow. And that goes for the hooker, too."

"What time will you be there for our statements?" Al asked.

"I'll be there when I get there. Have a good evening, boys." He turned to the nearest deputy. "Run a tape around the area and let's get started before it gets dark."

As Al and I walked back to the beach, I said, "I'm all for getting back to Madrigal's before the sun goes down, but there's no way we're telling everybody what we found."

"I assume you are going to tell the city desk what we found," Al said.

"Trish Valentine can read the story live in the *Daily Dispatch* tomorrow," I said.

"With photos taken live by Alan Jeffrey."

* * *

OBVIOUSLY THERE WAS NO WAY we were taking turns with Roxie, either. Our problem with Roxie was convincing her to keep her mouth shut. She was just dying to blab about our discovery to everybody who would listen. Al and I weren't about to let that happen.

"You have to swear that you won't tell anybody about that lifejacket or we will lock you in the closet in our cottage all night," I said.

"There's no lock on the closet doors," Roxie said.

"We'll barricade the door with every piece of furniture in the cottage. You won't be able to make a dime turning tricks tonight."

"That's the answer. You pay me what I get for an all-nighter and I won't tell anybody about finding the jacket."

"No way. You swear to keep quiet about the lifejacket or we keep you where you can't find an all-nighter."

"That's against the law," she said.

"So is selling your ass," I said. "How about I call the Brainerd cops and tell them that you're soliciting men here at the resort?" Of course this was a bluff. The resort was under the sheriff's jurisdiction and he was already aware of Roxie's illegal activities. And for some reason he was letting them continue.

The bluff fooled Roxie, and we were able to settle on a trade agreement. We promised to put Roxie's dinner and the next day's breakfast on our room tab in return for her silence until the story and pix were in print and online. It was obvious that her vow of silence was painful but we had convinced her that we'd put her out of business one way or another if she talked. We shook hands to seal the deal and then she insisted on hugging us both before heading for her cottage to shower and get dressed for her evening manhunt.

"Would you really lock Roxie in our closet all night?" Al asked when we were back in our cottage.

"You bet I would," I said.

"What if she started screaming?"

"I'd gag her with her own bikini."

"That wouldn't work. It's not big enough to cover her mouth."

"Then I'd use something bigger, like a band-aid."

I set up my laptop and sent an e-mail to the city desk telling them we had a page one story with pix coming.

"How are you going to explain our landing on the island?" Al said. "You can't write that I had to take a whiz."

"I'll say we wanted to stretch our legs after two hours of sitting cramped up in a boat," I said. "Most readers will accept that at face value, and guys who go fishing in boats will figure that we had to take a whiz."

"Are you including Roxie in the story?"

"Who is Roxie? I never heard of her—and neither will Martha or Carol."

"That's my boy," said Al. "You got to have moxie when it comes to Roxie."

Chapter Twelve

The Autopsy

THE FIRST THING I DID upon waking Monday morning was fire up my laptop and pull up the *Daily Dispatch* online edition. Halfway down the front page was my story, accompanied by Al's photos of the lifejacket lying uncovered in its intended grave and of Sheriff Val Holmberg leaning over the site. The pop out was a quote from Holmberg: ". . . we got no reason to believe that anybody connected to this vest was murdered."

"Looks good," Al said.

"Let's get over to breakfast and see if any of the troops have seen it," I said.

Apparently none of them had. Although the dining room was already crowded with men and women of the media when we arrived, nobody gave us a second look.

We found a table next to a window and scanned the room for Roxie, but she wasn't anywhere in sight.

"Lucky us, we get off free on the dinner and breakfast in exchange for a closed mouth deal," Al said. Roxie hadn't shown up Sunday evening to collect her free dinner so we assumed she had acquired a paying customer for the evening. Either her all-nighter was also providing breakfast somewhere else or the action was continuing in the bedroom.

"She can pay for a semester of grad school after this weekend," I said.

"Hats off for the working girl."

"And everything else off, too."

"I'd like to get off—for home," Al said.

"We'll be off as soon as the ME and the sheriff let us off."

"Oh, hey, here comes someone who looks pissed off."

The someone in question was Ann Rogers, who was headed our way at almost a gallop. The scowl on her face would have caused a raging, breast-beating gorilla to stop pounding its chest and back away. However, because we quiet, unassuming humans were seated against a wall of glass, we had no choice but to stand our ground. Or, actually, sit our ground.

Ann came to a halt inches from our table and tried to tower over us. Being only five-foot-four, her effort to create an intimidating image failed. Ann's eyes while standing were level with mine while sitting.

"What is this crap about a buried lifejacket with Alex Gordon's initials on it?" she said.

"Ah, you've been reading the morning *Daily Dispatch*," I said, smiling my brightest smile. "Good for you. And how are you this morning, Ann?"

"I'm ready to rip your eyes out, that's how I am," said the governor's new press secretary. "I ask you again, what is this shit?"

"Please, don't use words that I have to bleep out of my story when I quote you," I said. "It reflects poorly on your boss."

Her lips were forming another obscenity, this one starting with an F, when she stopped, puffed out her cheeks and held her breath until her face turned crimson. "You're right," she said as she finally exhaled. "I'll ask again very professionally and non-profanely, why wasn't I informed about this lifejacket before your story went in the paper?"

"I really wanted to ask you for a comment—and the governor, too—but I was afraid you'd broadcast it to everybody else in this room and there'd go my scoop. If you'd like to give me a comment now for the follow-up story I'll be writing today,

I'm ready to take it." I pulled my mini-tape recorder out of my shirt pocket and put my finger on the switch.

"I have no comment on your bull . . . on your story and the crummy, sensational pictures right now, and neither does the governor. I just wanted to know why we weren't informed and I guess you answered that with your selfish babble about a scoop. Did you also tell the sheriff not to contact us?"

"No, I guess I just got lucky there," I said. "The sheriff probably never thought about contacting you before he comes here to take our statements today. He had to work fast to finish processing the scene while there was still daylight, and anyway, he doesn't seem to be the publicity hound type."

"Did you say he's coming here to take your statements?" Ann asked.

"I did and he is."

"Well, he'll get my statement, too, whether he wants it or not, and he won't like what he hears, I guarantee you that."

"One of the hazards of his job," Al said.

The look Ann gave him would have sent the aforementioned gorilla away at full speed. "One of the hazards of your job might be that you won't hear about the governor's next photo op until it's over," she said.

"How will I survive?" Al said.

"Okay, you two, knock it off," I said. "Do you have any real questions, Ann?"

"Yes, I do," she said. "How about you filling me in on what you left out of the story?"

"I think I covered pretty much everything. The island, the hiding place, the lifejacket, the initials, the mark of another boat, the sheriff's comments. I don't know what else to tell you."

"You might start with the real reason you were tramping around in the woods on that island."

"To stretch our poor cramped legs," I said.

"Full bladder," Al said. "Like George Washington, I cannot tell a lie."

"Don't guys just go over the side, disgusting as that sounds?" Ann said.

"Two other boats close by," Al said. He pointed at me. "The old prude here didn't want me showing off."

"They might have reported us for polluting the fishing grounds," I said.

Ann's face turned a darker red. "I'm sorry I asked."

"Anything else you'd like to ask us?"

She thought for a moment before she said, "You played up the sheriff's statement that no crime was involved. Do you think that's true?"

"Correction: it was the city editor who played up the sheriff's statement, not me. I don't think Alex buried his lifejacket on the island. And why would someone else do it if he wasn't covering up a crime?"

"Oh, god, so you think Alex was murdered?" Ann said.

"I really can't think of any other explanation for the buried jacket," I said.

"Who would want to kill Alex?"

"I can think of several reporters who might. But seriously, I don't know. I need to find out more about Alex's life. What he might have done and who he might have done it to. Maybe you can help me there."

"Why would I help you after what you did to me this morning?" Ann said. "One day on the job and the governor thinks I screwed it up."

"I'll explain it to the governor. You'll help me because, I assume, you want to see justice done and the killer, if there is one, punished."

"I don't know that much about Alex outside of what he does in the office. You'd have to ask his wife about his home life, family, friends and all that."

"I intend to do that as soon as we get back to St. Paul."

"Why wait? She's in a cottage less than a hundred yards away," Ann said.

"Which one?" I asked. "We'll go see her right now."

"I wasn't serious. You wouldn't actually bother her in her grief today, would you?"

"That's what reporters do. That's why everyone loves the press. I'd have bothered her last night if I'd known she was here."

"If you spent more time working and less time entertaining those two cheap little whores from Bemidji you'd have known that Mari flew in while they were searching for Alex."

"Are the whores really cheap?" Al asked. "We haven't asked about prices yet."

Ann gave him another withering look and turned to me. "Is your photographer friend always such an asshole?"

"Not always. I think you offended him somehow," I said.

"It was the word 'crummy' used to describe my photos," Al said. "'Sensational' I don't mind. 'Crummy' is a gratuitous insult."

"Well, you guys insulted me this morning by running that sensationalized stuff without any prior notice," Ann said. "So I think we're even on that score."

"As I said before, there was no way to swear you to a night of secrecy, being as how providing equal access to information for everyone is in your job description," I said. "Actually, it was a compliment, because I assumed you would do your duty and spread the word."

"That's exactly what I'm going to do now," she said. "I'm going to broadcast the word to everyone in this room and let them tear you to pieces."

"Oh, god, they'll be swarming all over us asking questions about a story they haven't read and doing dumb TV interviews," Al said.

"Trish Valentine will be reporting live about us," I said.

"Give us a five-minute head start so we can get to the cabin and lock the door," I said.

"I'll give you as much head start as you gave me advance warning about that story," Ann said. She turned away from us and raised her voice to a shout. "Please give me your attention, everyone. Can I have your attention please?"

As we were pushing through the outside door we heard her say "*St. Paul Daily Dispatch*." We hit the blacktop running and set a record for the distance between the lodge and our cabin. This gave us time to throw the extra locking bolt before the first knock rattled the front door.

"This is Channel Five; we need to talk to you," said Barry Ziebart's baritone voice between knocks.

"No comment," I yelled through the door. "Talk to the sheriff when he gets here. He's coming to take our statements."

A voice I didn't recognize demanded an interview and I told him the sheriff had ordered us not to speak to the media.

"You *are* the media," the voice said. "And you splashed your story all over the Internet."

I had just told him that we weren't talking to reporters when a familiar female voice asked, "Will you talk to me?" The disconcerting thing about this voice was that it came from behind me. I spun around and found Trish Valentine standing in our living room. Tony, her cameraman, was a step behind her, aiming his lens over her shoulder.

"How the hell did you get in here?" I asked.

"Back door wasn't locked," she said. "Now tell me about finding a lifejacket buried on an island in Gull Lake." She pushed the microphone with the big square Channel Four logo on it to within two inches of my moustache.

I was so stunned that I actually responded. "We were on the island to stretch our legs and found what looked like a burial site. We dug away the sand and there was the lifejacket."

"Was it a Madrigal's lifejacket?" Trish asked.

"No, it was the kind you get at a sporting goods store."

"Do you know what brand it was?"

"REI."

"And it had initials written on it in ink?"

"Yes, A.R.G."

"And you think the 'A' and the 'G' stand for Alex Gordon, the governor's press secretary who drowned in Gull Lake Friday morning?"

At that point I finally came to my senses. "Wait a minute. Stop. That's enough."

"Trish Valentine reporting live from Madrigal's Resort on Gull Lake," Trish said. "Thanks, Mitch, that was great."

"You can't run that," I said.

"Why not?"

"I won't give my permission."

"This is America. Freedom of the press. You may have heard about that." Trish turned away, pushed her cameraman ahead of her and out the back door they went. Al was one step behind her and threw the locking bolt the second the door slammed behind the fleeing Channel Four invaders.

"I can't believe you gave her all that," Al said.

"I was in deep shock at seeing her," I said.

"You'll be in deep doo-doo when Don O'Rourke sees that interview."

"I'll plead insanity."

"I'll confirm it," Al said.

There was knocking and shouting at both doors now, along with faces peering in through every window. "Go away," Al yelled. "No interviews." He dashed from window to window, closing the blinds.

"You gave Channel Four an interview," a man yelled. "You owe us one at Channel Eleven."

"Channel Four broke in illegally and it wasn't really an interview," I yelled. "I'm having them arrested for B and E."

"We'll have you arrested for B and S," said Barry Ziebart. "Just give us a sound bite of what you found."

"Read my story out loud in front of the camera," I said.

More voices mingled in an unintelligible cacophony and then the racket ceased as suddenly as if someone had shut a soundproof door. Al looked out the window and said the mob was retreating. "I wonder why they're leaving," he said. "Looks like they're all headed for the lodge."

"Let's find out," I said. I picked up the phone and dialed "0." When the desk clerk answered I asked if something was happening at the lodge.

"The sheriff and the medical examiner just drove up," he said.

I thanked him, dropped the phone and headed for the door. "Grab your camera and let's go; the autopsy report is here," I said.

Dr. Louis Bordeaux was a roly-poly little man in his late sixties with a hairless dome that gleamed like it was polished and ears that stuck out like the handles on a sugar bowl. He was about five-foot-six in both height and width, and he wore a black suit with a pale lavender shirt and a pink-and-purple paisley tie. He also wore a three-inch-long white bandage that would have stretched from his right eyebrow to his hairline if he'd had either an eyebrow or a hairline.

"Must have really cracked that egg," Al said as Ann Rogers was introducing the doctor in the lodge's main meeting room.

"Humpty Dumpty had a great fall," I said.

"Don't you guys ever quit talking nonsense?" asked Trish Valentine, who as usual was right in front of us.

"Never," I said. "And that also goes for getting even with people who break into houses to steal intelligence."

"Number one, the door wasn't locked so I didn't break in," Trish said. "Number two, I didn't find any intelligence to steal."

I wanted to bop her on top of her little blonde head but the doctor was speaking so I didn't want to risk breaking my tape recorder.

After greeting the gathering, Doctor Bordeaux apologized for the one-day delay, pointed to the bandage on his glistening forehead and said, "This old egg got seriously cracked."

"What did I tell you?" Al said to Trish during the laughter.

"I give up," Trish said.

"You should," I said.

When the laughter ended, Doctor Bordeaux started reading from a written report. After the usual preamble giving name, age and date of death, the report began: "Although Mr. Gordon's body was recovered from the bottom of Gull Lake more than five hours after his boat was discovered in an unmanned condition on the surface of said lake, no lake water was found in Mr. Gordon's lungs." A chorus of exclamations from his audience caused him to pause.

When the room was quiet, the doctor continued. "This would indicate that Mr. Gordon was not breathing while he was under the water. Upon further examination of the remains, a small contusion was found under his hair on the back of his head at the base of the skull. It is my opinion that the contusion was caused by contact with a solid object and that the force of this contact was strong enough to cause a lethal injury to Mr. Gordon's brain. Therefore it is my official ruling that the cause of Mr. Gordon's death was the effect of blunt trauma to the head."

The reaction of the crowd was instantaneous and vociferous. People started shouting questions and Doctor Bordeaux started looking uncomfortable. As the doctor backed away from microphones being thrust closer to his face, Sheriff Val Holmberg stepped forward and loudly called for order.

"Back off and let the doctor finish his statement," Holmberg said when the roar had diminished to a rumble.

Gradually the room grew quiet and Doctor Bordeaux's eyes lost the deer-in-the-headlights look. "While it is possible that Mr. Gordon's head struck the side of the boat with lethal force as he fell out of said boat, the location of the wound suggests that it may have been incurred prior to the fall," he said. He added a couple of concluding sentences and backed away without calling for questions. Val Holmberg took the ME's place in front of the lineup of TV and radio microphones.

In a show of courage, the sheriff asked if there were any questions. Of course there were many, some cogent and some nonsensical, some answered by Doctor Bordeaux and some answered by the sheriff. Finally someone yelled, "Is it possible that the blow on the head and the lifejacket the St. Paul paper says you found buried on the island add up to a clear case of murder?"

"Not necessarily. First of all, you just heard the doctor say that it is possible that the blow on the head was incurred during the victim's fall from the boat," Holmberg said. "Second, we haven't yet confirmed the identity of the owner of the lifevest. The initials drawn on it are A.R.G., and while the 'A' and the 'G' could stand for Alex Gordon, we haven't been able to confirm what Mr. Gordon's middle name was. There was no middle initial or name listed on the identifying documents that we recovered from his wallet."

"It's Robert," shouted a woman in the back of the room.

Holmberg's head jerked back and he stared at the woman. "Are you sure of that, ma'am?"

"Absolutely," the woman said.

With a hint of indulgence in his voice, Holmberg asked, "And how do you know that for certain, ma'am?"

"I'm his wife. My name is Mari Gordon."

Chapter Thirteen

More Trouble

WELL, DIDN'T THAT START a stampede to the rear? All heads—and feet—turned toward Mari Gordon, leaving Val Holmberg abandoned and looking confused. *Damn,* I thought as I turned slowly away from the sheriff, *there goes my shot at an exclusive interview.*

Trish Valentine spun and went around me like a human cannonball and weaved her way toward Mari Gordon like a Vikings runningback heading for the Green Bay goal line. However, I put a full body block on Tony, leaving Trish waiting silently for her cameraman while two other TV teams were jamming microphones under Mari Gordon's nose. This gave me some satisfaction, but not quite enough to compensate for Trish's invasion of our cabin.

As for Mari Gordon, it was obvious that she regretted sounding off. She fluttered her hands in front of her face as she kept repeating the words "please, no comment" and "I can't answer that" to the reporters bombarding her with questions. First came the standard TV reporter's query: "How do you feel about your husband being murdered?" This classic was followed with a barrage of questions about her husband's possible enemies and who she thought might have killed him.

After a couple of minutes of chaos, Mari covered her face with both hands and broke into tears. At that point Ann Rogers, bless her heart, elbowed her way through the crowd, took Mari by the arm and steered her to the door and out of the room. With Mari gone, everyone in the crowd turned back to the sheriff. Everyone but Al, that is. "I'm going to follow the women and see where the widow is staying," he said. "I'll meet you in the lounge when this mess is over."

It wasn't long before Sheriff Val Holmberg raised his arms full length above his head and declared that the mess—he called it a press conference—was over. Dr. Louis Bordeaux had already vanished during the hubbub around Mari Gordon, and the sheriff, looking as stunned as a bombing raid survivor, started to follow in his tracks. I intercepted the sheriff halfway to the door and said, "Remember me? When do you want to take my statement?"

"Oh, god, give me a few minutes to cool down," he said. "You big city people are like wild animals. Tell you what. I'll meet you and your photographer buddy in the manager's office in half an hour. And bring your little playmate with you. I want to get her statement, too."

"Sure you just don't want to look at her boobs?"

"Right now all I want to look at is a hot cup of coffee. Like I said, you big city people are like wild animals." Having twice critiqued the big city media, Holmberg stepped around me and hustled away.

So now I had a half-hour to inform Al of the scheduled meeting and to find our young friend Roxie. The first was accomplished five minutes later in the lounge when he returned from his reconnaissance mission and reported on Mari Gordon's cabin number. The second proved to be more difficult. We didn't know Roxie's cabin number and we didn't see Angie anywhere in the lounge or the dining room.

"Do you think the desk would give us Roxie's cabin number?" Al asked.

"Do you know what last name to ask for?" I said. "All we know them by is Roxie and Angie."

"The sheriff can probably find out. All he has to do is ask where the cute young whores are staying and I'll bet the desk clerk can tell him."

"Good point" I said. "Should we try that approach?"

"Not me," Al said. "You never know who the clerk will tell about us looking for the hookers, and once the word got out it could spread all the way to St. Paul."

"Another good point. Let's leave it to the sheriff."

We settled into chairs in the lounge and I pecked out my story on my laptop while Al was sending some photos, including one of a row of microphones in front of the weeping widow with her hands covering her face, to the city desk. I had just pressed the send button when Angie walked in the door.

"We're saved," I said. I jumped up and waved to Angie and she came to us at a gallop.

"Where's Roxie?" The question was asked simultaneously by Al and me. And by Angie.

"You don't know where she is?" I asked.

"I haven't seen her all morning so I went to her cabin," Angie said. "The door was unlocked and cabin is a mess inside. Even more than usual."

"What do you mean by that?"

"I mean the whole place is torn up, not just the bed and the bedroom. Like they were going at it all over the kitchen and everything. I don't know where she could be."

"Did it look like there might have been a fight?" Al asked.

"Could have been," Angie said. "I'm scared for her."

This looked like another chore for Sheriff Val Holmberg. "Come with us," I said. "We're meeting the sheriff in two minutes."

Angie's eyes widened and her jaw dropped. When she recovered, she said, "I ain't going to the sheriff. He'll bust me for soliciting."

"If the sheriff was going to arrest you for prostitution he'd have done it a long time ago," I said. "He's been looking the other way, either because he doesn't want the hassle or he's been told by someone higher up the food chain to lay off. Some of your clients are prominent people and the politics could get messy."

Resort manager Martin Johansen ushered us into his office and bowed out, saying he was leaving us to talk in private with the sheriff. Two minutes later Sheriff Holmberg came through the door, looked us over and said, "That's not the same chippy that was with you on the island."

"This is her, uh . . . friend," I said. "The lady who was with us on the island is missing under rather unusual circumstances and Angie is here to lead us to Roxie's cabin."

"What do you mean 'unusual circumstances'?" Holmberg said. I tilted my head toward Angie. Shaking and talking in nervous spurts, she told Holmberg the same story she'd given us about what she'd found in Roxie's cabin.

"Take us there," Holmberg said. "We'll check this out and get your statements later."

Al and I looked at each other and groaned. We'd been counting on a quick session with the sheriff so we could get on the road to St. Paul.

Angie led Holmberg, a deputy who'd accompanied him, Al and me up the path to Roxie's cabin. The deputy stood beside the door while Holmberg knocked, announced himself and yanked the door open. He ordered us to stay put and stepped inside cautiously, followed by the deputy. They did a quick walkthrough and Holmberg called for us to enter.

Angie hadn't been exaggerating. The kitchen, sitting room and bedroom all looked like battle scenes, with articles of clothing, towels and small items strewn around, chairs out of place, a reading lamp lying on the floor and the small kitchen table tipped onto its side. Holmberg told us to stand still while he made a slower inspection tour.

He stopped by the overturned table and looked closely at the edge "Appears to be blood," he said, pointing to a brownish-red mark. Angie gasped and started to cry. "The son of a bitch hurt Roxie," she said.

"Do you know who she was with?" Holmberg asked.

"I don't know his name," Angie said. "She said he was one of those guys who came with the governor."

"Did you see him?"

"No. Roxie said he was kind of fat but not too bad looking."

"Did she mention an age?"

"No. Actually, all those guys look about the same age to us . . . to her."

Holmberg snorted a short laugh. "Their money all looks about the same, too, doesn't it?"

"I don't know what you mean," Angie said.

"Don't kid me, little girl, I know what you and your so-called friend are doing here this weekend, and I don't like it. I'd have both of you and all of your customers in court today if I hadn't been told to look the other way. When we find your friend you'd both better get your butts out of my county or by god I'll find a reason to put them in jail the minute the governor leaves Crow Wing County."

I steered the conversation back on course. "We need to go see Ann Rogers. She can tell us if anyone from the governor's party is also missing."

"And if nobody's missing, maybe she can tell you which guy is kind of fat but not too bad looking," Al said.

"We might need Angie to give us the working girl's perspective on which fat guy is not too bad looking," I said.

"Let's go," Holmberg said. Al and I followed him out the door but Angie hung back. "You, too, little girl," the sheriff said. "You're in this up to your tushy."

We found Ann back in the lounge talking to reporters. From the chatter, I gathered that most of the people were planning to stay a second additional night so they could talk to the sheriff individually, take a trip out to the island to see where we'd dug up the lifejacket and maybe get a shot at interviewing Mari Gordon. This meant we'd have to call Don O'Rourke to get our marching orders and pass along the additional revelation that our story was about to become further complicated by a search for a missing hooker.

Much as I dreaded being told to stay another night, I slipped outside and made the call to Don while the sheriff was talking to Ann.

Chapter Fourteen

Hunting for a Hooker

"DON'T TELL ME YOU'VE got a serial killer running loose up there," Don O'Rourke said when I gave him the news about Roxie's disappearance.

"No, I won't do that," I said. "One, we don't know that Roxie's dead. Two, even if she is, there's not enough similarity between a hooker and a press secretary to suggest a serial killer at work."

"You don't think there's any similarity between a political press secretary and a whore?"

"I won't deny a certain commonality between the two jobs but I doubt the average serial killer thinks that way."

"So what have you got?"

"We've got a dead man, possibly murdered by someone in the governor's office, and a missing woman, possibly murdered or imprisoned by someone else in the governor's office. I'm asking if Al and I should stay here on the scene or come home and cover the story, or stories, by phone." I knew darn well what the answer would be.

"The others are staying?" Don said.

"Sounds like most of them are."

"Well, it really doesn't matter what the rest of them are doing. You two might as well stick around for at least one more day," Don said. "You can't get pictures of the search by phone in St. Paul, and it looks like we'll be getting two stories for the price of one."

I sighed inwardly and told Don I'd send a story about Roxie as soon as we found out what the sheriff planned to do. I also said we'd try to get to Mari Gordon even though I thought we had about as much chance for an interview as a porcupine had for a hug.

I went back into the lounge and joined the sheriff, Al and Angie in a circle around Ann. Al's first question was, "Are we staying?" I nodded and he sighed.

Val Holmberg had asked Ann to round up all the men with any surplus poundage in the group from the governor's office, bring them to the lobby and line them up in front of the manager's office where Angie could look them over from behind the registration counter. The sheriff didn't expect to get a quick confession, but he planned to question the men one by one in the office. After the interviews he would ask Angie for an assessment of the men's relative good looks and call back any that she found to be "not too bad looking."

Ann said it was her duty to inform all the members of the media about the missing woman and the sheriff's plan to question a group of state officials and employees. Holmberg told her that she must keep all of the media, Al and me included, away from the lineup outside the office.

"I'll tape off the whole building if I have to," Holmberg said.

"That won't be necessary," Ann said. "I'm sure the media will honor your request without a problem." Oh, the naiveté of the governor's new press secretary.

"You'd better tape off the lobby," I said to Holmberg. "And have your deputy keep an eye on the short blonde from Channel Four."

"The one with the big knockers who's always up front?" he asked.

"That's the one. She's super aggressive. Your deputy might have to physically restrain her."

"I'm sure that'll break his heart." The deputy, standing just outside our little huddle, grinned like the proverbial canary-consuming cat.

Holmberg had radioed for additional deputies to come and begin the search. While Ann was rounding up prospective Roxie finders, I quizzed Angie and learned that Roxie's last name was Robideaux, that she was probably twenty-two years old and that her parents lived in the tiny town of Nisswa, just on the other end of Gull Lake. I incorporated this information into a brief story about her disappearance and the impending interviews to determine who she'd been with the previous evening. I did not explain the reason for her being with the man, hoping that most readers would consider it a normal relationship between two young people of the opposite sex. The time to report on her chosen profession would come later. It was still too soon to start damaging reputations—either Roxie's or those of the men being questioned.

The sheriff's tall, stern-looking deputy, whose name we learned was Leo, did close off the lobby with a long stretch of yellow plastic tape and the crowd was forced to watch at a distance as Ann Rogers brought the first of four men she had selected in through the back way and led him to the office door. Angie was in her station behind the registration counter where she could survey the men without being obvious. Photography of the interviewees had been strictly forbidden and Leo stood a step in front of the tape watching for any sign of a camera or a cell phone.

"Does that first guy look not too bad to you?" Al asked me.

"If I was a woman, I wouldn't date him," I said. "Not even for money."

"Me neither. Look at the gut on the guy."

"I think Ann went overboard. That one's way beyond 'kind of fat.'" I looked at the man again and realized that he was the state treasurer. I hadn't recognized him dressed in faded jeans and a Viking sweatshirt and minus the crummy hairpiece he usually wore. I couldn't imagine him being Roxie's all-nighter.

Ann Rogers opened the office door and gestured for the state treasurer to enter. Ten minutes later he came out looking somber. Ann led him back to where he'd entered, followed him out and returned with a second man. This one would never pass as "not too bad looking," but he was waved into the office. It looked like the score would be second down and two to go.

I took Al by the arm and pulled him out of the crowd. "I've got a better idea than standing here watching fat men go in and out of a room," I said.

"What could possibly be more fascinating than that?" Al said. "Do you have a pan of fudge we could watch harden?"

"Way sweeter than that. Which cottage did you say Mari Gordon is in?"

"Oh, that is sweet. She's staying down the beach, sort of out of the way of everybody else."

"Take me to that cottage. We can talk to the sheriff about his interviews later."

We quietly left the lodge and Al led me down the sidewalk that paralleled the beach. We passed a dozen cottages that faced the beach and then the sidewalk turned ninety degrees away from the shoreline, went up a short rise and dead-ended in front of the last cottage at the end of the path.

"To quote a famous Mormon, this is the place," Al said.

"You're sure?" I said.

"I watched Ann give her a hug and tuck her in."

I went up the front steps and knocked gently on the door. "Who is it?" asked the female voice inside.

"Warren Mitchell and Alan Jeffrey from the *St. Paul Daily Dispatch*," I said. "No microphones and no TV cameras. Can we talk to you for a minute about your husband?"

"Go away," she said.

"The governor thought you might talk to us since we're the hometown paper," I said. This bodacious lie drew a shake of the head from Al.

"Anders said that?" Mari said through the closed door.

"Yes, he did."

"I don't believe you."

"Call him and ask him." The ultimate bluff.

There was a pause and then the door opened. "Oh, shit, come on in. Quick, before the TV hound dogs get here."

I resisted correcting her grammar and quickly entered the cottage. Al quickly followed. She quickly shut the door and threw the sliding bolt in addition to clicking the lock on the doorknob. She turned and waved us toward a loveseat in the sitting room, followed us in and sat in a small armchair facing us.

Mari Gordon was in her late forties, slender and almost six feet tall. She wasn't pretty or cute, but she was attractive when she was gussied up for a public appearance. At this moment she was not gussied up. Her eyes were puffed from crying, she wore no makeup and her long, straight black hair was hanging in strings, as if it hadn't been combed in the three days since she first got word of Alex's demise. She was wearing baggy khaki cargo pants and a wrinkled blue denim shirt that wasn't tucked in. On her feet was a bizarre pair of slippers that looked like big furry gray rabbits, long ears and all.

"Thank you for seeing us," I said. "I'm sorry for your loss. We'll all miss Alex a lot."

"Really?" Mari said. "Alex said everybody in the press corps hated him."

"Not everybody," Al said. "We always got along okay." Another lie, but a charitable one.

Mari looked at the camera slung over Al's shoulder. "You're not going to take my picture." It was a command, not a question.

"Not without your permission," he said.

"Well, you won't get it. I know I look like shit."

"You've had some rough days," I said. "We don't need your picture; just some information."

"Like what?" Mari asked.

"Like do you know who, if anyone, really did hate Alex enough to, uh . . . do what they seem to have done to him?"

"I can think of a couple."

"Good." I took a small notebook out of my back pants pocket and a ballpoint pen out of my shirt pocket. "Name me some names and give me some motives." I sat back and waited with the pen poised and ready.

Chapter Fifteen

Naming Names

MARI GORDON OPENED her mouth to speak, closed it to think a moment and then said, "Are you going to put what I say in the paper?"

"No, this is strictly background," I said. "I'm looking for a place to start investigating. I suppose you've already given these names to the sheriff."

"As a matter of fact, I haven't talked to the sheriff since I've been here. From what I heard him say at the press conference, I don't think he's convinced that Alex was murdered."

"Don't be too hard on the sheriff. Alex's death didn't actually come together as a probable homicide until the autopsy report of the head wound was added to the discovery of the buried lifejacket. And right now the sheriff also has a missing woman to deal with."

"Who's missing?"

"A young woman named Roxie who had a date with somebody from the governor's group last night. The sheriff is questioning several men right now to find out who that was."

"What do you mean by a date?" Mari said. "Is Roxie one of those baby-faced whores who are rubbing their tits up against all the guys?"

"As a matter of fact, she is," I said. "I didn't know whether you'd noticed them."

"They're not exactly subtle. I saw them working the room after dinner last night. It was pretty obvious what they were selling. Just look at how they're dressed. I don't know how the brunette gets into those jeans."

"We know how guys do," Al said.

"I'll bet you do," Mari said. "What did it cost you?"

Before Al could respond, I said, "What I'm trying to tell you is that the sheriff has been, shall we say, distracted from investigating Alex's death by the immediate need to find out where Roxie might be. From the mess we saw in her cabin, it's possible that he'll have a second homicide to investigate."

"God, what fun the Governor's Fishing Opener has turned out to be," Mari said.

"It sure isn't the laid-back happy time we were expecting to cover," Al said. "We planned on fishing for walleyes, not fishing for a killer or two."

"Back to naming names," I said to Mari. "You said you have a couple."

"I do," she said. "Number one would be Dexter Rice, the previous governor's press secretary."

I had worked with Dexter when he held that job. He was outspoken and temperamental but he didn't seem like a man who would murder his successor. "Why him?" I asked.

"Dexter worked for the previous governor and he was sure he would be kept on when Anders, another Republican, was elected. When Anders hired Alex instead, Dexter was royally pissed off and told Alex he'd be sorry he took the job."

"Now Dexter's doing editorials on the evening news for Channel Five," I said. "He should be over losing the PR job to Alex."

"He's not over it. He's done everything he could to make Alex look bad in his editorials. And he told Alex in person once that he'd get him fired if he had to knock him on the head and give him amnesia."

"Very colorful," Al said. "Sounds like one of his editorials where he gets all red in the face and shakes his fist at what he calls the squishy-headed liberals."

"He's an asshole," Mari said. "Alex always thought he wasn't wound quite right, even when he was working for the governor."

I remembered clashing with Rice over a story I had written after a governor's press conference. Rice claimed that I totally misrepresented the governor's position and quoted him out of context. "He could get right in your face if he didn't like something you wrote," I said. "He once accused me of making the governor look foolish and damn near exploded when I said the governor didn't need my help to look foolish."

"But how could Rice have clobbered Alex?" Al asked. "He's back in the studio cranking out cranky editorials."

"No, he's not. He's here," Mari said. "I saw him with the Channel Five crew in the dining room. He made a point of not making eye contact with me."

"Sounds like a good one to start with," I said. "Who is your other candidate?"

"A man named Joe Weber who works in the secretary of state's office," Mari said. "I don't know what his problem is with Alex, but he's been sending Alex some really vicious, insulting e-mails. It might be a political thing; Weber's a far left Democrat."

"I don't know Weber," I said. "I wonder if he's one of the administrative bunch up here for the opener."

"Maybe Ann Rogers can tell us," Al said.

"Good thinking," I said. "We should get back to her and the sheriff to see what's going on." I turned to Mari and said, "Thank you for seeing us and for giving us this off the record stuff. Now is there anything you'd like to say on the record for my next story?"

"There is," she said. "You can write that I was devastated by Alex's death and now I'm even more devastated to learn that it looks like it wasn't an accident—that someone deliberately killed him. Also that I'm grateful for all the kind messages I've received and I hope the rotten bastard who did this awful thing is caught and rots in hell forever."

"The editor might bleep out 'bastard,'" I said.

"How about 'son of a bitch'?" Mari asked.

"I'll keep that as a second choice."

When we returned to the lodge the media crowd was breaking up. We didn't see the sheriff but we spotted Ann Rogers and made our way upstream through the departing multitude to reach her. She informed us that all four men questioned had denied being with Roxie Sunday night, but that she knew of two more possibilities who were currently out on the lake fishing. The sheriff had sent Leo out in a boat to hunt for them and bring them in for questioning. Meanwhile, a dozen additional deputies and local and state police officers had arrived to begin checking the cabins and surrounding area for any sign of Roxie. "They're looking for volunteers to help, if you're interested," she said.

"I've got a story to write, but we can join them when I'm done," I said. I was relieved that she hadn't thought to ask why we hadn't heard the sheriff's announcement. If Ann found out where we'd been and leaked the word that Mari Gordon had talked to us, every reporter and photographer at the resort would be demanding to know where Mari was staying, and they'd soon be beating on her door. I could envision Trish Valentine climbing in a window and reporting live from Mari Gordon's cabin before my story was posted on the *Daily Dispatch* online edition.

Actually, I had two stories to write—one to update the Gordon murder story with the quote from the victim's widow and another to update the story about the hunt for the missing woman. As I wrote the latter, I wondered whether one of the interviewed men had lied to the sheriff or if one of the fishermen being pursued by Leo had been Roxie's all-nighter. And of course there was the possibility that Ann Rogers hadn't brought in all the men who were kind of fat but not too bad looking. After all, Ann's perception of a man's shape and facial quality might not be the same as someone who looked at him as a potential purchaser of her services.

I finished my stories and sent them to the desk. Al had already e-mailed a couple of pix of the mess in Roxie's cabin. We both called our homes in St. Paul and left messages for our working women to call us as soon as they got home. Neither of us was looking forward to receiving those return calls.

We were ready to join the search party, but first we had to find the sheriff to get directions. We decided to start the hunt at Roxie's cabin, where we found Val Holmberg in the bedroom pointing out shots for his forensic photographer.

We greeted Holmberg and he responded with a grunt.

"I understand you didn't have any luck with the four guys you questioned," I said. "Are you sure they were all telling the truth?"

"The first three were for sure," Holmberg said. "I'm not sure about the fourth guy. If the two that Leo is bringing in from lake clear themselves, I might go back to number four."

"Can you give us a name?" I asked.

"Christ, no. You know better than that."

I'd been hoping that he didn't. "When are you seeing the other two?"

"Soon as Leo gets them off the lake and into the office." Holmberg went to the front door and looked out at the lake, which was partially visible through the pine trees that lined the path between the cabins. "Looks like it will be pretty soon. That's Leo herding them in."

We looked where the sheriff was pointing and saw two boats close together approaching the dock. They were too far away to see whether either of the two men in the leading boat was kind of fat but not too bad looking. The sheriff left the cabin and started walking toward the dock. We followed a couple of steps behind.

"One of these guys has to be the one who was with Roxie last night," Al said.

"Unless number four lied to the sheriff this morning," I said.

"If we knew who he is we could go beat on him 'til he told us the truth about Roxie."

"For a married man, you're awfully protective of Roxie. Did Mari's talk about getting into her jeans make you feel horny?"

"No, it made me feel like a worried father. If Roxie's really twenty-two, she's only four years older than my daughter."

As we neared the foot of the dock, Leo and the two fishermen climbed onto the far end of the dock from their respective boats and started walking toward us. From his gestures I could tell that one of the fishermen was giving Leo a hard time about being hauled in off the lake. They were met midway on the dock by Val Holmberg, where the angry man turned toward the sheriff and continued his harangue.

The angry man wasn't too bad looking and had only a moderate bulge around the middle. I had a very bad feeling about him.

Chapter Sixteen

On the Trail

APPARENTLY AL HAD THE SAME feeling of foreboding because he quickly raised his camera, shot a couple of pictures of the quartet walking toward us on the dock and lowered the camera to his waist without have been seen by his targets. We stepped aside as Holmberg, Leo and the two fishermen walked past and stayed a few steps behind as we followed them into the lodge.

The lounge was empty, and we could smell food and hear babble from the dining room. I checked my watch and saw it was lunch time. We followed the quartet to the lobby entrance but were halted there by Leo, who turned around and raised his hands. "This is as far as you go, boys," he said. "You can talk to the sheriff after he interviews these gentlemen."

"Do you know who they are?" I asked.

"No, and if I did, I wouldn't tell you. Why don't you fellas go sit in the lounge until the sheriff is finished?"

We mumbled in agreement and retreated. Looking past Leo, I saw that the man who gave me bad vibes was the first to go into the office with Holmberg.

"How'd you like to play bloodhound again?" I said when we reached the lounge.

"You mean follow that guy when the sheriff lets him go?" Al said.

"Exactly. I really think he's our man. Go hang out within sight of the lobby and see where he goes."

"What are you going to do?"

"Wait here and talk to the sheriff when he comes out. You come back when you've got a bead on our suspect's cabin."

Al went to hang out near the lobby and I plopped into a chair. Ten minutes later, Al was back. "Our suspect must be close," I said.

"Very close," Al said. "He went into the dining room for lunch."

I groaned. "Then we need to do the same. We'll get something we can eat fast so we're ready to follow him when he finishes."

"Okay, one fast lunch coming up."

"I hope it doesn't come up," I said.

"Yuck. Your humor is strictly from hunger," Al said.

In the dining room we spotted our man at a table near the exit. He had joined a group of men who were halfway through their meals. I didn't recognize any of them and I had no idea which state office they were from.

We decided to have ham-and-cheese sandwiches, and I was chewing my first bite when my cell phone rang. The ID said it was Martha Todd. I swallowed my food and answered.

"Well, aren't you the Twin Cities' biggest TV star?" Martha said. "That's quite a live interview you had with Trish Valentine."

"Oh, god, is that playing already?"

"It's playing on every Channel Four news break. You've been on the tube more than Katie Couric this morning."

"Don O'Rourke will kill me," I said. "I can't believe he hasn't called me."

"Maybe he's not speaking to you," she said.

"That isn't funny. Don's opinion of TV news is even lower than mine. And for me to be talking to Trish . . ."

"Then you'll probably hear from him later."

"Are my stories about the autopsy results and the missing woman playing on our online edition?"

"They're right up on top of the 'most read' list. Maybe that's why Don is sparing you."

"I'll try to keep him in a sparing mood with another update on the missing woman before he goes home."

"And I suppose that update and the new development in Alex Gordon's case are going to keep you up there on the lake for another day."

"Unfortunately, you're right. Don has already told us to stay. Luckily I brought along extra underwear and socks to put on in case I got wet fishing. But I'll be all out after tomorrow."

"Then Don will have to let you come home before you stink up the resort. He can't have you giving the paper a bad reputation in Brainerd."

"Good thinking. I'll mention that to him when he calls. What's new with you?"

"I'm working on getting asylum for Grandma Mendes. They've set up a court hearing for Wednesday, after which they could order her shipped off to Cape Verde if I don't convince them that she deserves a chance at citizenship. Would you believe it's a five-year process?"

"With our immigration laws I'd believe anything. Do you have any feel for how it will go in court?"

"None. But the only person in our firm who has dealt with an immigration case says the judge was not at all sympathetic."

Al leaned across the table and whispered, "Our boy is leaving. See you later." He got up and circled a couple of tables to put himself sufficiently behind the departing fisherman. In the doorway Al almost collided head-on with Val Holmberg, but he rolled around the sheriff like a running back spinning away from a tackler and disappeared. The sheriff made a quick stop, scanned the room and started walking toward me.

"The sheriff is coming to talk to me," I said into the phone. "I'll call you later. Love you." Martha made kissy sounds but the sheriff was too close for me to respond before she went away.

"Where's your buddy going in such a hellfire hurry?" Holmberg asked. He pulled up a chair from a nearby vacant table and sat down. He was looking at Al's plate, which contained a half-eaten ham-and-cheese sandwich.

I took a bite of my sandwich while I searched my brain for an answer. "He, uh, had to see a man about a horse," I said.

"He seems to have that problem a lot," Holmberg said. "What's he going to dig up this time when he pees?"

"Nothing, I hope. I mean, I hope that there's nothing buried in the men's room."

"I hope you're right. Especially no little brunette whore. I came to tell you that I'll be having a press conference on that investigation at about four o'clock."

"Was one of the men you just questioned with Roxie last night? The first guy kind of fits Angie's description."

"I'll be talking about that at the four o'clock press conference. I need to check out some alibis and talk to one of the men I questioned this morning again before I can give out any information. While I'm busy doing all that, I'm putting Leo in charge of the search."

"Does Leo have a last name?" I asked. "I'll need it for my next story."

"LeBlanc," Holmberg said. "With a capital 'B.' He's French-Canadian."

"Thanks. When Al gets back we'll go see Leo. How are you conducting the search?"

"We're knocking on cabin doors and we've got a couple of master keys to use when nobody's inside. We've also got people working the beach and the woods and the golf course. Be a bitch to find her in a sand trap." He rose and walked away, leaving me with a graphic image of a body in a sand trap in my mind—and without an appetite for the remainder of the sandwich in my hand.

My brain was wandering through the day's events when its journey was interrupted by another visitor. "You sneaky bastard, how did you get a quote from Mari Gordon?" asked Trish Valentine as she slid into the chair vacated by the sheriff. She was smiling at me like we were the best of buddies. She leaned toward me, giving me a generous view of the cleavage exposed by the always open buttons at the top of her blouse.

"My personal charm," I said. "Women just naturally want to pour out their hearts to me."

Trish leaned closer. More cleavage appeared as she poured out her heart externally. I observed a tiny brown mole I'd never seen before on her right breast. "Never mind the crap; tell me where she is." Still smiling.

"She's in a cabin at Madrigal's Resort."

"Which cabin at Madrigal's Resort?"

"Oh, shucks, I can't seem to remember the number," I said "Sorry about that. I hope it's not early Alzheimer's coming on."

She backed away and sat up straight. No more smile. No more cleavage on display. "I don't suppose you can remember the directions to her cabin, either."

"You're absolutely right. My mind is a total blank. But thanks for reading my story."

"You're not welcome. And I'll find Mari one way or another. Who needs you?" She popped up out of the chair like a spring-loaded jack-in-the-box and turned to leave.

"If you run across the missing Roxie Robideaux while you're searching for Mari Rogers, let the sheriff know, will you?" I said to her retreating back.

She flipped me the bird.

I was staring at the partially eaten sandwich on my plate, trying to decide if I'd done enough to get even with Trish for the impromptu interview, when Al returned.

"Your buddy Trish is really pissed about something," he said. "I said hi to her outside and she called me a name and flipped me the bird."

"Welcome to the club," I said. "Trish is in a bit of snit because I wouldn't tell her where to find Mari Rogers."

"She thought you'd give her a break like that after the sneak play she pulled on you this morning?"

"It's called chutzpah. Goes with being a TV star. She did give me a nice titty show before she gave me the bird."

"Well, she'll really be in a snit if the guy I followed turns out to be Roxie's customer last night. I followed him all the way to his cottage without any other reporters in sight. It's up the hill near the golf course."

"Why don't we go knock on his door?" I said, rising from the chair.

"Going to finish your lunch on the way?" Al said. He picked the remains of his sandwich off the plate.

"I lost my appetite talking to the sheriff."

"My god, what did he say?"

"Nothing you want to hear if you plan on eating that."

"Tell me what he said. You know I have a cast iron stomach."

"You'll be casting away that sandwich if I tell you, so let's just cast off for the possible bad guy's cabin."

Chapter Seventeen

Packing Up

AL LED ME ACROSS the parking lot and up the hill toward the golf course. At the crest, he pointed toward a cabin set in front of a grove of trees. A black Ford SUV was parked in front of it. "Again I quote the famous Mormon," he said. "This is the place."

"You seem to be awfully familiar with Brigham Young," I said. "Did you know him personally?"

"Young was old before my time. But I've visited the college of his youth."

"In other words, you're just Young at heart."

"But I'm an old school kind of guy. So now that we're at our prime suspect's cabin, how are we going to play this?"

"First I was thinking we'd play it dumb. Say we didn't know why the sheriff brought him in and wondered about it. But now I think we should go for the throat. Tell him the sheriff told us he's a prime suspect in Roxie's disappearance and ask him for a comment for my story."

"That should get a reaction," Al said. "I can probably get a picture of him with his mouth open when his jaw drops in surprise."

"Don will love that," I said. "And right now I can use anything that makes Don happy."

"The Trish thing?"

"Right. Well, come on. Let's go do it."

We marched to the front door and I knocked. No answer. I knocked harder and yelled, "Anybody home?"

"Who wants to know?" came the reply from inside. A deep voice. The tone of a man with authority.

"*St. Paul Daily Dispatch*. Mitch Mitchell and Alan Jeffrey," I said.

"What do you want?" This was not a friendly query.

"We want to ask you a couple of questions. It won't take long."

Heavy footsteps approaching, then the door opening about a foot. Behind it, peering through the gap, was our suspect. He was taller and broader of belly than he'd looked beside the sheriff. His face had no outstanding features other than a neatly clipped beard and a downturn at the corners of his mouth. His blond hair was clipped short and his face was pink from exposure to the sun. I guessed his age at a shade past thirty.

Not too bad looking, I thought. *The sour mouth is probably temporary.*

"What kind of questions?" he asked.

"We need to get your reaction to something Sheriff Holmberg told us," I said. "Can we come in?"

Behind the man I could see an open suitcase on the bed but I couldn't see what was in it. I also noticed a small patch of red on the floor underneath the bed. I thought maybe he'd dropped a sock or something. The man backed up and swung the door open all the way. I marched in with Al nearly in lockstep behind me. "Thanks," I said. "I'm Mitch and this is Al." I offered my right hand for shaking.

The man grasped my hand briefly but with substantial strength. "Ronald," he said. "But you already knew that."

"We did, but I'm glad you confirmed it. The sheriff wasn't sure exactly how to spell your last name."

Ronald's eyebrows went up. "Christ, how many ways are there to spell Jones?"

Oops, my cute little trick was backfiring. I paused a moment to consider how to remove my foot from the verbal mud I'd stuck it into. "Some people spell it with two N's," I said. "I knew a man like that. He said the first 'N' was silent so his great-grandparents decided to add the second one." I tried to project a smile of humor and self-effacing innocence. Al turned his back to us, pretending to survey the cabin while hiding his struggle to keep a straight face.

"You're shittin' me," Ronald Jones said. "Jones with two 'N's?"

"Swear it on a stack of style books," I said. I looked past him at the suitcase and saw it was partly full of crumpled clothes ready for the laundry. "Checking out today?" I asked.

"Yeah. Time to get back to doing the taxpayers' work."

"What do you do for the taxpayers?"

"The sheriff didn't tell you?"

"He didn't give us any details. Just that you work for the state, which describes almost everybody up here this weekend."

"He's got that wrong," Jones said. "I actually work for Ramsey County. For the treasurer. My job involves dealing with the state treasurer. I'm here because he invited me along on this crazy, fucked-up weekend."

"Lucky you," I said. "Have you been having fun?"

"Just loads of fun. First I watch a dead body being brought in and then I'm yanked off the lake by the sheriff to answer some stupid questions about a missing whore."

"That's what we need your statement about. The sheriff named you as the most likely person to have been with the missing whore last night."

Ronald's pink face turned several shades brighter. "That's a goddamn lie. I gave him a solid alibi."

"What was the alibi?"

"I was in Brainerd with three other guys last night. We all got drunk in a bar together. We even got stopped by a state cop on the way back to Madrigal's because the driver was so sloshed that he was weaving all over the center line. The trooper let us go without a ticket because we were from the governor's weekend. He made us change drivers, which didn't make a whole hell of a lot of difference because we were all equally shit-faced. Why's the sheriff handing out this crap? He said he'd check my story with the other three guys before he made any statements to the press."

"Maybe they were so drunk they didn't remember you were along," I said. "Obviously the sheriff thinks you're the man who can tell him what happened to Roxie."

"Well, I can't. I don't know nothing about anybody named Roxie. I'm a married man; I don't go around picking up whores." He held up his left hand to display a gold wedding band on the appropriate finger.

"If you're innocent, why are you packing up to go right home just minutes after talking to the sheriff?" Al asked. He'd been quietly shooting pictures while Ronald Jones talked.

"I'm leaving because I'm done here," Jones said. "I was going to hang around and fish for a couple more days but I've had all I can take of this goddamn nuthouse."

"Okay, let me get this straight. Your statement is that you were drinking in a Brainerd bar with three other men?" I asked.

"You could leave out the part about drinking in a bar. Just say I was in Brainerd with three other men. People don't need to know what we were doing."

"People being your wife?"

"Well, uh, yeah, that's part of it. But I meant nosy people in general that are going to read your story."

"And you know nothing about a woman named Roxie?"

"Absolutely not." His voice was getting louder with each response.

"Never were in her cabin?"

"Goddamn it, no!" Jones yelled.

"And she was never in your cabin?"

"No, no, no and double no." He was practically screaming now.

"Okay," I said. "Want some help packing?" I'd been thinking about the red object I'd seen under the bed from my vantage point outside the front door. It wasn't visible from where we were standing at the moment and I was curious about what it was. Jones didn't seem like the type of man who would wear red socks.

"I don't need any help," Jones said.

"You might be forgetting something you can't see." I went to the bed, swept my hand across the floor underneath it and came out holding a red item of clothing.

It was a woman's thong panty.

"You wear this very often?" I asked.

Chapter Eighteen

The Chase

RONALD JONES STARED AT THE THONG. I let it dangle full length from my thumb and index finger and jiggled it, waiting for an answer.

"I don't know where that came from," he said.

"I think I do," I said. "It looks like something a girl in Roxie's line of work would wear on a date with a paying customer."

"I told you, I don't know nothing about Roxie."

I turned to Al. "I think the sheriff should see this. Why don't you go get him? I'll keep Mr. Jones company while you're gone.

"Like hell you will," Jones said. He swung his fist and caught me on the left cheekbone with enough force to send me reeling toward a low wooden coffee table, which I fell across with my rib cage hitting the edge. The table collapsed with all four legs splayed out at the corners. I sprawled across the wreckage on the floor, from where I watched Jones slam Al to one side and dash out the door. Al bounced off the wall and followed Jones through the door. I hauled myself to my feet and got to the doorway in time to see the black Ford's wheels tearing up the gravel as it took off toward the blacktop road.

Al raised his camera and took a shot. "Got his plate," he said. "We can give the sheriff his number."

I felt a stabbing pain in my right side where my body had crashed against the coffee table. "You go get him. I need to sit for a minute." Bending over and holding my hand against my ribs, I hobbled to a chair and sat down.

"What's the matter? Did you break a rib on that table?" Al asked.

"I don't know. It feels like I might have. Go find the sheriff."

"You've got his number in your phone."

"That's his office number, not his cell."

"Okay, I'm off to see the sheriff. Sit tight 'til I get back."

I sat as tight as I could. Every time I moved, a shot of pain ripped through my right side like a jab from Sir Lancelot's lance. Between jabs, I felt something wet trickling down my left cheek. I wiped the spot with my left hand and my fingers came away wet—and red. Apparently my cheek was bleeding from Jones's sneak punch.

Just what I needed, I thought. *Won't I look great at my wedding Saturday, walking like a wounded scarecrow with either a scab or a bandage decorating my cheek?*

After what seemed like an hour, Al returned, accompanied by Sheriff Val Holmberg and Deputy Leo LeBlanc. While waiting, I had thought about picking up the thong panties from the floor where I'd dropped them but my ribs had advised against standing and stooping. Now I pointed at the small slip of red and said, "Looks like our missing lady left a souvenir."

Holmberg unfastened the billy club from his belt, stuck the business end through the thong and held it up for inspection. "We've got three cars chasing Jones and a BOLO out on the radio," he said. "We should catch him before he gets very far. Then he can tell us how he acquired this little number."

"Let's hope he'll also tell us where the owner is," Al said.

"And that the owner is still in need of underwear," I said.

"That would be good for her—and for me, too," Holmberg said. "I really don't need to be working two homicides at the same time."

That remark brought me back to my visit with Mari Gordon. "Do you have any suspects in the Gordon homicide case?" I asked.

"I've barely started the investigation," the sheriff said. "I'm a long way from having any suspects in this mess."

"Have you talked to the victim's widow?"

"Not yet. I've been sidetracked by this missing hooker crap. I might get to Mrs. Gordon one of these days, after we catch that bastard Jones and persuade him to talk." Holmberg's cell phone chimed and he answered it. As he listened to the caller, his face showed pleasure, followed by disbelief and finally by amusement. "I'm on my way," he said, shaking his head as he clicked off.

"They got him?" I asked.

Holmberg nodded. "He took off like a rocket when he spotted my deputies coming up behind him. They chased after him and about a mile later he missed a curve and went flying into the ditch and hit a tree. Before my guys could get to him he took off running and went into the woods. The deputies took off after him and when they were getting close and yelling for him to stop, you'll never guess what he did."

"He didn't shoot at them, I hope," I said.

"No, he doesn't have a gun. The son of a bitch climbed a tree."

"That beer-belly went up a tree?" Al said.

"It did. And the beer-belly's owner says he won't come down," Holmberg said. "I'm going out to help persuade him that it's healthier on the ground."

"I'm right behind you. I've got to get pictures of this," Al said.

"I think I'll stay here," I said. "The ribs can't take the ride right now."

"Oh, yeah, I meant to tell you," Holmberg said. "I called an ambulance to take you to the hospital in Brainerd to get those ribs checked out. And they should patch up that cut on your cheek while you're there."

"I don't need to go to the hospital," I said.

"Broken ribs are dangerous. They could puncture a lung. You need to get them x-rayed. Anyway, it's too late to call back the ambulance."

The sheriff was right, damn it. And that's how I missed all the fun at the tree. When Al picked me up later at St. Joseph's Medical Center, he told me what had happened in the woods while I was getting poked and prodded and questioned by a parade of nurses and doctors, looking at x-rays of my three cracked—but not broken—ribs and having a sterile butterfly patch put on the inch-long cut on my cheek.

Al said that Ronald Jones was at least thirty feet off the ground in a huge pine tree when he and the sheriff arrived at the scene. The sheriff ordered Jones to come down out of the tree and Jones told the sheriff to go away and leave him alone. The sheriff again ordered Jones down and Jones said he wasn't coming down and he wasn't going to talk to the sheriff any more.

Sheriff Holmberg huddled with the two deputies who had treed Jones, and one of them went back to his squad car. The sheriff gave the third order to come down from the tree and Jones remained silent. The sheriff then announced that he would have his men cut the tree down if Jones stayed up there. Jones told the sheriff to go to hell and take his men with him.

The deputy reappeared, carrying a bright orange chainsaw. The sheriff pointed out the chainsaw to Jones. Jones told the sheriff to stick the chainsaw up his ass. The sheriff nodded to the deputy, who pulled the rope. The chainsaw started with a roar. They looked up at Jones and observed that he was beginning to show some interest.

The deputy walked over to the tree and revved the chainsaw—*vroom, vroom, vroom*. Jones was showing intense interest at the sound. As the deputy pressed the moving blade of the chainsaw against the tree trunk, Jones yelled, "Hey, wait! I'm coming down."

"He slipped and fell the last ten feet and deputies grabbed him and handcuffed him," Al said. "He was scratched all over from the tree trunk and the branches, and he was all sticky with pine pitch. He even had gooey pine needles tangled in his hair. He looked like he'd lost a fight with a lion and fallen into a vat of glue. Wait till Don sees the pix I got. He'll forget all about your fiasco with Trish."

Holmberg and his men had taken Jones away for questioning and Al had driven to the hospital to pick me up. We were left with no word as to whether Roxie was being held captive somewhere or lying in a shallow grave.

When we got back to our cabin there was a message from Ann Roberts on the house phone: the sheriff's scheduled four o'clock press conference had been postponed until eight. I wrote my story and e-mailed it to the desk while Al e-mailed some photos. Fred Donlin, the night city editor, e-mailed back a "great job" to both of us and we gave each other a high five.

At 5:30 p.m., when Martha should have been home, I called her. Getting no answer, I called her cell phone, which went to voicemail. I left a message and went to supper with Al, who had called Carol and described our day. "Carol says she hopes you make it to the wedding in one piece," he said.

"So do I," I said.

The dining room was buzzing with speculation when we arrived for dinner. The sheriff had not explained the reason for the postponement of the press conference and nobody in the room knew about the chase and capture of Ronald Jones.

"What do you guys think the reason was?" asked Harry Winston, a reporter for the Minneapolis paper.

"Check out the *Daily Dispatch* online edition," I said. "That's where you can get all the news."

Harry found the page on his smart phone, read the first few lines of my story and yelled, "You bastard! Where'd you get this crap?"

"We followed our noses," Al said. "That's the best way to locate crap."

Harry held up his phone and began spreading the word around the dining room. Al and I gave each other another high five and sat down at a table near the windows. Minutes later Trish Valentine was standing beside us. Her eyes were practically shooting sparks. "I can't believe that sheriff," she said. "How could he blow off the whole press corps except you two clowns?"

"We two clowns found the joker who hid the princess," I said, cheerfully mixing three metaphors. "The sheriff had more important things to do than call in the audience for a briefing. Like getting the joker down out of the sky and into a jail cell."

"He could have called Ann Rogers," Trish said. "She could have spread the word."

"You can discuss public relations with Sheriff Holmberg at eight o'clock," I said. "Meanwhile, I have food on my plate and a stomach that's growling because it thinks my throat's been cut."

"I think you bribed the sheriff some way, and I'm going to ask at the press conference," Trish said. "Meanwhile, enjoy your greasy calories." She spun and strode away as fast as she could go.

We were just finishing our delectable deep-fried walleye and seasoned fries when I smelled cigar smoke. I looked over my shoulder and saw Aaron Ross approaching with an unlit cigar stub clamped in his teeth. The lieutenant governor pulled a chair over and sat down between us at the round table.

"I'm surprised you're still here," I said. "The fishing opener is officially over."

"The governor had to go back to St. Paul and he said for me to hang around another day to see what the sheriff knows about Alex Rogers," Ross said. "I can't believe somebody murdered the guy. There has to be some other explanation."

"Sure looks like murder to me," Al said. "Got any idea who hated Alex enough to whack him on the head and go to all that trouble to make it look like an accident?"

"Not a clue," Ross said. "I know he wasn't the most popular guy in the governor's office but like I said, I can't imagine somebody actually killing him."

"Tough on his wife," I said.

"Yeah, I feel for her. Hubby goes fishing and winds up swimming with the walleyes."

"Do you know if they were getting along okay?"

The cigar almost fell out of Ross's mouth. "What? You think Mari might have hired somebody to whack him while he was up here fishing?"

"Wouldn't be the first time somebody hired a killer to take out their spouse," I said. "And this would have been a perfect opportunity."

"Oh, god, I can't imagine that," Ross said. "I don't know anything about their marriage but Mari is just such a sweetheart." He paused and then said, "But like you said, it wouldn't be the first time."

"The spouse is always the prime suspect," Al said. "But like you said, she'd have had to hire somebody to do the job."

"So if it really was murder, who do you guys think might have done it—not including Mari?" Ross asked.

"We're like you, don't have a clue," I said. No need to tell him that we had a couple of possibilities thanks to Mari.

"Hey, maybe it's the perfect crime," he said.

"Maybe it is, but our experience has been that the killer has made some little mistake in every murder case we've covered," I said.

"In that case, I should be watching for your stories about Alex," Ross said.

"Of course you should. So, when are you going back to St. Paul?"

"I don't know for sure," Ross said. "I'm going to take a swing up to Bemidji tomorrow and then maybe go around the northwest part of the state on my way back to work. Got to schmooze some folks that I'm hoping will support me when I run for governor this fall."

"You seem very sure of the Republican nomination," I said.

"Who's gonna beat me? I don't think I'll even have a primary opponent."

"Lucky you," Al said.

"Damn right. Save me a pile of money if I don't have to run a primary campaign," Ross said.

"So you can buy more ads attacking the Democratic candidate," I said. Ross was noted for the viciousness of his campaign attack ads, which had skewered his past opponents while playing fast and loose with the truth.

"Damn right again," Ross said. "I'm sure I can dig up some dirt on whatever clown they pick to run against me."

"Something to look forward to," Al said.

"Hey, all's fair in love and politics," Ross said. "Well, I gotta go see if Ann has heard anything new from the sheriff. He's wasting way too much time chasing after that missing hooker, if you ask me. He should be concentrating on catching Alex's killer, if there really is one. Anyhow, it's been nice talking to you boys." He rose, shook hands with both of us and hustled away to find another victim.

"Hey, we can breathe again," Al said. "The second-hand smoke coming off his clothes nearly gave me emphysema."

"Think what the governor's office will smell like if he spends four years or eight years sitting there," I said. "The walls will be permeated just from his clothes."

"Old stogies never die, they just pollute your walls." Al sniffed the hand that had been gripped by Ross and made a face like Mr. Yuk. He dipped his dinner napkin into his water glass and sponged his hand with the wet cloth.

My right hand also smelled like stale tobacco smoke but before I could wash it, my cell phone rang and the screen said it was Martha. I answered, not knowing whether she would be worried, puzzled or angry. Turned out she was sympathetic. "Your story said you cracked some ribs when that man attacked you. Are you in bed or what?" she said.

"I'm ambulatory and taking nourishment," I said. "But ambulatory doesn't mean pain-free."

"Oh, you poor babe. I wish I was there to give you a hug."

"Not a good idea. The hug, I mean. You being here would be wonderful but physical contact will have to be minimal for a while."

"Are we still getting married Saturday?" Martha asked.

"I sure as hell hope so," I said.

"Then you'd better bring along some pain pills because there will be physical contact."

"I'll take two Oxycodones and call you in the morning."

"Oxydones? Is that what they gave you?"

"It is, and I'm feeling a little floaty. Fortunately I don't have to drive."

"That's my next question," Martha said. "When will you guys get to drive? I need you back in St. Paul. You have a suit to try on and I could really use some moral support." Because my only suit looked shabby—and had shrunk at the waistline since it was last worn at my college graduation—I had purchased a new one for the wedding. I needed to check the alterations in time to have them redone before Saturday if necessary.

"I'm sure the suit will be fine," I said. "What's with the moral support?"

"The feds are driving Grandma crazy, and because of that she's driving me crazy. Plus there are little last-minute wedding things to do."

"How do things stand with Grandma?"

"We had a hearing today and the judge took the case under advisement. We don't know for sure whether she'll be granted asylum so she can begin the permitting process or whether she'll be put on the next plane to Cape Verde."

"I'm hoping we can come home tomorrow, but we might be stuck here covering the missing-woman search if the guy they caught won't talk."

"Make him talk," she said. "I need you."

"If I had the power to make him talk I would," I said. "But I'm only a mere reporter, not a police interrogator."

As 8:00 p.m. approached, Ann Roberts herded us all into the conference room to await Sheriff Val Holmberg's press conference. When the sheriff arrived at 8:05, he walked into a room full of angry, frustrated people. Before he could speak he was bombarded with a volley of questions about his afternoon activities and with several complaints about giving exclusive information to the guys from the St. Paul paper. I was in my usual spot, directly behind Trish Valentine, when she accused Holmberg of taking some sort of bribe from us.

The decibel level in the room dropped substantially as Holmberg stared, or I should say glowered, at Trish for a long moment before responding. "Young lady, I have been sheriff of this county since you were in grade school and I have never, ever traded any information for a favor of any kind with any reporter from any paper, TV station, radio station, magazine or any kind of publication on God's green earth. For your information, the gentlemen in question were the ones who called our attention to the suspect and immediate action was necessary on our part. And now, unless you apologize for your ignorant accusation, this press conference is over."

Chapter Nineteen

No News Is Bad News

A CHORUS OF "APOLOGIZE" and "tell him you're sorry" arose around the room. Trish hesitated, but finally decided she'd overstepped. She offered an apology that sounded at least partially sincere, the sheriff accepted it and the press conference resumed with Holmberg clearly in charge.

He gave the group a description of the deputies' pursuit of Ronald Jones, the standoff at the pine tree and eventual surrender of Jones, who, Holmberg said, was thought to be involved in the disappearance of Ms. Roxie Robideaux. The sheriff said that nothing had been learned about Ms. Robideaux's whereabouts by questioning Jones because Jones had denied having any knowledge of where she might be and then "lawyered up," refusing to say anything more to the interrogators. Jones had complained of pain from a bruise on his head incurred when he fell from the tree, and was being held for observation under Brainerd police guard in St. Joseph's Medical Center. Upon release from the hospital he would be arraigned on charges of speeding, reckless driving and resisting arrest. Holmberg said the only evidence that could possibly connect Jones with Ms. Robideaux was a pair of women's panties found in Jones's cabin. There was, however, no proof that the panties belonged to Ms. Robideaux and therefore Jones could not be charged with any crime connected to her disappearance.

"The search for Ms. Robideaux has been suspended because of darkness and will be resumed at daybreak," Holmberg said. "We will attempt to question Mr. Jones again after the arraignment, presumably in the presence of his attorney. Now, are there any questions?"

"Can you describe the panties?" yelled Trish.

Holmberg's face reddened almost enough to match the item in question. "They're what is known as a thong, and they're bright red."

Trish persisted. "Are they the right size to fit Roxie?"

The redness in Holmberg's face grew even brighter. "I have no idea what size Ms. Robideaux wears. All I can say is that they're not very big." This drew a laugh from the crowd and I thought Holmberg's face might burst into flame.

When the laughter petered out, a voice in the back of the room asked a question that chilled the atmosphere. "Do you think the girl is alive?"

Holmberg was silent for a minute, and I could visualize the wheels turning while he constructed his answer. "I'm hoping with all my heart that she's alive," he said. "But my gut feeling is that if she was alive, and Mr. Jones knew where she was, he would be talking to us rather than remaining silent. And with that I'll say thank you all for coming and good night. I'll contact Ms. Rogers when there are any new developments."

"That didn't sound good," Al said as the crowd dispersed around us and we started toward the door.

"It's not what anybody wanted to hear," I said. "I'm afraid we'll be covering a search for a body and not a hidden hooker tomorrow."

At the door we were met by Angie Olafson, who was sobbing and wailing. "I heard what the sheriff said. That Roxie is dead."

"He's not positive of that," I said. "She could turn up alive and well tomorrow." I'm sure I didn't sound convincing.

"She's gone," Angie said. "That bastard killed her, I know it."

"Don't give up just yet," Al said. "He might be holding out for a deal before he tells the sheriff where he's got Roxie stashed."

"If she's locked up somewhere she'll starve to death before they find her," Angie said. "They need to beat the crap out of him until he talks."

"I'm sure they'd like to do that, but this is America," I said.

"I don't know what to do," Angie said. "I'm going crazy worrying about her."

She was so distraught that we invited her to come with us and sit in our cabin until she could stop crying and calm down. I had a story to write and Al had pix of the press conference to send. Angie walked between us, sobbing and sniffling all the way to our cabin.

The pleasant, high-sixties daytime temperature had been replaced by a forty-degree nighttime chill. Angie, wearing only a pink T-shirt and white shorts that barely covered her buns, was shivering and displaying a collection of goosebumps on her bare arms by the time we reached the cabin. We wrapped her in a blanket and sat her down on my bed. Al made a cup of hot chocolate with a packet he found beside the coffee pot and Angie sipped it while I tapped out my story and sent it to the desk.

Both Martha Todd and Carol Jeffrey called to say they were hoping that the search for Roxie Robideaux would end on the morrow so Al and I could finally get on the road for home. We reminded both Martha and Carol that there still was a murder case to be dealt with when the emergency search for the missing woman was over. Neither of us had given our statements about finding the lifejacket to the sheriff yet, and all the people who'd been present Friday morning, except the governor and lieutenant governor, were still under orders to remain at the resort until the sheriff had interviewed them.

"We could be here until Wednesday or Thursday if they don't find the woman early tomorrow," I said.

"Thursday?" Martha said. "How about Saturday? Will you be here then or am I getting married to a surrogate groom?"

"I will be there no matter what happens up here," I said. "I'll write out a statement for the sheriff if I have to, and I'll get Don to send up another reporter and photographer so my best man and I can make it to the wedding. I know Don will understand."

"Why can't you have a quiet, nine-to-five, five-day-a-week job that keeps you home in St. Paul all the time?"

"Because I would be bored stiff with that kind of job and you would be bored stiff with me and there wouldn't be any wedding to worry about."

"I suppose you're right. Just promise not to break any more bones or drown or get shot or stabbed or anything before Saturday, okay?"

"I promise," I said. "I swear on a stack of stylebooks that I'll be the most careful, cautious reporter on the *Daily Dispatch* staff for the rest of this week."

"What about after this week?"

"Can't promise a thing."

"Ooh, if I didn't love you so much I would hate you," Martha said.

"Lucky me," I said.

"Damn right you're lucky. Call me in the morning with some good news, please."

"I'll do my best. Love you." We made kissy sounds and clicked off.

By the time Al and I finished our respective phone conversations, Angie was almost asleep. She had slid down from a sitting position and was flat on her back as if preparing to stay for the night.

"Time for you to go home, Angie," I said. "You look like you could use some sleep."

"It's awful comfy here," she said in a small, drowsy voice.

"Sorry, but I'm not sharing the bed. I'll let you keep my blanket and walk you back to your cabin."

"You sure I can't stay? I promise not to rape you."

"Not a good idea to have you here. Come on, up and at 'em."

Grudgingly she sat up, swiveled on her butt and accepted my extended hand to assist her in rising. Still wrapped in my blanket, Angie kept hold of my hand as we walked to her cabin.

"Come in and I'll give you your blanket back," she said as she unlocked the front door. I followed her inside, where she unwound the blanket and handed it to me. Then she wrapped her arms around my neck, pulled my face down to hers and kissed me on the mouth for a long, long time. I confess that I did not resist when she added a thrust of her tongue before she pulled away. "Stay with me," she whispered. "I can feel that you want to." Her body was pressed tight against mine, which was responding the way a male body responds to that kind of kiss.

"Can't happen," I said. "I'm getting married Saturday."

"How will she know if you don't tell her?"

"Al will know. I won't be able to face him."

One hand crept to my crotch. "I need you," she said. "I'm afraid to stay here alone."

It was all I could do to pull her hand away. A miniature tug of war around the zipper on my fly was interrupted by a loud banging on the back door. We stepped apart and stared at the door where the banging persisted.

"Expecting company?" I asked. The banging continued.

"No way," she said. "I wouldn't be grabbing your dick if I thought somebody was coming." More banging at the door.

"You open it and stand off to the side, and I'll deal with whoever is there," I said. The banging was growing weaker.

Angie went to the door and I stood squarely in front of it, about ten feet back. She snapped open the lock, grabbed the knob and yanked the door open. A woman stumbled in, staggered toward me and flung her arms around my neck, sending a bolt of pain shooting through my cracked ribs. I instinctively wrapped her in my arms.

I was holding Roxie. And she was naked.

Chapter Twenty

Roxie's Tale

ROXIE WAS GASPING AND SOBBING and babbling all at the same time. All I could make out was, "Help me. He's going to kill me."

I wrapped her in the blanket I was holding and half-carried her to the bed with my ribs complaining all the way. "You're safe," I said. "He's in the hospital with a cop outside his door. Where were you?"

"On the beach," Roxie said, still gasping for breath. "Under boat."

"He put you under a boat?"

"No, no. I got away. Hid under boat."

"Catch your breath and then tell us what happened," I said. "Angie, get her some water."

Angie ran to the sink and filled a glass from the faucet. She gave it to Roxie, who gulped it down and promptly tossed it back up all over my blanket. "Oh, shit, sorry," she said.

I grabbed the glass and handed it back to Angie. She refilled it and brought it back. I took it and held it in front of Roxie. "Go real easy on this one," I said.

Roxie nodded and I gave her the glass. She took cautious little sips while her breathing slowed to normal.

I sent Angie back to our cabin to get Al and waited for Roxie to finish the water and blow her nose on a tissue from the bedside table. "You said he's in the hospital?" she asked.

"He was packing up to leave this afternoon but I found your thong under his bed," I said. "He took off in his car but the sheriff's deputies chased him and he went off the road and ran into the woods. He climbed a tree, would you believe, and wouldn't come down until they started sawing through it. He fell part of the way down and hit his head so they put him in the hospital for observation. He claimed he didn't know where you were."

"He didn't. I got away and hid under the boat. Did you say that fat-ass climbed a tree?"

"Any port in a storm. When Al and Angie get back here I want you to start at the beginning and tell us everything that happened."

"It was awful," she said. "He wanted me to do pervert stuff, things I would never do, so he tied me up."

I told her to relax a minute and wait for the others. My mini-tape recorder was still in my shirt pocket from taping the sheriff's press conference so I took it out and rewound the tape. Angie and Al, carrying his camera, came rushing in the front door.

"I don't think pictures are a good idea," I said, and Al nodded his agreement. "Now, Roxie, take a big breath and tell us what happened, beginning with you meeting Ronald Jones last night."

"Can I have some more water?" Roxie said. "And is there anything to eat? I haven't had any food since dinner last night."

Angie found a box of crackers in the kitchen cupboard and carried it to Roxie along with another glass of water. I reminded her not to gobble and gulp, so she nibbled at the crackers and sipped the water slowly while she told her story.

"He seemed really nice at first," she said. "He said his name was Ronny and that he was the Ramsey County treasurer. He took me to dinner in a nice place in Brainerd and then we came back here to my cabin to spend the night. We took off our clothes and went to bed and did it once in the regular way, and then he started asking for some kinky stuff. Some of it I didn't mind, but then he got into some other stuff—I won't even tell you what—and I said, 'No way, I won't do that.'

"Well, that pissed him off. He said I was a dirty little whore who'd taken his money and I had to do anything he wanted me to do, and he threw me on the bed and put it to me real rough and hard. Then he said, 'Now you're going to do what I want,' and I said no, I wouldn't. I told him I was done with him and started to put my clothes on—you know, the thong you found and my shorts and sun top. He watched me do that and then he said we were going to his cabin for the rest of the night. I said I wasn't going there and he came after me, chased me around the cabin knocking furniture over and throwing things at me, calling me awful names. Finally he caught me and twisted my arms behind me so it really hurt and said if I screamed he would break my neck and kill me.

"He was pretty strong, and after he pushed me out the door he held my hands behind my back with one hand and clamped his other hand around the back of my neck. He pushed me like that all the way to his cabin, and when we got there he threw me onto the bed and pulled off all my clothes. He said that now I was going to do everything he wanted whether I liked it or not.

"He roughed me up some and did something disgusting that I won't tell you about. And then he used some rope that he had in the kitchen to tie me to the bed. That was one of things he wanted that I didn't want him to do—tie me up and spank my ass. I was spread-eagled naked, face down on the bed and tied to the four legs of the bed. He swatted my buns with both of his hands until they really burned, and then he put his clothes on and said he was going out with some friends and would be back to have some more fun. He said if I tried to get away he would kill me and sink my body in the lake with cement blocks.

"I was trying to breathe and I was crying and he whacked me on the ass about six more times and turned out the lights and left me tied up like that in the dark. I was hurting all over and scared about what would happen when he came back. Could I have some more water, please?"

She handed the glass to Angie, who refilled it and brought it back. After a couple of swallows, Roxie resumed her tale.

"I tried to get loose but he really had me tied up tight and I couldn't. I finally got tired and gave up, and I was almost asleep when he came back. He turned on a light, took of his clothes and flopped onto my bare back. His breath stunk like booze and he slobbered all over me and tried to jab his dick between my legs but he was so drunk he couldn't get it up That made him mad and he swore at me and said I was a two-bit whore that wasn't worth the money. He started choking me and kept it up until I thought for sure I was going to die. Finally he let go and got off me and went into the bathroom where I could hear him puking.

"He came back out and sat in a chair. I could just turn my head far enough to see him. I guess he passed out because he didn't come at me again until it was just starting to be daylight. He was still naked and he said he was going to fuck me one more time before he went out fishing. When he finished, I told him he had to let me up to go to the bathroom. He told me to go ahead and wet the bed and I said it would be a lot more than wet and his cabin was going to stink like a dirty outdoor biffy.

"That convinced him to untie me and let me go to the bathroom. I went in and locked the door as fast as I could. The room had a little window and I could just barely squeeze through it. There I was, standing outside naked, wondering where to go. I knew he'd be checking the bathroom pretty soon, and I only had a few minutes before he'd be putting some clothes on and coming out to look for me. I ran into the trees and kept going until I saw the beach and an old boat that was tipped over upside down. I managed to pull one side up far enough to get under it and I laid in the sand there all day praying he wouldn't find me. I heard him walk past the boat one time but he didn't look under it. I guess he finally gave up, I don't know . . ."

"He did go fishing with another man," I said. "The sheriff had them brought in off the lake for questioning and Ronny told him that he'd never heard of you. We wanted to talk to him so we followed him to his cabin, I pulled the red thong out from under the bed and he knocked me down and ran. But go on with your story. Why did you lay under the boat all day?"

"Well, duh!" Roxie said. "Number one, I didn't know where Ronny was, and number two, I was naked and all beat up. I decided to stay there 'til it got dark and then try to work my way to Angie's back door. The problem was it got cold when the sun went down and I was freezing when I came out from under the boat. I'd have got here sooner but I just snuck along slow, trying to stay out of any light, and for a while I kind of got lost. You're sure that crazy bastard's being guarded by a cop?"

"Sure as we're sitting here listening to you," I said. "Now we should call the sheriff and get him back here. While he's on his way, you're going to put some clothes on and I'm going to write a story about your little adventure and get it in our online edition before the rest of the media mob finds out that you're alive."

"Remember who will be reading that story," Al said. "Have fun explaining to Martha why you were in Angie's cabin at ten o'clock at night."

Oh, god, I hadn't thought about that.

Chapter Twenty-One

Circus Time

YOU'VE PROBABLY HEARD the term "media circus." Well, this one was large enough for three rings and a big top.

I called the ringmaster, Sheriff Val Holmberg, who arrived at the lodge twenty minutes later in a convoy of two squad cars and two SUVs with all lights blazing—strictly showbiz. Ann Rogers had been in the lobby talking to the manager when the sheriff walked up to the desk and asked where to find Angie's cabin. Naturally, the governor's new press secretary had asked Holmberg what was going on. Naturally, he had told her where Roxie had been found. And naturally, Ann had done her job, which was to spread the word to every reporter and photographer on the scene.

She'd found most of the troops partying in the bar, which should have made her job easy. But, being thorough, she'd also put out phone calls to every media-occupied cabin to make sure those not in the bar were alerted. The result was a stampede to Angie's cabin.

Luckily for Roxie, Val Holmberg had learned a few things about handling the mass media over the weekend. He and six deputies had outrun the crowd to the cabin and had strung yards of yellow plastic police tape around the building to create a twenty-five-foot perimeter before the first TV crew came puffing up the path. Within minutes, two dozen people were playing ring around the tape, yelling out questions and shining bright lights through the windows of the cabin while Holmberg talked to Roxie.

Where were Al and I? Inside, of course, since we were part of the rescue team and were required to give our statements. If the folks behind the yellow tape had known this they probably would have tried to crash through the barrier. As it was, Roxie had put on those skin tight jeans and a sweatshirt that was a size too small around the bust line, giving Al the opportunity to take some photos of her bruised and scratched face. He e-mailed them to the desk immediately, and the city editor's selection appeared in the online edition beside my exclusive story while the people outside the cabin were clamoring for their first look at the rescued kidnapping victim.

Oh, yes, my exclusive story. I managed to blur the arrival of Angie and me—I was walking her home because she was so distraught that we feared for her wellbeing—with the assault on the back door by Roxie. In my version, no real time passed between Angie opening the front door and Roxie banging on the back door. No time for hugging, kissing and the arousal of anything male. I was hoping that this would negate the arousal of any curiosity in the mind of a certain St. Paul female.

With Roxie seated more comfortably in a chair, Holmberg led her through a repetition of the story she had told us. While she was talking, Ann Rogers arrived, took a military stance on the front doorstep and tried to quiet the crowd. This only led to more high-volume complaints about abrogation of the First Amendment and denial of freedom of the press. To her credit, Ann remained stoic throughout the verbal assault.

When Roxie finished her story, which got a bit more explicit the second time through, Holmberg said he had an ambulance on the way to take her to the hospital for a checkup. As everyone does when they hear the word "hospital," Roxie stood up and protested, saying she was kind of beat up and hungry but that she would be fine without going to the hospital.

"You won't be fine," Holmberg said. "My men and I won't be here to hold back those people outside, so they'll be yelling at you and beating on your door and looking in your window all night if you stay here. In the hospital you can have your wounds treated and get some food and rest. You are going to the hospital and you will stay overnight for observation, and you'll be under police guard."

Properly chastised, Roxie resumed her seat in the chair. The sheriff went to the front door, opened it a crack and spoke to Ann Rogers's back. She turned her head and said something and Holmberg closed the door.

"Ms. Rogers is telling the media that I will be making a statement in a minute and then Ms. Robideaux will be put in an ambulance and taken to the hospital, where she will be treated for minor injuries and kept overnight for observation," Holmberg said.

"They'll be on you like a pack of wolves," Al said. "Better stay way back from the tape."

"I'm staying on the steps until the ambulance crew arrives. Once they're here we're going to have to walk Ms. Robideaux through the crowd because the ambulance can't get up to the door. You two can help us build a moving shield around her."

"They'll kill us when they see us come out the door," Al said. "They'll tear us apart."

"That's the idea," the sheriff said, with a smile playing at the corners of his mouth. "You'll be a buffer for my deputies and me as we help Ms. Robideaux to the ambulance."

"Hey, we found both the kidnapper and the victim and now you want us to sacrifice our lives to save yours?" I said.

"That's about it. Wish me luck; I'm going out to face them now." He opened the door and stepped out beside Ann Rogers. A roar went up, followed by a sharp reduction in the decibel level when Holmberg raised his arms above his head.

Holmberg did a nice job of delivering an abbreviated version of Roxie's story. I couldn't help thinking he'd be an asset on the *Daily Dispatch* copy desk when a long and salty story had to be trimmed and made fit to print in a family newspaper. He didn't censor the fact that Roxie had been hired by Ronald Jones to provide sexual favors for money, but he glided smoothly over the reasons for Jones's anger and the graphics of the subsequent sexual assaults.

Of course the news mavens were not satisfied with the sheriff's stripped-down picture of the Roxie horror show. They wanted more detail and were demanding it loudly when flashing lights in the distance signaled the arrival of the ambulance. The sheriff was trying to disengage from the crowd and the crowd was trying to keep him answering questions when inspiration struck me. I popped through the door, held up my arms for silence and yelled, "If you want all the details, read my online story in the *St. Paul Daily Dispatch*."

The decibel level rose to a crescendo as every reporter on the other side of the tape started screaming at me. I was called many unpleasant names as they questioned my presence in the cabin, the accuracy of my story and the marital status of my parents at the time of my birth. Trish Valentine was actually bouncing up and down with anger and frustration, which gave me the pleasant feeling that I had more than gotten even for her sneak attack in the morning. While this was going on, the sheriff disappeared into the cabin and four deputies followed him in.

Holmberg and his men formed a solid ring around Roxie as they walked her down the steps and through the cordon of shouting faces, microphones and tape recorders. Al took a position on the left side of the ring of lawmen and I walked on the right. My media compatriots were unsparing in their defamatory remarks but I held my temper until the EMTs from the ambulance had taken charge of Roxie. I finally blew off some steam when a TV reporter from Duluth said, "Hey, Mitch, what were you guys doing in that cabin with those two hot little babes before the sheriff got there?" The sneer and the implication were obvious.

I knew the man was reporting live, so I grabbed his wrist, pulled his microphone up to my chin and held it there while answering his snotty innuendo: "You asked me what we were doing? We were chasing down a hot little news story while you and your buddies were sucking up cold martinis in the bar at company expense. That's what we were doing." I let go of his wrist and he shrunk back like a terrified turtle drawing its head and legs into its shell. *Warren "Mitch" Mitchell reporting live.*

The ambulance pulled away, bound for the hospital in Brainerd with Roxie riding in the front seat beside the driver. The sheriff and his deputies split up, with two following the sheriff to Roxie's empty cabin and three others going to Ronald Jones's abandoned cabin. Al and I followed the sheriff, along with half the media mob. The other news crews followed the deputies. All of us were disappointed when all the sheriff and his men did was string yellow tape around both cabins and warn us to stay outside the perimeter.

"See you tomorrow, folks," Holmberg said. He led his men back to their vehicles with all of us trailing along behind. As he got into his van, Holmberg added, "We'll be searching those cabins for evidence in the morning so you'd better not mess with anything around them. And we'll also be interviewing people about the death of Mr. Alex Gordon. Anyone remember him?" Oh, yeah. The original reason we hadn't all gone home after breakfast Sunday morning.

After the sheriff's entourage disappeared into the night, Al and I kept walking toward our cabin. The media mob split up, some following us and some heading back toward Angie's cabin. I hoped she had followed our advice to lock all the doors, close the curtains and turn off the lights.

We arrived at our cabin with a dozen people trailing behind us. On the doorstep, we turned and faced them and the TV lights lit us up like high noon on a Hawaiian beach. Reporters began shouting questions and I held up my hands for quiet. Instantly, three microphones appeared beneath my nose, including one bearing a big number four.

"You folks have been calling us names and cussing us out all night, so obviously we are not reliable sources to answer your questions," I said. "That means it's good night from Mitch Mitchell and Alan Jeffrey, reporting live from the shores of beautiful Gull Lake." Al was holding the door open. We walked in, slammed the door faster than the spring on a mousetrap and snapped the lock.

After shouting a few final insults, the group outside grew quiet. I peeked out a window, half expecting to see Trish Valentine's face staring back at me. To my relief, all I saw were the backs of people walking away from our cabin. Before I could celebrate, my cell phone warbled and again it was Martha Todd.

"I just got through watching Trish Valentine reporting live from the cabin where the missing woman turned up," Martha said. "Then I went online and read your story. You guys have been pretty busy."

"It's been crazy," I said. "We've gone from covering a report on what we thought was an accidental drowning to a homicide to a possible second homicide to a captured suspect to a returning kidnap victim, all in about twelve hours."

"You must be exhausted."

"You've got that right."

"Tell me something. You didn't come right out and use the p-word in your story but I get the impression that the missing woman and her friend are working in the world's oldest profession. Is that correct?"

"That is correct."

"So tell me something else," Martha said. "What were you doing in that working girl's cabin at ten o'clock at night?"

I knew she would ask that question and was ready with a plausible explanation. I told her that Angie had been terribly distraught about the probability of her friend being dead, that we had taken it upon ourselves to calm her down and that I had walked her home because she was afraid to go alone. "She was barely in the front door when Roxie, the missing woman, started hammering on the back."

"Barely in the door?" Martha said.

"You know what I mean. Barely in the sense of very recently, not in reference to a state of dishabille."

"But the victim who came in the back door, the one you call Roxie, was, as you put it so cleverly, in a state of dishabille?"

"Just for a few seconds. We immediately wrapped a blanket around her."

"We?"

"Angie and I."

"Oh, yes, Angie," Martha said. "How did you and Al happen to the ones who calmed Angie down and escorted her home?"

I could feel myself sinking deeper into a morass. I decided stating the truth would be the best way out. "She and Roxie solicited us the first day and we told them we weren't interested in buying what they were selling. They were very disappointed because, as you know, we are a couple of hot-looking stud muffins, so we bought them each a drink to make them feel better about their missed opportunity. We had a nice friendly conversation that day, sort of like big brothers and kid sisters, and when Roxie didn't come home Sunday night Angie came to us looking for advice. Then later, when the sheriff all but told the press he thought that Roxie was dead, Angie heard it and went ballistic. We happened to be there and we did what friends do. You know, it is possible for a man to talk to a hooker without purchasing her product."

Al, who was listening to my end of the conversation, was covering his mouth with both hands to keep from laughing out loud.

"So you're asking me to believe that you and Al have been spending time strictly as friends and never as customers with two prostitutes you describe in your news stories as young and quite attractive?" Martha said.

"Well, yes," I said. "That's exactly what I want you to believe because that's exactly what's been happening, although I wouldn't say we've been spending very much time with them. You can ask Al; he'll tell you the same thing."

"I imagine he would. After all, Don O'Rourke swears that you two are connected at the funny bone."

"It has nothing to do with how we're connected. It's the honest-to-god truth, Martha."

Beads of sweat were forming on my forehead and I must have sounded desperate because Martha said, "Oh, Mitch, take it easy. I'm just pulling your chain. I can't imagine either of you two cheapskates ever paying a woman for sex."

I realized I'd been holding my breath and let it whoosh out. "I'd rather you believed me because of the high quality of my character than the thriftiness of my nature," I said.

"Whatever toasts your bread, sweetie," she said. "Just be glad I believe you for any reason at all because if I didn't, you'd find your things out in the front yard when you got home—assuming you're ever going to get home."

"Tomorrow they're going to search the cabins of Roxie and her kidnapper and interview those of us who are stuck here until the sheriff lets us go. I'm hoping the sheriff gets to Al and me before we have to spend another night."

"What are going to do all day if he doesn't? Spend some quality big brother time with your new kid sisters?"

"No, no, of course not. We probably won't even see them. We'll be reporting on the search results and whatever else the sheriff does. And we've got a couple of leads on the Alex Gordon murder that we can check out."

"You're not going to get bludgeoned, shot or stabbed by one of those so-called leads, are you?" Martha said.

"No way. I've already cracked some ribs, and that's all the physical damage I can take for one assignment."

"Be sure it is. I don't want to spend our wedding night hugging Sherlock Holmes."

I remembered how my ribs had hurt when Roxie threw herself at me and almost said something about letting Sherlock stand in, or lie in, for me. Wisely, I took a different path. "Don't worry, Sherlock will spend the night in the kitchen," I said. I was counting on my friend Oxycodone to help me make it through the night.

Al was still grinning when I put down the phone. "Sounded like Martha put you through the wringer," he said.

"And hung me out to dry," I said.

"Speaking of hanging out to dry, don't get scared when you go into the bathroom. I washed out some skivvies and hung them over the shower rod."

"Think they'll mind if I hang mine alongside them?"

"No problem. Just don't connect them at the funny bone."

Chapter Twenty-Two

Fishing for Comments

THE SUN WAS SHINING and the temperature was rising toward a normal spring level when Al and I went to breakfast Tuesday morning. As we entered the dining room, Angie Olafson gave us a come-hither wave from a table by the windows.

"I suppose we should join her," I said.

"I seem to remember someone saying that's what friends do, big brother," Al said.

"I seem to remember you laughing like a kid at a clown show while I was trying to save my impending marriage on the phone."

"You should have seen the look on your face while Martha was grilling you. I almost took your picture."

"Either that picture would have been deleted or you'd have been debilitated," I said.

"It would have been delivered to Martha, who would have been delighted," he said.

Angie had managed to put herself together physically, but not so well emotionally. Her blonde hair was neatly pony-tailed with a purple scrunchy and she looked fresh and ready to go in short red shorts and a tight white T-shirt with a full-color leaping walleye on the front. If one ignored the fact that walleyes don't leap, it was appropriate for the occasion.

Her eyes were covered by a pair of sunglasses to hide the effects of crying, but there was anguish in her voice when she spoke. "You know what's really rotten about this whole mess with Roxie?" she said after we sat down.

"Well, what Ronald Jones did to Roxie is pretty rotten," I said.

"The way Roxie spent the day yesterday was also pretty rotten," Al said.

"What are you thinking of as number one on the rotten list?" I asked

"I think it's really rotten that the news stories have been calling Roxie a prostitute, a hooker and a call girl," Angie said. "It's going to kill her parents."

"They didn't know what she's been doing?" Al said.

"Are you kidding? She told them she's serving the customers here," Angie said. "They thought she was waiting on tables."

"What she's doing does involve customer service," I said.

"Different method of delivery," Al said.

"You guys are so not funny," Angie said with tears trickling from under the shades. We both apologized for trivializing the situation and said we hoped that Roxie could straighten things out with her parents.

"They've been humiliated," Angie said. "I don't think they'll give her a chance."

"She's still their daughter," Al said.

"You city guys don't understand the people up here," Angie said. "They're still living by the Bible."

"There were prostitutes in the Bible," I said.

"Yeah, and people were ready to stone them," Angie said. "I'll bet Roxie's parents are out picking up rocks as big as baseballs this morning."

"Are her parents without sin?" I asked. "Remember, Jesus called for anyone without sin to cast the first stone."

"So they'll go to confession," Angie said. "Believe me, Roxie ain't got a chance with her parents."

"That's too bad," Al said. "You two are the nicest bad girls I've ever met."

"Tell that to Roxie's father," Angie said.

We were interrupted by Ann Rogers, who came to our table and said the sheriff wanted to talk to Angie. "The poor man is working two high-visibility cases at once," Ann said. "After he interviews Ms. Olafson he plans to finally begin talking to people who were here when Alex was killed. I'm sure that includes the two of you."

"That can't happen too soon," I said. "I've got a wedding to go to in a few days."

"Hope you make it," said Ann. She took Angie by the arm and led her away without even asking whose wedding I needed to attend.

"Time we checked out those people Mari Gordon mentioned as possible suspects," I said. "We need to get to them before the sheriff does or they'll be on the road for home."

"What's our excuse for talking to them?" Al said.

"That's easy. We're doing a roundup of people's reactions to this crazy weekend. It might even be true. Let me check it out with Don." I took out my cell phone and punched in Don's direct number.

"Don't tell me you've got another dead body," Don said by way of a greeting.

"Nothing that exciting," I said. "This involves live bodies." I floated the idea of a reaction roundup story and he liked it. This was good. It meant we would be talking to more than just our suspects, which would make the suspects less suspicious of our motives.

"Who's up first?" Al said.

"I'm glad you didn't ask who's on first," I said. "To answer your question, I see Channel Five's editorial maven at a table by the door. I suggest we start with him."

"Okay, Dexter Rice it is. I'll let you do the bit about the roundup story."

Dexter Rice, a paunchy, balding man in his late fifties, was in a discussion with two other men, neither of whom looked familiar. We walked up to their table and waited until all three looked our way before saying good morning. I told Rice that we were fishing for comments about the weird events during this Governor's Fishing Opener and asked if he'd like us to wait until his conversation with the other two gentlemen was finished. The three of them agreed that they were finished and the other two left without an introduction or a handshake.

"Couple of network guys from New York," Rice said as we sat down. "They're tired of waiting for the Hicksville sheriff and are flying off to fry some bigger fish today."

"We haven't provided enough bait with a murder and a kidnapping with sexual overtones?" I said. "What are they looking for, a sex-addicted gunman to shoot up a convent full of nuns?"

"They're used to dealing with high speed New York cops. Our sheriff moves way too slow for them. I don't know if it's true, but I've heard that this is his first homicide case ever."

"Wouldn't surprise me," I said. "I think he's doing fairly well, considering the major distraction thrown in by Ronald Jones kidnapping and beating up a woman."

"I can't picture Jones going off like that," Rice said. "Not that I know him all that well, but he seemed like the quiet type."

"It's always the quiet man who surprises you with a criminal act," Al said. "How many times have you heard a killer's neighbor tell a reporter, 'he was a quiet man'?"

"Well, you don't have to worry about me then, do you?" Rice said. "People are always telling me to shut up."

"Good point," I said. "But we're here to let you talk. What do you want to say about this weekend's activities?"

Rice sat back, removed his wire-rimmed glasses and thought for a moment. "If I had to describe them in one word I guess that word would be 'bizarre,'" he said. "I've been to quite a few fishing openers and never imagined anything like this could happen."

"That's right, you were the governor's press secretary for a couple of terms," I said. "You had Alex's job with Governor Patterson, didn't you?"

"Yes, I was Governor Patterson's press secretary for eight years, so I prefer to think of it as Alex having my job with Governor Anderson."

"I'll be careful how I phrase it."

"I wish you would," Rice said.

"Were you surprised that Governor Anderson, being another Republican, didn't keep you on as press secretary when he took over from Patterson?"

"Nothing surprises me in politics. But it would have made sense to keep me."

"Did Anderson tell you why he was making the switch?"

"Not really. He gave me the old crap about wanting to bring his own team on board but I don't think that's the whole reason."

I liked the way this was going. "What else might it be?" I asked.

Apparently Rice did not like the way this was going. "I'd rather not say any more about it," he said. "It was the governor's prerogative to hire whomever he wanted to; let's leave it at that. I thought you wanted to ask me about this weekend, not ancient history."

Damn, I thought. "Right," I said. "What else would you like to say about the weekend?"

"How about this: Instead of the weekend of the walleye it was the weekend of the weird. First you had a killer bungling his attempt to make a murder look like an accident and then you had a sex pervert screwing up . . . no, better make that botching up . . . a night with a prostitute. And did the idiot really climb up a tree?"

"Al got pictures of him thirty feet off the ground," I said. "What are your feelings about Alex's murder?"

"Tragic. He was a hard worker and a fine press secretary and I'm sure we'll all miss him." Rice put his glasses back on. "Now, if that gives you enough, I've got to see a man about a horse. Morning coffee is hitting bottom."

"That's fine," I said. I made a show of turning off my tape recorder and said, "Do you mind telling me off the record what you really thought of Alex Gordon?"

Rice frowned. "You guarantee it's off the record?"

"Swear it on a stack of stylebooks."

"That's your bible?"

"That's my bible."

"Good enough. Off the record, Alex Gordon was an ass-kissing, self-serving little prick with a put-on Harvard accent. Have a good day, gentlemen."

"No tears shed over Alex by that one," Al said as Rice strode off.

"He's more likely to wet Alex's grave with what he's putting in the urinal," I said.

"Well, he certainly had both motive and motivation to murder."

"And if he came up Thursday like the rest of us he had the opportunity Friday morning. Who knows, he might have started the morning as Alex's fishing partner."

"Possible. But how would he get to shore after dumping the body out of the boat? He doesn't look like he could swim that distance in lukewarm bath water, much less ice-cold lake water."

"That whole scenario has puzzled me from the start. If the killer dumped the body out of the boat and left the boat circling, how did he get to the island to bury the lifejacket and how did he get back to Madrigal's?"

"A second boat?"

"Possibly," I said. "If so, was it provided by a second person?"

"You think we might be looking for two killers?" Al asked.

"Maybe. Or at least an accomplice after the fact."

"This could get complicated."

"It already is complicated."

"So what we do now?"

"Now we look up our other prospect, Mr. Joe Weber of the secretary of state's office," I said.

"Didn't Mari say she wasn't sure if he was here?"

"If he is here, we can get his cabin number from Ann Rogers and go knock on his door."

"And you're hoping we'll find a killer behind that door?"

"I'm hoping to at least find a clue behind that door." Al looked at me with a question in his eyes. "What?" I asked.

"Mr. Obsessive Grammarian, didn't you just split an infinitive?" he said.

"Damn, you're right. Cracked it wide open. Whatever you do, don't tell Don."

Chapter Twenty-Three

All About Alex

Not only was Joe Weber at the resort, he was inside the cabin that Ann Rogers pointed to on Madrigal's map. He answered our knock with a "who's there?" and opened the door wearing only tight white undershorts when our response indicated that his visitors were both male.

He was a tall, wiry man with a long face, a nose like a hawk's bill and dark circles under his pale blue eyes. His brown hair was disheveled, as if it had been recently slept on. He confirmed this by saying he had been trying to catch a few winks after lunch so he'd be fresh for the drive home.

"Has the sheriff talked to you?" I asked.

"Not yet, but I'm near the top of his crazy, bass-ackwards list," Weber said. "What do you guys want?"

I explained our reaction story mission and asked if he would comment on the weekend. He thought a moment and decided to invite us in. Once inside we saw that his luggage was packed and sitting near the door, ready to be moved to his car.

Weber waved us toward a couple of chairs and he sat on the end of the bed facing us. He ran the fingers of his right hand through his straggly hair and asked, "Is there any particular thing you want me to comment on?"

"Not really," I said. "Just give us your feelings about the weekend in general compared to what you expected, and that might lead me into asking a question or two." I took the tape recorder out of my pocket and turned it on.

"Well, what can I say? I mean, we all came up here expecting to have a lot of fun fishing and drinking and shooting the shit . . . uh, I mean, bull . . . with our buddies. And what did we get instead? One crazy thing after another. A drowning that turned out to be a murder and a kidnapping of a hooker who turns up naked the next night. We could have stayed home and had all that."

"Surely not in St. Paul," I said.

"Well, you might have had to go to Minneapolis for the naked hooker but there have been a few murders in St. Paul. I read the *Daily Dispatch* every day and I think I recognize your name from stories about the guy who got poisoned at the state fair last summer. Am I right?"

"You are. And I'm flattered that you remembered my byline."

"I'm a detail oriented person," Weber said. "I have to be in my job."

"That's my next question. What is your job?"

"I'm the assistant to the secretary of state. That means I keep things in order and make sure the office staffers do their jobs."

"Your boss is a Democrat, isn't he?" I asked.

"He is. One of the blessed few left in state office right now."

"So do you have much contact with the Republican side? Did you know Alex Gordon very well?"

Weber's face went grim. "Too damn well," he said. "Please don't put that remark in your story."

"Sounds like you weren't very fond of Mr. Gordon."

"I have no comment on Mr. Gordon."

I shut off the tape recorder and stowed it in my pocket. "How about off the record? Did you have a problem with Alex?"

"Everyone who wasn't a rightwing Republican had a problem with Alex," Weber said. "You're in the news business, you should know that."

"I know he was very one-sided when he talked politics with reporters but I didn't know it affected the work of people in other offices," I said.

"In my case the problem wasn't the job. It was the election that got us into that office. Do you remember how nasty the campaign was two years ago when my boss won in a recount?"

"I remember a lot of attack ads, mostly from the Republican side."

"Right. And the most dishonest, biggest-lie attack ads were written by none other than Mr. Alex Gordon."

"Some of them were really vicious," Al said.

"Those were the ones written by Alex," Weber said. "I called the son of a bitch up a few times and offered to break his goddamn nose. He laughed about it and went right on lying and slinging mud. It turned out okay in the end. I actually think my boss won because Alex's ads turned off so many independent voters."

"That was two years ago," I said. "Have you or your boss had any problems with Alex since then?"

"The governor has been totally unresponsive to our office and I think it's because of Alex. He and I have e-mailed back and forth and some of them have been pretty nasty. I guess I started it by rubbing his nose in the election results but he was as vicious with his e-mails as he was with his ads. It started with our political differences but it got really personal. He even slandered my husband."

After a moment of surprised silence, I said, "Your husband?"

"I'm married to a man," Weber said. "We were one of the first couples in line when gay marriage became legal in Minnesota."

"And Alex made that an issue?"

"He said things about my marriage to Raymond that I won't even repeat. I cut off all contact with Alex after that. I was just too damn mad to even write an e-mail. If I'd had Alex there I'd have . . . Oh, my god, you promised this is off the record, didn't you?"

"I did and it is," I said. "I imagine you weren't terribly sorry to see them carrying Alex in a body bag the other morning."

"If they catch whoever killed the little bastard I'll blow him a kiss at his trial," Weber said.

I couldn't resist asking, "What if the sheriff thinks you did it after you tell him all this?"

"No way," Weber said. "I hated Alex but I'm not smart enough to pull off a stunt like leaving his boat running around in circles, like he fell out and couldn't get back in."

"That was pretty creative but the trick didn't work," Al said.

"Only because the guy hit him too hard," Weber said. "If he'd just knocked Alex out instead of killing him he would have drowned."

I was trying to form my next question when we heard a knock at the door. "Who is it?" Weber yelled.

"It's me, Ann Rogers," said a woman's voice. "The sheriff wants to talk to you in the office. He's taking people in reverse alphabetical order, you know. You're right after Gabriel Zymanski."

"Tell him I'll be there in a couple of minutes," Weber said. "I've got company and I need to get dressed."

"That's more information than I need," Ann said. "See you in the lodge."

"Oh, god, that didn't sound good, did it?" Weber said. "She must think I've got that other little whore in here."

"Not if she knows you're gay," Al said.

"I'm not sure about that. Anyhow, I'll explain it was you guys when I get to the lodge," Weber said. "And you've got me thinking I should be careful what I tell the sheriff about my problems with Alex."

"I'd recommend telling the truth," I said. "It has a way of coming back to bite you if you try to hide anything."

"He might make me a suspect."

"He might have good reason to make you a suspect."

He rose from the bed. "What? Do you think I did it?"

I stood up to answer. "To be honest with you, I wouldn't count you out."

Weber's face grew red and he clenched both fists. "Get the hell out of my cabin," he said. "And don't you print anything I said or I'll come after you."

"Not even what you said on the tape?" I asked.

"Not even that. I don't want my name in your goddamn rag if you think I killed Alex."

Al and I stood and went to the door. "Have fun with the sheriff," I said as we stepped out into the sunshine.

"Kiss my ass," Weber yelled before slamming the door behind us.

"Could be our man," I said as we walked toward the lodge.

"Like our other person of interest, he's got motive and motivation," Al said.

"And a very quick temper to go with them."

"The kind of temper that could make him hit a guy too hard."

We returned to the lounging area in the lodge, looking for other fishing opener weekenders to interview. As luck would have it, the first person we ran into was Joe Weber's boss, Secretary of State Harold Svendsen. He gave us a couple of quotes that were similar to Rice's and Weber's, but added that the diversion, although unfortunate for the individuals involved, was actually in a way welcome because the fishing had been way below par.

"So Alex Gordon's death relieved your boredom?" I said.

"Oh, god no, I didn't mean it to sound like that," Svendsen said. "Please don't put it that way in the paper, Mitch. Of course Gordon's death was a tragedy for his family."

"How about for the people he worked with? How do you feel about Alex's murder?"

"I'd rather not comment on my personal feelings about Alex Gordon."

I turned off the tape recorder and pocketed it. "If we go off the record would you comment just for our enlightenment?"

"It's better that I don't. We were miles apart politically and philosophically and I'm going to leave it at that."

"I understand that Alex wrote some of the most vicious attack ads during your campaign for office."

"Who told you that?"

"Your assistant, Joe Weber. Don't worry, his comments on Alex were off the record and won't be reported.

"Joe was ready to kill Alex over those ads," Svendsen said. "Oops, maybe I shouldn't have said it that way under the circumstances. I meant 'kill' figuratively, not literally."

"Do you think Joe might be capable of doing it literally?" I asked.

"Oh, Mitch, what a crap question! Of course not. I'm amazed that you'd even ask that. Joe Weber is a level-headed public servant who would never even think of doing such an outrageous thing."

"Just touching all the bases. Thanks for your comments and your time, Mr. Secretary."

"You're welcome," he said. "And please don't print anything I said in connection with Joe Weber and Alex Rogers. Rogers is gone and there's no reason to pursue that battle against a dead man."

As we moved on looking for another interviewee, Al said, "Do we think that the gentleman doth protest too much?"

"Methinks he did sort of go overboard when I asked that, as he called it, crap question," I said. "He must be aware of Joe Weber's quick temper and hatred of Alex Rogers."

Our next catch was State Treasurer Mathew Hardcastle, an old-school conservative whose name fit the tightfisted fiscal policies that he championed. He was tall and thin—almost gaunt—with a long chin and close-cropped snow white hair. His response was a familiar tune until I asked how he viewed the death of Alex Rogers.

"Terrible loss to the state and to the citizens," Hardcastle said. "A very bright young man with a great political future in the Minnesota Independent-Republican Party."

"You saw him as a rising star?" I asked.

"Absolutely. He'd have been a great candidate for state office. I'd bet you that he could have knocked that left wing loony Harold Svendsen out of the secretary of state's office next time around. Alex wrote some powerful campaign ads last time and he'd do even better delivering those ads in person."

"I've heard that Alex's ads actually turned off a lot of independent voters and cost his man the election," I said.

"There's no proof of that piece of leftwing poppycock. You probably heard that from that scumbag Joe Weber."

That caught my attention. "Scumbag?"

"Yes, scumbag. You can quote me on that if the subject ever comes up, not that I expect it to in this story. But think about it. With all Weber's leftwing populist blabber, why wasn't he running for public office? Check him out."

"Maybe I'll do that," I said. "Thanks for the tip."

"My pleasure," Hardcastle said. "Now if you don't require anything further of me, I'll be on my way. Have a good day, gentlemen."

"It'll be really good if we get to say goodbye to Gull Lake before the sun goes down," I said in response.

"You may be seeing another sunrise over Steamboat Bay," Hardcastle said. "The sheriff is talking to a lot of people, and the way he's doing it puts Mr. Jeffrey's last name seventeenth in the reverse alphabet."

I counted backwards on my fingers from W to J as Hardcastle walked away. "He's right," I said. "I'll be waiting around for you."

"If he'd gone the normal way I'd be waiting around for you, so what's the difference?" Al said. "What we need to do is convince him to take us together as one big M for Mitchell, which would put me three letters closer."

"I'll tell him we have to stay together because we're joined at the funny bone," I said.

"He should get a laugh out of that."

While we waited for my turn with Sheriff Holmberg, we buttonholed three more opening day holdovers for comments on the proceedings. We now had six that could be put in the paper so we went back to our cottage where I could write about the comments and Al could send his mug shots of my subjects.

Before I started to write what was turning out to be a less-than-absorbing story, I called a man with whom I'd worked on several St. Paul murders. "Homicidebrown," he answered, all in one word as he always does.

"*Dailydispatch*mitchell," I replied, all in one word as I always do.

"Mitch, old boy," said Detective Lieutenant Curtis Brown, chief of the St. Paul Police Department's homicide division. "How are the walleyes biting?"

"Haven't had much time to look for walleyes," I said. "We've been too busy looking for bodies, both dead and alive."

"Yeah, I've been reading your stuff in the paper. It sounds like you're involved in some kind of TV reality show up there. Did the kidnapper really climb up a tree?"

"You must have seen Al's pictures of him sitting way up high and later falling on his stupid head."

"I did, but they could have been photo-shopped."

"Never happen to a *Daily Dispatch* news photo," I said. "Feature photos might be tweaked, but not a news shot."

"That's good to hear, but I'm sure you didn't call to fill me in on the ethics of the *Daily Dispatch* photo department," Brown said. "What's on your mind?"

"I want to ask a teeny tiny little bitty favor of you. If you say yes you could be helping solve the murder of a public employee on Gull Lake."

"Gull Lake's not in my jurisdiction."

"Doesn't matter whose jurisdiction it is. Truth knows no boundaries."

"Who said that, George Washington? So tell me, what is this teeny tiny little bitty favor, and is it legal?"

"I'm asking you to check if there are any rap sheets for a couple of people. I'll let you decide on the legality."

"Oh, come on, Mitch, you know I can't do that for you."

"My question is not can or can't, it's will or won't," I said.

Brown was silent for a moment. "Who are the people?"

"Their names are Dexter Rice and Joseph Weber."

"Are you shittin' me?" Brown said. "Rice is a very prominent person and Weber is a government official, for god's sake."

"They're also high on the widow Gordon's list of people who possibly hated her husband enough to kill him."

"I can't believe you're serious."

"Have I ever played games with you?"

"About a dozen times that I can think of," Brown said. "Do you want to hear the list?"

"All I want to hear, or see, are the results of a rap sheet check. I will dispose of all evidence immediately after reading."

"Sorry, no can do. Have a nice day, Mitch." The phone went dead.

"Will he do it?" Al asked as I put down my phone.

"I think so," I said. "All his phone calls are recorded so he had to say no, but knowing Brownie, I'm betting that he'll find a way to come through. He is, first and foremost, a homicide detective."

Chapter Twenty-Four

Q and A with the Sheriff

It was 3:04 P.M. when I finally was summoned to the office by Ann Rogers to take my turn with Sheriff Val Holmberg. Al tagged along and when we suggested to Ann that we give our statements as a team she said she would ask the sheriff if that was acceptable.

When she emerged from the office she shook her head in the negative and I went in alone. I decided to try again with the sheriff, saying that we'd both be telling the same story.

"That's what I want to check," Holmberg said. "That's exactly why I want to question you separately." I knew that, but I needed to find out if he did. Apparently he'd gone to the same school as the big city cops, who always separate their witnesses.

"Do you think you'll get to Al by the end of the day?" I asked. "We're both getting tired of washing out our underwear every night."

Holmberg smiled. "From all the bitching I've been hearing, you're not the only ones doing that. I'll get to your buddy when his turn comes up and I can't promise it will be today. Now then, first I'm going to ask you about finding the lifejacket on the island, and then I'm going to ask you about your relations with those two little hookers."

"I haven't had relations with either of those two little hookers." Jeez, I was sounding like President Clinton.

"Poor choice of words on my part. What I want is a complete rundown on how you met them and how you happened to be in Ms. Olafson's cabin when Ms. Robideaux appeared. So let's get started with the lifejacket story, and remember to include how Ms. Robideaux came to be in the boat with you and your buddy that day."

I told the story of meeting Roxie and Angie as fast as I could, and moved on to telling about the fishing trip that ended up on the island. Holmberg kept interrupting me with questions and backtracks until I thought I'd never get to the accidental discovery of the lifejacket's burial site. When my story finally reached the point where Holmberg and his deputies joined us on the island, he turned the questioning to the disappearance of Roxie Robideaux.

Holmberg seemed intrigued by our reason for following Ronald Jones to his cabin. "You say you followed him just because you had a bad feeling about him?" the sheriff asked.

"That's right," I said.

"No other reason? Purely on a gut feeling?"

"He fit Angie's description and I just had a bad feeling about the guy in general."

"Man, I should hire you on as a deputy. With instincts like that you could really cut down the time needed to apprehend a suspect. Care to try solving the Gordon murder case, then?"

"I'm already working on it."

"You're working on it? How?"

"By being a reporter. I don't have enough to back up my suspicions yet but I'll let you know when—better make that if—I do. How about you? Any suspects?"

"No. At this point I don't even have a person of interest," Holmberg said. "The governor was no help and the lieutenant governor exercised what he called 'executive privilege' and left for Bemidji and points west to start his campaign for governor. I'll have to track him down when he gets back to St. Paul if I want a statement from him."

"Wear your gas mask when you question him or the second-hand cigar smoke will give you virulent lung cancer," I said.

"Yeah, the air around him does seem kinda thick. But let's get back to your story. I believe we left off with Mr. Jeffrey following Mr. Jones to his cabin."

I picked up the story with me knocking on Ronald Jones's front door and continued from there, again with stops for questions and requests for repetition. It was almost 4:30 when we finally reached the point of the sheriff's arrival on this scene. Holmberg thanked me for my cooperation and ushered me to the door. As I went out he instructed Ann Rogers to send in the next person on the list. I heard him say, "That'll be the last one for today. I'm talked out." I emitted an agonized groan but I don't think he heard me.

When I entered our cabin I was greeted by the sight of Al lying facedown on his bed with Angie Olafson straddling his buttocks and leaning forward with her hands on his shoulders and her boobs dragging on his back.

To my relief, both were fully clothed. Still, I thought the situation warranted an explanation, so I requested one as calmly as I could.

"Massage," Angie said as she continued to knead his shoulders. "Don't get your knickers in a twist."

"M' back was killing me," Al mumbled with his face in the pillow. "'M I up yet?"

"We're washing out another day's worth of underwear," I said. "The guy who followed me in will be the last one for the day."

Al pushed himself up onto his elbows, freeing his mouth and nearly toppling Angie backwards. "I'm sick of washing out underwear," he said. "The shorts I've got on didn't even get all the way dry."

Angie giggled. "You can borrow some of mine."

"My body parts won't fit in a thong," Al said.

"Just thinking of you in a thong is wrong," I said.

"I'd sing a song in a higher key wearing a thong too tight for me," Al said.

"Oh, stop it," Angie said. "I was only kidding." She sat back, resting her butt on Al's calf muscles.

"No need to apologize," I said. "To offer a thong is to do no wrong."

"Please," Angie said. "You sound like Doctor Seuss." She swung one leg across Al's legs and got off the bed. I was working up a suitably Seussian reply when the phone beside the bed rang. Al skootched forward on his belly, answered the phone and listened to the caller. "Oh, goddamn it, no!" he yelled. "Why in hell would he do that?" He rolled to the edge of the bed and stood up, still listening. "Thanks anyway for the head's up," he said. He put the phone down and looked at me with wide eyes and an open mouth.

"What?" I asked.

"The sheriff just called Ann Rogers and she's alerting the press. Ronald Jones has disappeared from the hospital."

"Oh, my god, we'll never get home," I said. I flopped into a chair ready to sink into deep depression and despair.

"Do you think he'll come after Roxie for revenge?" Angie said.

"Isn't she in the same hospital?" Al said.

"She got out at noon. I picked her up and she's sleeping in my cabin," Angie said.

I jumped up out of the chair. "Go wake her up. She needs to move to a protected place."

"Like where?" Angie said.

I searched a moment for an answer. "Like, damn it, here."

Angie dashed out the door.

My cell phone rang. It was Martha Todd.

Chapter Twenty-Five

Guarding Roxie

"ARE YOU GUYS on the way home yet?" Martha Todd asked. "Trish Valentine just reported live that the sheriff has been taking statements from people all day."

"He got mine but he quit before he got to Al," I said. "We're stuck here for at least another day."

"What do mean by 'at least'? Surely he'll get to Al tomorrow."

"Don't bet on it. The creep who kidnapped the woman here has disappeared from the hospital. The woman hunt is over but the manhunt is on."

"Oh, no! I don't believe it."

"Well, do believe it. Trish Valentine will be reporting it live any minute now. I just hope they catch him soon."

"Are they checking the tree tops?" Martha asked.

"I'd be going out on a limb to answer that," I said. "Actually, I don't know where they're looking. The news was relayed through the governor's press secretary and she didn't branch out with any details."

The front door swung open and Roxie and Angie dashed in, greeting us loudly as they did. I motioned for them to shut up but it was too late.

"Do I hear women's voices?" Martha said.

I was tempted to say it was the TV, but I decided that telling the immediate truth might save me from later embarrassment. "Yes, you do," I said.

"So who's there? Some other reporters?"

Ooh, there was a good way out. I could tell her that Trish Valentine was in our cabin reporting live. Instead, I confessed that Roxie and Angie had just come in.

"The hookers?" she said. "Are you telling me that you and Al have those two hookers in your cabin?"

"I am. Angie was afraid that the creep might come after Roxie for revenge so we offered to hide her momentarily until the sheriff can move her to someplace safe."

"Oh, aren't you the gallant big brothers, protecting your little sisters? And how long do you expect 'momentarily' to last?"

"Probably, oh, say, less than thirty minutes," I said. "The sheriff or one of his deputies should be here by then."

"I thought you said you didn't know where the sheriff and his deputies were looking," Martha said.

"Well, yeah, but he's got to send somebody to the resort to take care of Roxie."

"You're sure of that?"

"As sure as I am about anything that's happening here."

"In other words, you don't have the faintest idea how long you will be playing house with two young prostitutes."

"I would hardly call it playing house, Martha. We're just keeping our little sisters safe."

"My question is whether *you're* safe," she said. "And I don't mean from the revenge-seeking kidnapper."

"What? You think we're going to be seduced by two young girls half our age?"

"They might be that desperate."

"Thanks so much for the compliment."

"You're so welcome. Tell you what: give your phone to Roxie."

"What are you going to do?"

"Never you mind what I'm going to do. Just give your phone to Roxie."

I called Roxie over, told her my fiancée wished to speak with her and handed her my phone. After "hello," Roxie said nothing. She just listened, and as she did her eyes grew wider and her jaw dropped.

When Roxie handed back the phone I asked Martha what she had said. "Girl talk," she said. "No need for you to know."

We talked for a few more minutes, mostly about Martha's efforts to straighten out her grandmother's problems with the immigration office. She also reminded me that we had a wedding scheduled for Saturday and said it would be appreciated if I were in attendance. When we were finished I asked Roxie what Martha had said to her.

"Girl talk," Roxie said. "I can't tell you what all she said. All I know is you'd better be awful damn careful when you marry that woman." I was already aware of that.

Now, because of Martha's questions, I had begun to wonder whether the sheriff really would send a man to Madrigal's. I decided to find Ann Rogers and ask her what she knew. "I hope you're safe here alone with these two women," I said to Al as I opened the door to leave.

"I have a feeling my phone will ring as soon as Martha passes the word about our guests to Carol," Al said. "That should keep me busy while you're gone." I heard his cell phone sound off as I pulled the door shut behind me.

I found Ann Rogers in the lodge, pinned against one of the fireplaces by a dozen people carrying notebooks and cameras. She was telling them that she had no details other than that the sheriff and his deputies were organizing a search to find Ronald Jones.

"How'd he get away?" Barry Ziebart asked. "Wasn't there a guard on his room?"

"The guard went to the men's room," Ann said.

"How long was he gone?" Trish Valentine asked.

"I'm not sure. However long it takes for a man to do what he had to do."

Knowing that this would depend on several variables, such as the nature of the mission, the quantity of the mission and the guard's efficiency in accomplishing the mission, I decided to take a different track and asked where Jones might have found transportation to get away from the hospital.

"Probably caught a taxi," Ann said. "The Brainerd police are checking with cab drivers and also with bus drivers to see if anybody remembers picking up a man of Jones's description."

"What was he wearing?" Trish asked. "Seems like they'd remember seeing him if he was running around in his Johnny."

"I'm not sure what he was wearing," Ann said. "I just assumed he put on his clothes."

"Any trees near the hospital?" said a voice behind me. This produced a round of laughter.

"Funny man," Ann said. "I doubt Mr. Jones is back to climbing trees. Now if you folks are done asking serious questions I'll see if I can get in contact with the sheriff and get some more information." As the mob parted like the Red Sea before Moses, Ann strode through the gap and headed for the office.

I settled into an armchair and sent an e-mail describing the latest turn of events to the *Daily Dispatch* city desk. Fred Donlin, the night city editor, e-mailed back a request for a brief story to post on the online edition. He also asked if Al had a mug shot of the missing man. I was sure he had some from the interview that preceded the kidnapper's tree climbing adventure so I went back to the cabin to pass the word to Al.

To my amazement, he was alone. "Where are the girls?" I asked.

"Deputy LeBlanc came knocking on our door and took them away," Al said.

"How'd he know to knock on our door?"

"He said he tried both of their cabins and when he found them empty he guessed that we would be, as he put it, 'entertaining them here.' I think we're getting a reputation."

"Oh, great. There's nothing like being known for 'entertaining' prostitutes. Speaking of which, what did Carol have to say?"

"She said she trusted me completely." His expression told me there was more.

"But?" I asked.

"But she talked to Roxie. And Roxie was impressed."

"More secret girl talk?"

"Exactly. I'd sure like to know what she said."

"Maybe you'd rather not know. Anything that scares Roxie has to pack a potent punch. Anyhow, right now we need to pack some copy and some pix off to the city desk." I sat down to write the story and Al flipped through his file to find the best mug shot of Ronald Jones.

When I booted up my laptop again I discovered that I had mail from an unknown sender. I gambled on opening the message, planning to delete it if it carried an attachment or contained a link to something else. It had neither, and the return address was that of a public library. The sender didn't identify himself but the content of the message told me who it was.

Chapter Twenty-Six

Finding a Pattern

LOOK AT WHAT I GOT from A Nonny Mouse," I said to Al as I turned the computer screen to face him. What he saw was this brief message: "JW fnd glty asult w/ddly wpn, 8/15/12. Srvd 30 days + 90 prob + 60 pblc srvc. Male vic w/concussion."

"Whoa!" Al said. "No wonder Weber wasn't running for office. Imagine what fun the Republicans would have with this."

"We owe Brownie for this one. Maybe you can shoot a really good angle of him with the next VIP who comes to town." Getting a really good photo angle on Brownie was difficult because he is nearly bald and his ears stick straight out like the mirrors on the cab of an eighteen-wheeler.

"I suppose I could Photoshop his ears."

"I just told the sheriff we never do that with news copy, only features," I said.

"Brownie's ears are a feature," Al said.

"They're a double feature. Like a pair of movie screens."

"I'll see if I can turn them into a short feature next time I shoot him."

"I wonder who the victim was and what prompted the assault," I said. "I wish Brownie had included that bit of info."

"Maybe there was a story in the paper at the time."

"Now why didn't I think of that? Maybe you should be the reporter."

"No thanks. I feel safer hiding behind my camera."

I called the *Daily Dispatch*, punched in the extension for the morgue and got Alice Strait, the keeper of all things historical. I asked her to look up anything she could find on Joseph Weber and e-mail copies to me. A few minutes later a message from Alice that included several attachments popped up in my e-mail. The most interesting attachment was a crime short saying that Joseph Weber, age forty-one, had been charged with assault with a deadly weapon after a fight in Finnegan's Bar on Payne Avenue in St. Paul. According to the story, Weber allegedly struck a man named Peter Vanfleet on the head with a beer bottle with enough force to shatter the bottle.

We flipped through the other attachments and found briefs about Weber's appointment to the secretary of state's staff, a citation for speeding and reckless driving and the court appearance that Brownie had sent us.

"We need to talk to Peter Vanfleet," I said.

"Could it wait until after supper?" Al said. "My stomach tells me it's that time."

"So does my watch. Let's go."

The dining room was filled with grumbling reporters and photographers who either hadn't been interviewed by the sheriff or had been ordered by their bosses to stay and cover the search for the escaped kidnaper. Everyone was voicing loud support for a quick capture and immediate confinement, preferably solitary, in an extremely secure facility. The pain that rippled through my ribs every time I moved gave me an additional interest in the pursuit. I couldn't help but hope Ronald Jones would experience some physical discomfort at the time of his apprehension. A bullet in the soft part of his posterior would not make me weep for him.

We all sat around in the lounge after dinner hoping for a report from the sheriff via Ann Rogers. It didn't come until almost eight o'clock and it didn't give us much to work with. A man answering the description of Ronald Jones had taken a cab to a car rental agency near the airport, where he acquired a gray Chevrolet sedan. Nobody knew which way he had gone but every paved road that led out of the Brainerd area was being watched.

I asked Ann how a hospitalized man who'd been scheduled for a court appearance the morning he disappeared was able to keep his wallet with cash and credit cards. Ann shrugged and said the wallet had been left with his clothing in a closet in his hospital room. "Just one of those dumb little mistakes that people sometimes make," she said.

With no more immediate news on the horizon, the group broke up. Al and I adjourned to our cabin, where Al started taking off his clothes while I called information and obtained a number for one Peter Vanfleet in St. Paul. For some reason the name seemed familiar but I couldn't attach it to any personal meeting or news story.

A woman answered, said she was Mrs. Vanfleet and told me that her husband was at a meeting and wouldn't be back until nine o'clock. I identified myself as a reporter and asked her to have him call me no matter how late he got home.

"A reporter? What's this about?" she asked.

"It's about an incident in Finnegan's Bar a few years ago," I said.

"You're not going to drag all that crap out and put it in the paper again, are you?"

"No, it definitely will not be in the paper. It's strictly for background. The man who hit your husband might be in trouble again."

"Wouldn't surprise me," she said. "That man's a walking time bomb."

"Apparently he went off on your husband."

"Did he ever. Who'd he whack on the head this time?"

"I'm sorry, but I can't say. I don't have enough evidence yet."

"I hope the bastard goes to jail," she said. "I'll have Pete call you when he gets home."

Al was sitting in bed with two pillows behind his back talking to Carol and the kids on his cell phone. I stripped to my underwear and went into the bathroom to brush my teeth. A pair of wet white undershorts hung over the shower curtain bar. A few minutes later they were joined by another. They hung side-by-side like two white flags of surrender to the forces holding us captive at Gull Lake.

My cell phone warbled at 9:15 p.m. and I picked it off my bedside table. The caller was identified as Peter Vanfleet. I greeted him, and he asked what Joe Weber had done this time.

"It's too early to prove it was Weber," I said. "But I'd like to hear about your adventure with him."

"You promise you're not dragging this up to put in the paper again?"

"Swear it on a stack of stylebooks."

"Whatever those are. Well, basically my story is that we got into an argument over politics in Finnegan's and he settled it by whacking me with a full bottle of beer. The bottle broke and I wound up with eighteen stitches and one bitch of a concussion, not to mention being soaked with cold beer. My civil lawsuit against him is still in court. His claim is that he just meant to scare me with a tap and accidentally swung too hard."

"You say you argued over politics?"

"That's right. He's a big-spending leftwing socialist and I'm a solid conservative Republican, as you must know."

"I should know your politics?"

"I was Anders Anderson's campaign chairman the first time he was elected governor," Vanfleet said.

"That's where I've heard the name," I said. "Well, it's no wonder you got into an argument with Joe Weber."

"So how is this helping whatever story you're working on?"

"It's showing me a behavior pattern that could verify my current suspicion."

"Wait a minute," Vanfleet said. "Didn't you say your name was Mitchell?"

"That's right."

"I read your paper every day. You've been writing about the Alex Gordon murder. Are you thinking that Joe—"

"I'm just following a hunch," I said, cutting off his question. "Please don't start any rumors because of this call."

"Oh, boy, wouldn't that be something? I hope you get enough to hang it on him. And don't worry; I'll keep my mouth shut until I see that he's been charged. I wouldn't do anything to screw up sending Joe Weber to Sandstone."

"I'd appreciate that. Thank you for the info and your time."

"Have a good night," Vanfleet said.

"You may have just made it better," I said.

I put down the phone and ran the conversation past Al, who had finished his phone call and was listening to the end of mine.

"Interesting," he said. "Here we have a man who hit another man on the head much harder than he intended."

"Could be a pattern," I said.

"Yeah, a pattern etched in fractured skulls."

* * *

WEDNESDAY MORNING I AWOKE before Al and went into the bathroom. While brushing my teeth my thoughts turned to home and I shivered a bit realizing that I was only three days away from becoming a married man. *Surely we'll get out of here today,* I thought. *Surely Ronald Jones will be caught and Don O'Rourke will say, "Come home, oh good and faithful servant."*

There was a knock on the bathroom door. "You about done in there?" Al asked.

"Innamintch," I said through the toothbrush. I finished brushing, rinsed my mouth and took my undershorts off the shower curtain rod. When I pulled them up to my waist they felt like a cold, damp octopus grasping my family jewels. No wonder babies cry when their diapers are wet.

At breakfast the dining room was half-filled with crabby, disgruntled people who were swearing never to cover another Minnesota Governor's Fishing Opener. The governor was back in his Summit Avenue home, the lieutenant governor was contaminating the air with cigar smoke somewhere on a campaign tour while we were all trapped in a multiple crime scene at Gull Lake with no clean clothes to put on. In addition, it was raining. Drizzling, actually. Just enough to make it unpleasant to be outdoors.

Ann Rogers walked into the dining room and the muttering rose to a clamor. She raised her arms for silence and waited. "The sheriff is on his way here to continue his interviews of those who were here last weekend," she said when the questions and complaints died out. "His deputies, local police and state police are continuing to search for Ronald Jones, who is driving a gray Chevy Impala. You may quote the sheriff as saying he is sure that both Mr. Jones and the person who murdered Alex Gordon will be brought to justice very soon. I thank you all for your patience and I will notify you as soon as I know anything further about either case." She went directly out the door without even looking in the direction of multiple questions shouted her way.

"Tough way to break into a new job," I said.

"If she survives this week she should get a raise," Al said.

"Watch what you're saying. That's our tax dollars you're talking about."

"From what we've been hearing, it's better that Ann gets the money than Alex Gordon."

"Be careful, you're speaking ill of the dead."

"No problem. Once the ill are dead they can't sue me," Al said.

"Maybe they can haunt you," I said. "And speaking of haunting, here comes that spooky editorial writer from Channel Five."

Dexter Rice greeted us and pulled up a chair between us. "Solved the Gordon murder mystery yet?" he asked.

"We think the butler did it," I said. "We're just waiting for the DNA report to confirm our suspicions."

"Always the wise-ass, aren't you?" Rice said. "Do you have any real theories?"

"If I did, I certainly wouldn't share them before they were good enough to publish. How about you?"

"Not a thing. You know, after thinking about our conversation yesterday, I had the feeling you might have suspected me."

"Should I have?"

"Of course not," Rice said. "Why would I do such a damn fool thing?"

"He took away the cushy state job you thought was secure for another two terms. And it was easy to see that you hated him."

"A lot of people hated him. In fact, if you lined up everybody who hated Alex Gordon end-to-end it would stretch halfway from here to St. Paul. And I actually walked into a better job where I could get my kicks knocking Alex Gordon's boss on TV whenever I felt like it. No, Mitch, I had absolutely no desire to kill Alex Gordon. I was having too much fun throwing stink bombs into his life. I'm one of the few people who'll actually miss the little shit."

"Can I quote you on that? I have to file some sort of story this morning."

"Absolutely not," Rice said. "I have my dignified TV image to maintain. If you really want a quote, you may say that I am frustrated with the inordinate amount of time it is taking the state and local authorities to apprehend the perpetrator of this heinous crime. Who knows who might be the deranged killer's next victim?"

"How do you know the killer is deranged?" I asked.

"Only a madman—or woman—would think they could get away with murdering a man who spoke directly for the governor. Indeed, his or her next target might be the governor himself. Have a nice day, gentlemen."

Rice rose and walked away, leaving Al and me shaking our heads. "Was that the performance of a man with murder on his conscience?" I said.

"If it was, he gets a bravo for bravado," Al said.

"Or at least a hurrah for chutzpah. I'm certainly not deleting Dexter from my tiny little list of suspects."

We walked briskly through the drizzle back to our cabin. When I booted up my computer, I found an e-mail from Don O'Rourke, who was looking for stories on both the murder and the kidnapping, and wanted them pronto. I put what little new information we had—that Jones was still on the loose and the sheriff had no suspects in the Gordon murder case—together with some background filler and sent it off. As expected, Don's reply was not complimentary, but what could I do? Although Joe Weber looked like a prospective killer, neither I nor the sheriff had enough evidence to even hint at having found an unnamed person of interest. And I had nothing much beyond wishful thinking on Dexter Rice.

I e-mailed back that Al would almost certainly be interviewed by Sheriff Holmberg today and then we'd be heading home.

"No, you won't be heading home unless the fugitive kidnapper is caught," was Don's reply.

Al heard me groan and said, "Don't tell me Don wants us to stay."

"Come here and read it then so I don't have to tell you," I said. "I'm going to ask him to fly us a suitcase full of clean shirts and underwear."

I sent an e-mail to that effect and Don sent back a suggestion that we run a load at the local laundry. I replied, "Send us two rolls of quarters."

He responded, "Try the Brainerd bank." I gave up and closed the laptop.

"So now we're supposed to just sit here on our butts and twiddle our thumbs waiting for the troops to bust Ronny Jones?" Al said.

"That's what the boss wants us to do," I said.

"We can't even go fishing in this crappy weather. And I finished reading the book I brought along. Six hundred pages."

My cell phone warbled. It was Martha Todd.

In the cheeriest tone I could muster, I said, "Good morning, my love." Her response sounded borderline hysterical.

"Mitch, you've got to come home. You'll never believe what happened this morning."

Chapter Twenty-Seven

Hot News

I QUICKLY RAN THROUGH the possibilities that could have put Martha in such a state of panic. I finally decided on one. "Are they deporting Grandma Mendes?"

"No word on that yet. Like I said, you'll never guess."

"You lost your job?"

"Worse. You lost your pants."

"How's that again?" I asked.

"Harry's Haberdashery had a huge fire last night."

At first I was puzzled. "What's Harry's Hab . . . ?" Then it hit me in mid-query. "Oh, my god, that's where I bought my wedding suit."

"That's right. The suit in which you were to become my lawfully wedded husband three days from today is part of the pile of water-soaked ashes where Harry's used to be. You need to get home now—today—and buy another suit and get it tailored."

"I doubt Don O'Rourke will accept that as a reason to abandon the story of a loony tunes fugitive who climbs trees and runs away from hospitals," I said.

"Why can't Don send somebody else to take your place if he's so dead set on covering that story?" Martha said.

"Your choice of the word 'dead' reminds me of another reason for staying here. There is also an investigation of the murder of the governor's top flack going on. Remember? The sheriff is questioning people again today and probably will have a press conference just in time for the evening TV news."

"So let Trish Valentine report live and somebody from your paper cover it by watching her, or by phone or by e-mail or . . . or . . . or by Facebook."

I couldn't believe she said Facebook. Letting Trish Valentine stand in live for me was the most odious thing I could think of, but Facebook was the most ridiculous. "You're not serious," I said.

"I am serious. What are you going to get married in?"

"I could wear the old suit that shrunk around the waist. I could cover up the top button that won't fasten with a cummerbund or something."

"Get real," Martha said. "If you think I'm walking down the aisle beside you with your pants unbuttoned, you've got another thought coming."

"Would save time on the honeymoon," I said.

"Oh, stop being the clown for a minute. You need to get back here and go to a clothing store, pick out a suit and get it tailored to fit you in the space of two days. Call Don. Tell Don the problem. Plead with Don. Tell Don to send another reporter."

"Do I leave my best man here or plead for him, too?"

"He's got a little more time. And he at least owns a suit that buttons around his belly."

"Okay, okay, I'll run it by Don but I don't expect a lot of sympathy from him. I may have to get married in the navy blue blazer and gray pants combo that I wear to funerals."

"It'll be your funeral if you don't get home pretty soon," Martha said. "Let me know what Don says, okay?"

"Okay. Talk to you later, my love." We made kissy sounds and hung up.

"What the hell was that all about?" Al asked.

"There was a hot time in the old town last night," I said.

"What kind of a hot time?"

"A fire that made Martha hot under the collar." I gave him a rundown on what had happened in St. Paul. Al laughed and wished me luck with Don.

Before I could call and verbally prostrate myself before our practically peerless city editor, the bedside phone rang. It was Ann Rogers spreading the word to all the media that Sheriff Val Holmberg would be holding a press briefing in ten minutes. I asked if that meant they'd caught Ronald Jones but she'd already hung up.

My pleading with Don O'Rourke for a replacement would have to wait. We grabbed computer and camera and trundled off through the drizzle to the lodge, where we joined the crowd assembling in the meeting room. I worked myself into my usual spot right behind Trish Valentine.

"Morning, Trish," I said. "Are we still buddies?"

"I never knew we were," Trish said without turning her head even halfway in my direction.

"Until this cockeyed murder and kidnapping mixture started our rivalry has always been friendly. Let's call it even and start over."

She still looked straight ahead but she shrugged. "I've got no problem with that."

"Good," I said. "Then I won't bop you over the head when you beat me to asking the first question."

"Trish Valentine reporting live," she said. The cheery tone was back in her voice.

Sheriff Holmberg appeared about five minutes later than scheduled and was greeted with a barrage of shouted questions. He raised his hands and waited for silence. When all the questioners finally realized that Holmberg really wouldn't speak until everybody shut up, the room grew quiet and he spoke.

"I'm here to report that the North Dakota State Police have found our fugitive and have him surrounded," he said.

"North Dakota?" somebody yelled.

"North Dakota," Holmberg said. "He stopped for gas in a town called Rugby, about 150 miles west of Grand Forks. The woman behind the counter had seen his picture on TV less than an hour before. She called the local police, and they called the state police, who set up road blocks on U.S. Highway 2 and State Highway 3, the two major roads out of Rugby. Mr. Jones encountered the western roadblock on Highway 2 and turned off the road into a farmyard. There he abandoned his car beside the barn and ran into a very tall silo, where he climbed up the ladder inside."

"Are you serious?" Trish said.

"The guy sure loves to climb," said Barry Ziebart.

"Maybe he has friends in high places," Al said.

When the laughter subsided, Holmberg continued. "The silo is empty because its contents were used for cattle feed during the winter," he said. "Mr. Jones is about thirty-five feet up and is threatening to jump to his death if the police don't back off and promise to let him go."

"He's gone out of his mind," Trish said.

"It was a short trip, believe me," I said. I could still feel twinges of pain in the ribs that were cracked when he knocked me down onto the coffee table, and my cheek still wore a scab where his punch had broken the skin.

"What are the cops going to do?" asked a man behind us.

"They have called for a negotiator to try to talk the fugitive down safely," Holmberg said. "They've also called for firefighters with a safety net. So far it's a standoff, with the state police watching the fugitive and the fugitive repeatedly telling them to leave or he'll jump."

"Damn," said Al. "Would that be a great picture or what? I wonder how far away from here that is."

Trish Valentine asked that very question and Holmberg said it was about 350 miles by roadways, not as the crow flies.

"He's covered a lot of ground," Trish said.

"He'd been driving all night on straight, flat highways," the sheriff said.

Having grown up on a dairy farm, I could picture Ronald Jones hauling himself up the U-shaped steel rungs embedded in the concrete silo wall. It made my stomach flutter to imagine him standing on one rung and gripping another while looking down at a concrete floor littered with moldy remnants of the chopped cornstalks that had once filled the tower. Obviously we would never get to Rugby in time to see the stalemate end, either with a surrender, a spectacular safety net catch or a leap that left Ronald Jones splattered on the concrete slab. At that point I didn't much care which way it went. I just wanted the fiasco to be finished so I could go home and buy a wedding suit.

Holmberg brought the briefing to an end with the announcement that the State Highway Patrol was sending a helicopter to carry him to Rugby. Immediately every person in the room began yelling requests to hitch a ride on the chopper. "Oh, sure, I'm going to pick one of you over all the others," Holmberg said. "Wouldn't I be popular?"

"We could draw straws to see who would be the press pool photographer," someone yelled. "Like they do in a battle zone."

"Too late," Holmberg said. "Hear that?" We did. It was the sound of a whirring rotor passing overhead at treetop level. "He's picking me up in the golf course parking lot." The sheriff dashed out of the room with everyone but me in hot pursuit. I was busy with my cell phone, punching in 411 to get the number of the Rugby, North Dakota, Police Department.

A woman answered the Rugby PD phone and identified herself as Officer Peterson. While wondering to myself how many Officer Petersons there were in Minnesota and the Dakotas, I told her who I was and asked if the local police were involved in the standoff in the silo. She said almost the entire Rugby police force was at the scene. This would have been a great time to rob the bank in Rugby—if there *was* a bank in Rugby.

"Are you in contact with the chief?" I asked.

"I'm in radio contact with him, yes," she said.

"Do you think he would call me on my cell phone?"

"Would his name be in your paper?"

"It would."

"He'll call you." I gave her my number, punched off and waited. Three minutes later I was talking to Rugby Police Chief Lester Wanamaker. He spelled his name for me, making sure that I understood it was Wanamaker with only one 'N.' I asked him how many officers were on the scene and he said at least ten North Dakota state troopers, the Pierce County sheriff with five deputies, and eight men from his department. The negotiator who would try to persuade Ronald Jones to come down the ladder had just arrived and was entering the silo.

"How big a town is Rugby?" I asked.

"About twenty-nine-hundred," Wanamaker said. I heard him spit and wondered whether he was chewing tobacco.

"Is it pretty much a farm town?"

"Pretty much. Only thing we're famous for is bein' the geographic center of North America."

"Rugby is the geographic center of North America?"

"'At's right. Got a monument in town that says so."

"What kind of monument?" I asked.

"Looks like a skinny pyramid," he said. "'Bout twenty feet tall and mebbe six feet across at the bottom." I heard another spit.

"How long has it been there?" I asked.

"Date on it says August 1932. Put there by the U.S. Geological Service."

"That's very interesting. So, tell me what's happening at the silo right now."

"Ain't much of anything I can see from outside. The state cops' negotiator is inside by himself tryin' to talk the nut cake down off the ladder. I don't need to see what happens if the nut cake decides to take a swan dive." Another spit.

"No, I don't blame you," I said. "It would be a real mess."

"Least my boys won't have to clean it up, then," the chief said. "We're outside Rugby city limits so it's in the sheriff's territory. Oh, oh, I gotta go now. The state police captain is callin' a meetin' over by the silo."

"Please save my number and call me if there's any change—like the nut cake coming down, one way or another."

"I'll do that," Chief Wanamaker said. "Nice talkin' to ya, then." I heard a final spit before the connection was broken.

Al returned a moment after the chief's closing expectoration. "God, what a scene," he said. "Everybody wanted to get on the chopper. People were actually grabbing at it. One fool would've walked into the rotor if I hadn't grabbed him. It looked like the evacuation of Saigon back in the seventies."

"Sorry I missed it," I said.

"So what have you been doing while I was standing in the rain shooting battle scenes?"

I told him who I'd been talking with and said, "Did you know Rugby, North Dakota, is the geographic center of North America?"

"Can't say that I did, but that's a middling good angle. I'll bet Don will just jump right off the center of his chair when he reads that fascinating piece of folklore in your story."

"And I'll bet neither Trish Valentine nor any other TV star will be talking about that fascinating piece of folklore when they're reporting live tonight. It's the little things like that that lift an otherwise mundane story out of the ordinary and make the reader feel fully informed, my friend."

"Well, if anyone knows about mundane stories it would be you," he said. With friends like that, etc . . . ?

We were back in our cabin and I was working on my extraordinary story when my cell phone sounded. The caller was Rugby Police Chief Lester Wanamaker.

Chapter Twenty-Eight

Party's Over

I ANSWERED THE PHONE and thanked the chief for calling.

"No problem, Mr. Mitchell," he said. "I just wanted to tell you that the party's over."

"Is the guest of honor safely down?" I asked.

"Yup. He come down peaceful as a lamb just a couple minutes ago. Funny thing was, he slipped off a rung and fell the last fifteen feet. Landed in some muck leftover from the silage and either sprained or broke his ankle. EMTs are lookin' at it now."

"Is he in pain?"

"Oh, yeah. He's all wet and stinky and hurtin' like hell." A louder, lustier spit than any of those previously heard.

I smiled and caressed my fractured ribs with my fingertips. My wish for a painful ending to the pursuit of Ronald Jones had been granted. "So what's the next move?"

"They'll put the screwball in an ambulance and take him to the hospital in Minot, I guess The state police theory is that Minot was where he was headed because he has family there. Now the family can visit him in the hospital. Hope they chain him to the bed."

"That's a good idea." I asked the chief if he knew the name of the man who had persuaded Jones to descend the ladder. He did not, but at my request he corralled the state police captain who did know the name, which was Polish and contained an intricate combination of C's, Z's and W's.

"How'd you ever learn to spell that one?" I asked. He replied by spelling out his own name, which was also Polish and contained an intricate combination of C's, Z's and W's. I thanked him for his help, and he gave the phone back to Chief Wanamaker, from whom I obtained the name of the people who owned the farm. This one was Irish and much easier to spell.

I got the farmer's number from 411 and had a nice chat with Molly O'Malley, who said her husband Sean was outside talking to the policemen. She said she'd been hiding in the house the whole time because she was afraid the crazy man would escape from the silo and do God knows what to anybody who got in his way. I asked her some questions about the size and products of their farm and even found out how many cubic feet of silage the silo would hold. It's details like those that lift a story out of the ordinary and make the reader feel fully informed.

"I can't believe how friendly and cooperative these people are," I said to Al after my conversation with Mrs. O'Malley. "They answer every question and act like they're willing to talk to a reporter forever."

"Out there they don't have to deal with clusters of TV microphones poked into their faces and having to answer the same dumb questions a dozen times," Al said. "They haven't learned to hate us yet."

"Good point." I wrote by far the most readable story I'd produced all week and e-mailed it to Don. Al sent along some shots of the mob scene at the helicopter. Don replied with an e-mail saying the story and pix were just what he needed for page one, and that my including the bit about the geographical center of North America was a nice touch. I took a deep breath and prepared to ask him for permission to go home.

I put together an impassioned but not panic-stricken request for a replacement at the Gull Lake scene, carefully explaining my need to get home and purchase a wedding suit to replace the one lost in the fire. I e-mailed it to Don and received an instant reply: "Has Al given his statement to the sheriff?"

I e-mailed, "No. He's scheduled for this afternoon."

Don's response was: "Stay on scene until he does. Then call me and you probably can come home."

"Hallelujah!" I said in a voice loud enough to have been heard by the walleyes swimming in Gull Lake.

"Don's letting you go home?" Al said.

"He says we can both go as soon as you've had your turn with the sheriff this afternoon. Let's pack our bags," I said.

"I'll pack everything but the underwear I've got hanging in the bathroom."

"Martha would've burst a blood vessel if I'd had to tell her we were still stuck here for another night."

"In that case, you could have asked Martha to call Don and use her feminine wiles."

"Don's been city editor for so long he's immune to every kind of wily trick, feminine or otherwise."

"I can't believe that any living, breathing male is immune to Martha Todd."

"Good point. But I'm glad that won't be necessary. I suppose we could use the time we've still got here to continue helping the sheriff solve the Alex Gordon murder."

"So what do we have to base a solution on?" Al asked.

"Damn little. We have two men who had both motive and opportunity. Dexter Rice lost his job to Alex and hated him for that. Joe Weber, who argued with Alex and thought he was a political troglodyte, has a history of using violence to settle political arguments. But we have no way of putting either of them in a boat with Alex last Friday morning. Also, the mysteries of how the lifejacket was buried and how the empty boat was left circling in the bay remain unsolved."

"So we're up Gull Lake without a paddle," Al said.

"Paddle, schmaddle; we don't even have a canoe," I said.

"And it's too rainy to check out a boat. Hey, wait a second. How about the guy who checks out the boats? It's possible he saw somebody with Alex that morning."

"That's worth checking. Once again, I have to admit that you might be a good reporter."

"And once again, I have to admit that some day you might be a good reporter, too."

The drizzle had turned to a soaking rain so we put on our hooded plastic ponchos for the long trek to the marina. When we got there we found the door to the rental office closed. With the all-day rain, this was no surprise. I knocked and got no response. I knocked again, louder. The door opened a crack and a young man peered through the opening. "You want a boat in this weather?" he asked.

"No boat," I said. "I just want to ask you some questions."

He opened the door and gestured us into the office, which wasn't much bigger than a broom closet. There was a desk with a single chair, which he offered with a gesture, apparently expecting us to flip a coin or arm wrestle to decide who would sit. We both remained standing and introduced ourselves. "I'm Pete," the man said in return. His blond hair was almost white, and he looked young enough to be a high school kid. He wore a long-sleeved shirt and jeans, and somehow his face had acquired a suntan that would have looked natural in July.

"What can I do for you gentlemen?" Pete asked when the introductions were finished.

"Were you working here last Friday morning?" I asked.

"You mean when all hell broke loose because of the empty boat?" Pete asked.

"Before that. I'm talking about before sunrise. Did you rent the boat to Alex Gordon that morning?"

"No, sir. Mr. Gordon took the boat out Thursday evening, just before I closed for the night. He wanted to get out on the lake before we would be open Friday morning, just like he did last year."

This was not helpful. "Was anyone with him when he was here?" I asked.

"No, sir, he was alone," Pete said.

"Did he say anything about who might be going with him in the morning?"

"No, sir. He went out alone last year and I figured he was doing the same thing this year. I remember him complaining that he couldn't talk anybody else into getting out of bed that early Friday morning because they all got shit-faced . . . uh, I mean, drunk . . . the night before."

"So as far as you know, he was going out alone Friday morning?"

"Yes, sir.

"And you didn't see him leave Friday morning?"

"No, sir, I was still sleeping when he went out. I didn't need to be here until six o'clock."

"Looks like we struck out on this one," Al said.

"Yes, damn it, it does," I said. "Just one more question, Pete. How did you get such a deep suntan this early in what's been a cold, rainy spring?"

Pete laughed. "It's actually been fading since I got here. I got tan skiing out west. Spent all winter in Colorado and got a pretty good burn on sunny days with a lot of snow to reflect it."

"So you work here in the summer and ski out west all winter?"

"Yes, sir. I make enough in pay and tips in the summer to be a ski bum all winter."

"Nice life," Al said. "Enjoy it while you can. Some day you'll be saving your money for your kids' college tuition like I am."

"Not unless I adopt some, sir," Pete said. "I'm gay."

"That was more than I wanted to know," I said when Al and I were once again outside in the rain.

"At least you can't fault him for hiding in that closet he calls an office," Al said.

We slogged back to the lodge, where we were greeted by Ann Rogers. "Where've you been?" she asked. "The sheriff just got back from Rugby and he was looking for you, Mr. Jeffrey. You missed your turn to be interviewed and now you're at the end of the line."

"How long until he gets to me?" Al asked.

"He said he was tuckered out from being up all night and left for home," Ann said. "He won't get to you until tomorrow morning."

"Son of a bitch!" I said so vehemently that Ann took a step back. "Sorry," I said in a calmer voice. "We were counting on going home today."

"At least we didn't pack our stuff," Al said.

I could have pointed out that if we had stayed in the cabin and packed our bags, the sheriff would have found Al in time for the interview, but some things are better left unsaid.

Chapter Twenty-Nine

Martha's Misery

"HERE GOES NOTHING," I said as I pressed Martha Todd's cell phone number. The call went to voicemail and I left a message.

"She's not answering. The condemned man has a little while longer to live while waiting for a return call."

"It's time for the feminine wiles thing I was talking about earlier," Al said.

"I'll suggest it but I don't think it will sell."

I was on the bed, half asleep with a true crime novel resting on my chest, when Martha called. I told her about the postponement of Al's interview with the sheriff, being careful to put the blame on the sheriff and not on our absence from our cabin, and held the phone a couple of inches away from my ear.

Al heard the shriek fifteen feet away. "He can't keep you there. He's got to let you come home."

"He's the sheriff," I said. "He can keep me here."

"There are freedom laws. There are anti-cruelty laws. There are common decency laws. I'll go to court and get a writ of *habeas corpus*." Each sentence came out in a higher note and a greater decibel level. By the end of the third one, I was holding the phone at arm's length.

I pulled the phone back to its normal position. "Do you want to try talking to Don?" I asked in my calmest, most deliberate manner. "Maybe you can persuade him to send up a replacement for me so I can go home tonight. He's left work by now but I have his home number."

Martha was close to tears. "Yes . . . no . . . maybe. Oh, forget it. Get married in your damn old funeral blazer and slacks. It's you I care about, not the stupid clothes."

"I'm relieved to hear you say that. If we get home tomorrow, there'll still be time to buy something."

"There won't be time to tailor it. You'll have to turn up the cuffs with safety pins."

"Okay, I'll be your pin-up groom."

"Oh, Mitch, I don't need this on top of all the other crap that's been going on today. The woman at Immigration called and said they're going to deport Grandma Mendes."

"Good god, why? She's been in this country forever."

"They say they can't grant her asylum because there's no evidence that her life is in danger if she goes back to Cape Verde. The perverse woman I've been dealing with, her name is Ms. Wong, says we have to prove Grandma's life is in danger if she goes back there."

"Ms. Wong isn't wight. Your grandmother is too old and frail to survive away from her family. Wait a minute. What's Ms. Wong's first name?"

"I think it's Grace. Yes, I'm sure it is."

"Grace Wong? I think I know her. Give me her phone number." Martha recited the number and I wrote it on the notepad beside the bed. "I'll call her tomorrow and see if it's who I think it is."

"Oh, sweetie, if you can get those people to change their decision I'll . . . I'll marry you if you have to wear a ragged pair of jeans and a paint-spotted T-shirt with holes in it to the wedding."

"Be careful what you're promising," I said.

* * *

I DID KNOW GRACE WONG. She was a regular attendee of my Monday night Alcoholics Anonymous meetings.

My first encounter with Grace had been two years earlier when I covered the deportation hearings for a ninety-five-year-old German immigrant accused of having herded prisoners into gas chambers in a World War II Nazi death camp. The process dragged on for more than a year while the man's attorneys tried every trick they could think of to thwart the effort to return him to Germany for trial.

Grace Wong was an investigator on the case and served as the spokesperson reporting to the public. I had interviewed her an hour after the issue was finally resolved and the man had been escorted out of the courtroom and into a van headed for the airport. She was so shaky and distracted during the interview that I finally asked why she was so severely affected by the case. Grace replied that her grandfather had been an officer in the Chinese army during World War II and had been captured by the Japanese. His captors had tortured him so severely that his mind had reverted to his early childhood when he returned to his family at the end of the war.

"Listening to the evidence against Otto Bergsdorf brought all that back to me," Grace had said. "I'm so shook up and sick that I'm absolutely dying for a shot of whiskey."

When I'd said that a calming drink was not unusual or inappropriate, she had surprised me by telling me that she was only six months out of treatment for alcoholism and was afraid she was about to fall back. "I'll lose my job," she had said. "I saved it by going into treatment at Hazelden, but now I'm craving alcohol and if I go back to drinking they'll fire me for sure. I am really worthless when I'm drunk."

I was stunned to hear something so deeply personal from a woman I didn't know, but I had a ready response. "You need AA, and you need it now," I'd said, and immediately called my sponsor. Between us we had staved off the immediate crisis and gotten Grace started with my group. She had been there every Monday since, and never failed to express appreciation for the rescue.

The question now was: how could I use this relationship to keep Grandma Mendes in St. Paul? I would have to approach Grace as a supplicant and hope she felt a need—and could find a way—to repay me for steering her into AA.

"You're thinking awfully hard about something," Al said.

"I am," I said. "And it's something I really can't discuss with you."

"I'm assuming it has something to do with the phone number you wrote down."

"It does. I'll let you know if the problem gets resolved to everyone's satisfaction."

It was after five o'clock. The Immigration office would be closed. The call to Grace Wong would have to wait until the next morning.

* * *

THURSDAY DAWNED BRIGHT AND CLEAR, with the clean sweet smell of wet grass in the air as Al and I walked to the lodge for breakfast. On Tuesday night we had decided to wash out two sets of underwear at a time so that one set would have an additional day to get dry if we were still stuck at Gull Lake. Here we were on Thursday, and for the first day since Sunday I hadn't been forced to put on slightly damp underwear. How could life be better?

Well, maybe by putting on a fresh shirt that hadn't been worn three times without washing. Or best of all, by being told we could go home.

Ann Rogers was also still stuck at Gull Lake. I had no idea what the governor's press secretary was doing about underwear and I wasn't about to ask. She was making the rounds of the media-occupied tables, spreading the word that Sheriff Val Holmberg would give us a briefing at 11:00 a.m. He was planning to give updates on both the case of the tree-and-silo-climbing kidnapper and the case of the mysterious death of Alex Gordon.

"Has he got a suspect in the murder case?" I asked when Ann reached our table.

"He didn't say," she said. "All he said was that he'd give you folks an update."

"Be nice if the update was that the killer is in jail," Al said.

"We should be so lucky," Ann said.

"I can't believe you're still stuck here with us," I said. "How is the governor operating without a press secretary? Has he been breaking in a new assistant for you?"

"He's using the lieutenant governor's press secretary," Ann said.

"I thought the lieutenant governor was on what he called a pre-campaign tour," I said. "Is he touring northern Minnesota without a press secretary?"

"He can't use a state employee on any kind of campaign tour, pre or otherwise," she said. "If he's got a press secretary with him it's not anyone your taxes are paying for."

"Where is Old Smokey, anyway?" Al asked.

"I don't really know," Ann said. "I've been too busy with all the crap that's going on here to try to keep track of Aaron Ross. He said he was going to start the tour in Bemidji but that was several days ago, so he could be most anywhere by now."

"I haven't seen anything in the paper about cities having local air pollution alerts," I said. "That would be an easy way to track him."

"Frankly, I don't really care where he is," Ann said. "The thought of having him in the governor's office is almost enough to make me vote Democrat for the first time in my life. I know darn well that I won't be working in that office anymore if he gets elected."

"Sounds like there's more than cigar smoke involved in that decision," I said, hoping for printable tidbit about dissension in the Republican ranks.

"It's just that he's . . . oh, forget I said anything at all. Please. I can't get into personal feelings in this job." She turned and walked quickly away to another table.

"I'd like to know what that's all about," I said.

"She certainly has no love for our next governor," Al said. "She wasn't just blowing smoke."

We returned to our cabin, and I e-mailed Don O'Rourke about the sheriff's upcoming update, ending with the unequivocal statement that Al and I would be heading home immediately after the briefing.

Don's reply said, "Upcoming update noted. Upstart homecoming note deleted." And he complained about Al and me dropping an occasional smart-ass pun.

Al was reading our online edition on his laptop when I stepped outside, sat on the front steps and called Grace Wong. After wading through a series of prompts longer than Pinocchio's nose, I reached a living human being who said, "Ms. Wong's office, how may I help you?"

I gave her my name and asked if Ms. Wong was in. She asked if I was calling about a current problem or something new and I said it concerned a current case. After a moment's pause, a familiar voice said, "This is Grace Wong. How may I help you?"

"This is Mitch," I said. "I want to talk to you about the Mendes case."

"I'm sorry, sir," she said. "Do I know you?"

"Would it help if I said my name is Warren Mitchell and I'm an alcoholic?"

"Oh, Mitch," she said. "I didn't hear you clearly. What can I do for you? Aren't you up north somewhere on a fishing trip?"

"I am up north somewhere on the fishing trip from hell, but I want to talk to you about a woman who is in St. Paul, has been in St. Paul for almost sixty years and is about to be sent to her certain death in Cape Verde."

"You said the name is Mendes, right?"

"I did. She happens to be the grandmother of my fiancée and I'm hoping to persuade you to look for a way to avoid deporting her."

"Martha Todd is your fiancée? The woman you rave about at our meetings as the most wonderful woman on earth?"

"That's the one," I said.

"Oh, man, she is very nice but she's also very persistent. I really haven't been in charge of that case. I've mostly been the spokesperson. You know, the messenger that people want to shoot."

And that people call "perverse," I thought. To Grace, I said, "That's because you're the bearer of bad tidings."

"That's true, but I'm not the one who decides what the tidings will be."

"Well, I'm not going to shoot you. I just want you to get the department to listen to reason and find a way to resolve this without sending Grandma Mendes to her certain death."

"How is it certain death? No one is waiting there to kill her."

"No one is waiting to greet her, either. She has no family in Cape Verde anymore. No friends. No home. No place to live. She's so frail that just the long plane ride could do her in."

"I'm sure the people handling the case have heard all that," Grace said.

"How about letting them hear it again? How about looking for some little crack in the wall to let her slip through? It was done for a president's Kenyan uncle not too many years ago. I'm asking you to do this as a friend."

"As a friend who helped save my life. Are you pushing that button here?"

"If that's what it takes to get your help, I'm pushing it."

"You should be ashamed of yourself," she said. Before I could muster a reply she laughed and said, "But the department should also be ashamed to do this to an elderly woman who has harmed no one. I'll do some checking and get back to you, Mitch. What's your number up north somewhere?"

Chapter Thirty

No Suspects

SHERIFF VAL HOLMBERG FOUND himself facing a smaller sea of faces, cameras and microphones when he stepped up before us at 11:00 a.m. All the network TV crews had gone in search of meatier stories and some of the smaller Minnesota newspaper, TV and radio representatives had decided to rely on second-hand sources for subsequent reports.

With the end of his bizarre climbing adventures, Ronald Jones had become small potatoes to national news outlets lusting for steak dinners. Simultaneously, the lack of investigative progress in the Alex Gordon murder had reduced public interest in online updates and live TV reports on that case proportionately. As I stood behind Trish Valentine, I was hoping my city editor's interest would sag as well.

Holmberg opened with the news that Jones had been treated for a severely sprained ankle and a bruised shoulder in a Rugby hospital, after which he had been released into the custody of federal agents. The feds were taking charge because Jones had crossed a state line, which meant he was now residing in a much more secure facility than St. Joseph's Medical Center.

"It is actually a pleasure to get back to a simple homicide investigation after chasing Mr. Jones up one tree and down a silo," Holmberg said with a smile. The smile vanished when he followed with, "If only it was a simple homicide investigation."

He paused for a breath. "Ladies and gentlemen, it is anything but a simple investigation. All I can tell you is that my interviews with all the people who were present when Mr. Gordon was apparently hit on the head and thrown out of his boat have yielded very little information. I've had some thoughts about a couple of people, but we haven't gathered anywhere near enough evidence to arrive at a probable suspect. I am going to interview one person further but at this time I'm not even classifying that individual as a person of interest. As far as I'm concerned, that's all I can tell you today, but I will answer any questions that I can."

"Is this person a man or a woman?" asked good old Trish Valentine.

Holmberg took a moment to study Trish's V-necked blouse, which featured three unfastened buttons at the top, before he said, "Yes."

"Yes, what?" I asked.

"Yes, the person is a man or a woman," Holmberg said.

"Well, which one?" said Barry Ziebart.

"I'm not saying at this time," the sheriff said.

"Is the person a state official?" a Duluth newspaper reporter asked.

"I'm not saying at this time," Holmberg said. "There's no use asking me for details about the person because I'm not giving out any details at this time."

"Well, what kind of questions are you answering?" Trish asked.

"I guess maybe no kind," he said. "Have a good day, everyone. I'll be in touch with Ms. Rogers if anything develops." With that he put on his Smokey Bear hat and stalked out of the room.

"Now what?" Al said. "Are we going home?"

"Maybe later," I said. "Right now we're staking out Joe Weber's cabin to see if he's the sheriff's anonymous second-time interviewee."

"What are we going to do? Hide behind a tree?"

"Two trees. One for me and one for you."

"Aren't we kind of going out on a limb?"

"Leaf the details to me."

"I'm rooting for you. Let's go."

We took an oblique route to the rear of Weber's cabin, staying well off the blacktop path and watching in all directions for the sheriff or any of his deputies. We were not followed by any of the other news gatherers and I suspected they would all be packing up to leave Gull Lake. Much as I wanted to do the same thing, I couldn't walk away without knowing whether or not Joe Weber was the person of near interest.

We each selected a tree from behind which we could see anyone approaching Weber's cabin. The minutes ticked by with my chosen tree seeming to get harder and the bark rougher the longer I leaned against the trunk. At last a man approached on the path, looked around as if to see if anyone was watching, climbed the steps to Weber's cabin and went in. It was Weber.

A second after Weber's door banged shut I heard a slap. I looked at Al. He mouthed the word "mosquito." I put a finger to my lips to signal silence. Another man was walking along the path toward Weber's cabin. This one wore a light blue uniform with dark blue shirt pockets and a big shiny badge. Al and I watched as Deputy Leo LeBlanc went up to Weber's door and knocked. The door opened and LeBlanc went in. A few minutes later Weber emerged with LeBlanc a step behind him. They walked up the path to the parking lot.

When Weber and LeBlanc were out of sight, Al and I left our hiding places and followed in the direction they had gone. "I'm glad to finally get away from that tree," Al said. "It felt like I was getting Dutch elm disease."

"You're barking up the wrong tree," I said. "That was an oak you were leaning against, not an elm."

"Is there such a thing as Dutch oak disease?"

"The only thing in an oak that you have to worry about is a squirrel that might take you for a nut."

A hundred feet ahead of us we watched Joe Weber and Deputy Leo LeBlanc get into a black SUV with a sheriff's department logo on the door and drive away.

"Weber's our man," I said. "Now we have to find a way to keep the story alive until we can identify him."

"Don't keep it so alive that it kills our chances of getting out of here today."

"I'll send Don a teaser about the sheriff questioning a political opponent who admittedly hated Alex Rogers, after which I'll say we can follow up with the sheriff by phone from the newsroom of the *St. Paul Daily Dispatch*."

"I hope Don doesn't tell us to follow up with the sheriff in person in, uh, wherever the hell the sheriff's office is."

"It's in Brainerd. Don't worry, I know how to handle Don on this one. Trust me. Have I ever let you down?"

"Dozens of times, but go ahead and try to get us a ticket home. I'll pack my stuff while you're writing your story."

"Oh, no, don't do that," I said. "It's bad luck. Like packing up your bats before the last out of a baseball game."

"Okay, okay," he said. "Let's sit in the lodge and I'll read a six-month-old fishing and hunting magazine from the rack in the lounge while you knock out your story."

Into the lodge we went, and Al sifted through a stack of year-old outdoors magazines while I wrote and e-mailed my story. Next I crafted a carefully worded note making it clear that the sheriff would be holding no more briefings for the press until he had a suspect in custody.

Don's reply was a shocker. "What is this crap? Trish Valentine is reporting live that the sheriff has a woman in custody in Brainerd."

I blinked and read Don's e-mail a second time. "Al, we got a problem," I said. I showed him the e-mail and he agreed.

"See if Trish is saying who it is."

I asked Don that question and he replied that the sheriff had not identified the woman. "Get your butts into Brainerd and check it out," he added.

"On our way," I replied.

"I guess it was bad luck to even think about packing before the last out," Al said.

"Let's check with Ann Rogers before we drive to Brainerd," I said. "Maybe she knows who the woman is."

We went to the registration desk and asked the woman on duty there to call Ann Rogers's room for us.

"No point in that," the woman said. "Ms. Rogers left here with the sheriff about half an hour ago."

Chapter Thirty-One

Tomorrow, Tomorrow

AL AND I ASKED EACH OTHER the same question as we hurried toward our car: Was Ann Rogers in custody or had Trish Valentine made a mistake? It was possible that Ann had gone with the sheriff either to give him information about Joe Weber or to gather information about Weber's interrogation for dispersal to the press.

"I can't imagine Ann killing Alex Gordon," Al said.

"She did inherit his job," I said.

"Flacking for a lame duck governor is not the kind of job anybody kills for. And it's going to be very short term if she's serious about not working for Smokey Ross, assuming he's elected."

"Could be something personal between Ann and Alex. Maybe they were having an affair. Maybe one or the other of them broke it off and they had a fight. Who knows what goes on behind closed doors?"

We wandered around Brainerd a bit before we found the Crow Wing County Sheriff's office. We parked beside a panel truck from Channel Four, went in the front door and were met in the small lobby by Trish Valentine, who looked like the cat who'd swallowed the canary and washed it down with the cream. She was even wearing boots.

"About time you guys got here," Trish said. "I thought a crack news team like you two would have been right behind us."

"We were ahead of you in a different place," I said. "What's going on here?"

"The sheriff is questioning Ann Rogers. Apparently she's the prime nonperson of interest he was talking about. She followed him out of the meeting room and he turned around and took her by the arm, said a few words and away they went. Tony and I followed them here but we haven't been allowed to talk to anyone beyond the woman at the desk. All she'll tell us is that the sheriff is interrogating an adult female. She won't even say why."

"Hard to picture Ann killing anybody," I said.

"You never know," Trish said. "She is kind of a hard-assed bitch, if you ask me."

"What about Joe Weber?" I asked.

"Who?"

"A deputy picked up Joe Weber back at Madrigal's and put him into an SUV. Didn't he bring him here?"

"I don't know anything about that. I wouldn't know your Joe Weber from Joe Sixpack. Who is he?"

Realizing I'd already told Trish more than I wanted to, I said, "He's a state employee who didn't like Alex Gordon."

"There was a long line of people who fit that description," Trish said. "Why would the sheriff pick this guy out?"

"I haven't a clue," I said, hoping my nose wouldn't grow from the lie.

There was nothing to do but stand around in the lobby and wait. I e-mailed Don O'Rourke and informed him of the situation. He replied with instructions to sit it out and talk to the sheriff ASAP. *Hard to sit it out without a chair,* I thought. I called Martha Todd's cell phone and left a message on her voicemail. Al called Carol's cell and did the same.

After thirty minutes of watching the four of us pacing and leaning against the wall in the small foyer, the woman at the desk, whom I'd learned was the Shirley I'd talked with on Sunday, made a phone call. Minutes later a deputy brought out four folding chairs and we all sat down. After another thirty minutes the front door opened and we were joined by the tired-looking crew from Channel Five.

"We were halfway home when they called us and said Trish was here and we should get our butts back to Brainerd," Barry Ziebart said. None of us offered the new arrivals a chair.

A few minutes later Roy Winston, a reporter for the Minneapolis paper, and a photographer I didn't recognize joined our bevy of slack-faced, droopy-eyed sentinels. The crowded space looked like a hospital waiting room filled with next-of-kin expecting the worst results from a loved one's heart transplant surgery.

Al's phone chirped and he went outside to answer the call. "Carol is taking it like a trooper," he said when he returned. "But she says there will be payback later this summer."

"What does that mean?"

"I'm guessing that I'll be left to feed and manage the kids while Carol and her sister go somewhere fun for a week."

"If Martha still wants to marry me, I'll probably be left to feed and manage Sherlock Holmes while she and her friend Lisa Maseratti go away for a month," I said.

The hands on the clock above Shirley's head crept onward. Those of us seated offered to give those standing a turn in the chairs. Those standing said thanks but they were doing okay. When the clock's little hand arrived at three, we offered our seats again and this time received unanimous acceptance.

Everybody switched again at 3:30 and again at 4:00. I'd had an e-mail from Don saying he was done for the day, and an e-mail from Fred Donlin, the night city editor, saying he was waiting for my story. Al had e-mailed a couple shots of Ann Rogers taken on Friday when she was telling us that Alex Gordon was missing.

Neither Martha Todd nor Grace Wong had called me by 4:22 p.m. when a door on our left opened and Sheriff Val Holmberg stepped through.

"Jesus Christ, they told me there were reporters here but I didn't expect a mob scene," Holmberg said.

"There are more on the way," Trish said. "By now everybody has seen my live report."

"Who have you been questioning?" asked Barry. Other voices echoed him in a cacophony that rattled off the walls of the small room.

"Okay, okay," the sheriff said, with his arms raised for silence. "Here's what we have at this time. We have questioned a woman who was seen with the murder victim, Alex Gordon, before dawn on the day the victim was allegedly struck on the head and tossed out of his boat sometime before 6:15 a.m. The witness is a male member of the governor's fishing party who says he couldn't sleep Thursday night because he felt sick from drinking too much at the party in the bar that night. He went outside to get some fresh air and to dispose of the remaining booze in his stomach. His cabin is near the marina and the moon was quite bright. He'd been upchucking in the shadows, but he says he saw the victim and the woman walking together toward the boat dock in the moonlight."

"Is she under arrest?" asked Trish.

"I have not placed the woman under arrest but I am holding her for further questioning. If I decide to proceed with an arrest and a court appearance I will identify her for you."

"Come on, Sheriff, we all know who she is," Roy Winston said.

"Regardless of that, your paper will be opening itself to a libel suit if you name her before she's arrested," Holmberg said. "It still may turn out that we have no case."

"What about the witness?" I asked, knowing full well who it was.

"I'm not releasing his identity at this time, either," the sheriff said.

"Again, we all know who it is," I said.

"No, we don't," Winston said. "Who the hell is it?"

"No comment," said the sheriff. "You guys can duke that one out between yourselves, but I wouldn't identify the witness yet if I was you."

"Does the woman have a lawyer?" Ziebart asked.

"She does. That's one reason the interrogation has been taking so long."

"Did the witness see the woman get into the boat with the victim?" I asked.

"The witness saw them walking together toward the dock, but he did not see them together either on the dock or in the boat because his vision of that area was partially blocked and clouds covered the moon just as the couple reached the base of the dock," Holmberg said.

"So it's possible the woman never went with him to the boat?" Trish asked.

"That's the sticky part," the sheriff said. "The witness cannot place the woman in the boat or even for certain on the dock."

"How close to the dock were they when he last saw them?" Winston asked.

"They had just reached the base of the dock when the moon was obscured."

"So they could have parted company there," I said.

"Like I told you, that's the sticky part," Holmberg said. "Now if you would all excuse me, I'm going back to ask some more questions. If you leave a contact number or e-mail address at the desk, I'll get in touch with you in the morning."

"In the morning," Al said after I handed my card to Shirley. "Another night at good old Gull Lake. I hope they haven't cleaned out our cabin and thrown our dirty clothes into the toxic waste dump."

"Whatever they've done, I'm dead meat," I said. "Martha will cancel the wedding and I'll go live with my mother and grandmother and become known as the Hopeless Hermit of Harmony."

Our cabin was just as we'd left it—in a mess of scattered clothing, books, magazines, newspapers and various articles of trash. I wrote and e-mailed a story that ended with a note begging to be replaced the next morning in Brainerd, and Al sent a couple of photos of the sheriff and the crowd in the police station. Fred Donlin's reply was: "Hang tight. We'll see about getting you home."

My phone played its tune and I saw it was Martha Todd calling. "Missing persons," I said when I answered.

"When will my missing person be found in St. Paul?" Martha said.

"Tomorrow. Fred Donlin promised tomorrow. Like Orphan Annie's song about tomorrow, it's only a day away."

"And the day after tomorrow is only two days away. I have something marked on the calendar for that day but it may have to be cancelled."

"Don't do anything rash," I said. "I'm heading for home tomorrow whether the desk sends up a relief reporter or not. I will be at your Saturday occasion and I will be wearing something better than jeans."

"In other words, you also struck out with Ms. Wong," she said. Ooh, I'd forgotten that Martha had said I could wear jeans to the wedding if I rescued Grandma Mendes.

"Not yet. I mean, maybe not. She was sympathetic but she hasn't gotten back to me yet."

"Do you think there's any hope?"

"I'm assuming that the full day's response time means they haven't rejected the request and they're looking for a way to keep Grandma Mendes in America."

"Speaking of grandmas, yours is arriving with your mother tomorrow. What should I tell them about your arrival time?"

"We'll be on the road right after talking to the sheriff in the morning. We'll have dinner with Mom and Grandma Goodie at the restaurant of your choice."

"Cross your heart?"

"I swear it on a stack of stylebooks," I said.

"I'll make a reservation for four and ask them to be flexible on the time," she said.

* * *

AS WE ENTERED THE DINING ROOM for yet another dinner at Gull Lake, we were met by the manager, Martin Johansen. "Back again?" he asked. "Are you guys here for the summer?"

"We'd be long gone if you hadn't been harboring a murderer," Al said.

Johansen's face grew red, his spine stiffened and he said, "That was through no fault of ours. Do you know who it is?"

"Yes, but we can't tell anybody until the sheriff makes an arrest. Let's just say that Alex Gordon's killer has been under one of your many roofs, including this one, ever since the murder," I said.

"Give me a hint," Johnansen whispered, leaning an ear my way.

"The suspect was seen with the victim by the light of the silvery moon," I said.

"That could be anybody that was here."

"Exactly. See you tomorrow when we finally check out of your crime-ridden establishment."

"Oh, please, don't use that word when you write your stories," he said.

I couldn't resist pulling his chain. "I'll have to mention that you were harboring a killer," I said.

"Then please don't mention us at all." He walked away shaking his head.

With the entire Governor's Fishing Opener party gone, the dining room was only about half full. Most of the diners were men who would be skipping work on Friday to start a long weekend of chasing walleyes. Trish Valentine and the others who'd been with us at the sheriff's office apparently had decided to eat somewhere else. The only familiar faces we saw appeared at our table a few minutes after we'd sat down.

We were discussing the possibility of Joe Weber accusing Ann Rogers in order to divert suspicion from himself, a trick that criminals sometimes use, when two familiar voices chirped, "Mind if we join you?"

"Of course," we said in unison and pulled out chairs for Roxie and Angie. They were dressed for business in those painted-on jeans and form-fitting T-shirts with no visible bra lines.

"What are you guys doing still here?" Roxie asked.

"I was going to ask you the same thing," I said.

"You first," Roxie said.

We told the young women where we'd been and what had happened, without naming any names. "I'll bet it's the woman that got the dead guy's job," Angie said. "She's a tough bitch; tried to get us arrested for soliciting. Imagine, us soliciting?"

"So now it's your turn to tell us why you're back here," Al said.

"New crop of clients," Angie said, sweeping her arm toward the other tables that were occupied mostly by men.

We asked them where they'd been and they said they'd been working a resort a couple of miles down the road. "It's the one you can see on the point across the bay," she said. "It's called Crabtree's."

"Yeah, nobody there from the governor's weekend," Roxie said.

"Well, there was one," Angie said.

"Oh, yeah, the guy that smokes cigars all the time," Roxie said. "He's over there with a really high maintenance broad."

"Wait a minute," I said. "Are you talking about the lieutenant governor?"

"I'm talking about the tall guy with the pot belly who's always got a cigar in his mouth and stinks like his clothes are on fire," Angie said.

"That would be the lieutenant governor," Al said.

"Let's get this straight," I said. "When did you see the man with the cigar at the other resort?"

"Right after I got away from that crazy maniac that kidnapped me," Roxie said. "The sheriff moved us over there and we saw the cigar guy that night. They put us in a cabin way on the end, as far from the main lodge as possible so nobody would find us. The cigar guy was in the next cabin—the very end one."

"And you say he was with a woman?"

"Was he ever. Gorgeous big-ass blonde with tits you wouldn't believe," Roxie said. "Designer blouses and decorated jeans that must have cost megabucks. They stayed in the cabin together and never went any place beyond sitting on the porch. A guy from the kitchen delivered their meals."

"Could the woman have been his wife?" Al asked.

"She didn't look like a wife, if you know what I mean," Roxie said.

"A one-night stand, perhaps?" I said.

"She's been shacked up with him at least since the night we were moved there . . . what was it? Tuesday, I think it was. So that's three nights going on four. It looks to me like it's a long-term kind of deal. Probably costing him a lot of money but I'll bet she's really something in the sack."

Now this was news worth checking. Aaron Ross, who had proclaimed himself the state's next governor, was officially on a pre-campaign tour of northern Minnesota, but he'd been hiding with a woman at a Gull Lake resort most of the week. His campaign tour hadn't generated any noticeable publicity, but we'd chalked that up to the concentrated coverage of the goings-on at Madrigal's and its surroundings.

And Ross's hidden playmate was a beautiful "big-ass blonde" who in the eyes of a discerning sexual practitioner was not his lawfully wedded wife. Oh, baby, wouldn't I like to write this story and see it run with Al's pictures of Ross and the blonde.

This had to be played coolly and cautiously, with stealth equal to the raid that killed Osama bin Laden. We swore Roxie and Angie to secrecy and asked them if they knew the lieutenant governor's cabin number. They not only gave us the number but also drew us a map on a table napkin (it was cloth; the *Daily Dispatch* would be owing Madrigal's for one missing napkin).

We decided the first thing we needed to do was make certain that the woman with Aaron Ross was not his wife. That would require a phone call to their home on Friday morning. We could only hope that the wife would (a) be home and (b) be willing to talk to a reporter.

After that, assuming Roxie's assessment of the big-ass blonde was accurate, we had to get a look at Ross and the woman. Al would have to do the paparazzi thing and get some sneaky pictures of the couple together. Finally, we would have to decide how to approach Aaron Ross with the photos and the revelations gleaned from our two little informants.

Of course, all our careful planning could be thrown into disarray at any time by a phone call from the sheriff announcing a press conference in Brainerd. Whatever we did concerning Aaron Ross and his female companion, we couldn't get ourselves trapped in a corner that interfered with our coverage of the Alex Gordon murder. The murder story was, after all, our reason for being where we were.

Oh, yes, there was also the little timing problem of a Saturday afternoon wedding in St. Paul.

Chapter Thirty-Two

Stealth

WE SLEPT ON IT, our theory being that the morning sun would clarify our thinking. Besides, there was nothing we could do until we were positive that the woman sharing Ross's cabin was not his wife.

There were no familiar faces in the dining room at breakfast Friday morning. Apparently the rest of the group chasing the Gordon murder story had taken cheaper overnight quarters in Brainerd. We hadn't been instructed to do that and the only move we planned to make was toward St. Paul.

I e-mailed Don O'Rourke to let him know we were bright-eyed and bushy-tailed and eager to excel. "What have you been smoking so early in the day?" was Don's reply. We finished breakfast a few minutes after nine and decided it was a decent enough time to call Mrs. Aaron Ross.

A woman answered and identified herself as "Frances speaking." Having no clue who Frances might be, I asked for Mrs. Ross. "Who may I say is calling?" Frances asked. I told her and she asked me to wait a moment.

Soon she was back with another question. "What do you wish to speak with Mrs. Ross about?"

I was ready for that one. "Her husband has declared himself the next governor of Minnesota and is on what he calls a pre-campaign tour. My editor has tasked me with asking Mrs. Rogers for her reaction to her husband's decision to begin his run for governor." Again Frances asked me to hold for a moment. I crossed the fingers on my free hand and waved them at Al. He responded with a similar gesture.

A new voice spoke into my ear. "Good morning, Mr. Mitchell, this is Karen Ross. I understand you're looking for my reaction to my husband running for governor. Is that correct?"

"Good morning, Mrs. Ross," I said. "That is correct. Did you know he had made this decision? And how do you feel about him taking this step? It's a much bigger obligation than lieutenant governor."

"Please call me Karen, Mr. Mitchell. As far as Aaron running for governor, I've always supported his political ambitions even though I'm not a political person myself, and I'll support him on this one. Actually, when he ran for lieutenant governor it was sort of understood between us that the next step would be governor."

"And please call me Mitch," I said. "It will be difficult to have him gone on the campaign trail for the summer and most of the fall, won't it? I mean, already you haven't seen him for more than a week now, what with the fishing opener and the pre-campaign trip and all."

"Oh, yes, it does get lonely. The trip he's on now came as a surprise, but he calls me every night from wherever he is and he's even been sending me pictures from his smart phone. Last night he called me from Alexandria and sent a couple pictures of where he was staying by a very pretty lake."

Pictures already. Now there was a nice touch. "Where all has he been since he left Gull Lake?" I asked.

"Let's see now," she said. "He sent a picture of Paul Bunyan from Bemidji and something from Detroit Lakes. There was one other place; I can't remember off-hand. Maybe Waconia, wherever the heck that is. Would you like me to get my iPad and look it up?"

"No, no, that won't be necessary." I was already feeling like a sneak from the *National Inquirer* so I didn't want to put her through any more work than necessary. However, I did lead her through a series of additional questions to make it sound like I really was gathering material for a story. All through the interview she was pleasant and cooperative and supportive of her cheating son of a bitch of a husband. When our conversation ended I felt genuinely sorry for what my story about her husband and his phony pre-campaign would do to her.

"The military would call it collateral damage," Al said when I told him how I felt about the pain we were about to inflict on Karen Ross. "Knowing what we know, we can't let that scumbag off the hook unless you want to see him as your honorable governor."

Al was right. It was our job to inform the voters of Minnesota about the tomcat morals of the man who wanted to be their governor, no matter what the fallout was on his wife.

"Sending her pictures of the places he's supposedly been is a really nice touch," I said. "I wonder how he does that."

"Probably has them stored in his smart phone from a previous visit," Al said. "I could send you a picture of Yellowstone National Park taken when we went there last summer and tell you I was there today and you'd never know the difference. That's one of the wonders of the digital age."

"Some of those wonders really get misused."

"I won't argue that. So what's next on the scandal trail?"

"I guess it's you playing paparazzi and getting some real-time pictures of the happy couple at their hideaway in the woods."

"Sounds good, but why don't we check with the sheriff to see what his schedule might be before we set up surveillance on Smokey and his big-ass blonde?"

I made the call and talked with Shirley, who had no information about Sheriff Holmberg's plans. "The person he was interrogating was released a few minutes after all you press people left," Shirley said. "I think it was a case of her lawyer saying either arrest her or get off the pot, if you know what I mean."

"Do you know if Sheriff Holmberg has ever investigated a homicide before?" I asked.

"I don't think so. I can't remember another killing around here in the last twenty years. I think he's kind of feeling his way along on this case. Oh, hey, you aren't going to print that, are you?"

"No, your job is safe. I just had the feeling that despite his many years as sheriff he was new at homicides—come to think of it, he may have mentioned it at some point—and of course the sideshow of the climbing kidnapper hasn't helped."

"Yes, he's had a lot to deal with all at once. I hope there's peace and quiet for a while after he cleans this up."

Oh, man, I thought as I put away the phone. *Wait until the fireworks start with the lieutenant governor. Holmberg won't have to deal with that as a criminal case but it will give folks in Crow Wing County plenty to talk about.*

"I guess we're clear to start Operation Smokey," I said to Al. "Ann has been released and there's nothing on the sheriff's schedule for the press this morning."

Al slung his camera bag over his shoulder. "Let's go play tabloid journalist," he said.

* * *

CRABTREE'S RESORT TURNED OUT to be considerably larger than Madrigal's. The office, the main building and the cabins were spread out along high ground with a steep drop to the water. An upper row of cabins looked down over the rooftops of the beachfront cabins. The main building was three stories tall and looked like a giant motel.

We were glad we had the map because it would have taken half an hour to find the lieutenant governor's cabin, which was at the far north end overlooking Gull Lake. We parked the car with the giveaway *Daily Dispatch* logo on it at the south end of a one-row parking lot and started hiking north along the blacktop road. As soon as we found an opening we abandoned the road and slipped into the grove of pine trees, throughout which the northern cabins were scattered.

Our informants had told us that Aaron Ross and his blonde were in the very last cabin in the line. When we saw the last cabin in the distance we ducked behind a pine with low sweeping branches and stopped to study the layout.

Our hope was to get some shots of the two cabinmates together on the porch Roxie and Angie had talked about. Said porch turned out to be a very handsome deck that faced the lake. Our lucky break was that the developers had left a line of trees in front of the cabins, removing only those that directly blocked a view of the lake. This allowed Al to hide behind the sweeping, ground-touching branches of a huge pine tree at a forty-five-degree angle from Ross's cabin, and zero in on the deck through a gap in the branches with his biggest telephoto lens.

"Just like a duck hunting blind," Al said. "Only in this case, we're shooting weasels."

"I was going to say skunks," I said.

"We can let Mrs. Ross decide on that."

"Oh, please don't mention her. I feel like such a bastard doing this to her."

"Collateral damage, Mitch. Unavoidable collateral damage."

Al fastened his camera atop a short-legged tripod, set it under a low pine branch, sprawled on his belly to peer through the viewfinder and lined up the lens to cover the cabin deck. "We're going to get a low angle shot, but I don't dare jack it up to a height where they might see me from the deck," he said.

"Whatever angle you need. Just be sure to get their faces."

"Be even better if I get their faces joined in a passionate, tongue sucking kiss." I almost gagged at the thought of anyone swapping tongues with our cigar-smoking target.

Al lay on his belly behind the camera and I sat on the ground behind the tree trunk. The ground was covered with a layer of dead brown pine needles but the cool dampness of the earth gradually seeped through. The minutes ticked slowly away. We'd been there long enough for my calves to start cramping when my phone, which I'd had the foresight to set on vibrate, vibrated. I whispered "phone" to Al and crawled away to a more distant tree before taking the phone out of my pocket. It was the sheriff's office calling.

Chapter Thirty-Three

A Touchy Situation

SHERIFF'S GONNA TALK to the press in one hour," said Shirley.

"Has he arrested the woman?" I asked.

"Can't tell you anything more," she said and hung up.

We were about a twenty-five-minute drive from the sheriff's office and it would take us at least ten minutes to pack up the camera and walk back to the car. Our Friday morning skunk and weasel hunt was over.

"When we come back I'm going to bring a blanket to lay on," Al said on the way to the car. "My belly button got so cold it crawled inside and snuggled up to my backbone."

"I know what you mean," I said. "My calves were mooing for a warm barn."

"Okay, you've milked that one for all it's worth."

* * *

SHERIFF VAL HOLMBERG had rounded up all the usual suspects, so many in fact that we were told to remain outside for the briefing. Trish Valentine was right up front as always and, also as always, I pushed into a spot behind her. Barry Ziebart was to my right, and Roy Winston was behind him. We had some new arrivals from Twin Cities Channel 11, along with TV and newspaper teams from Duluth, Bemidji, St. Cloud, Moorhead and of course Brainerd. The Alex Gordon murder had relevance again, at least with the Minnesota media.

I had e-mailed Don about the event, which was to begin at 11:00 a.m., and he had replied: "When you're done with that, come home." So now we had a dilemma. Did we go home immediately or did we tell Don about Operation Smokey and stay until we either got photos or the sun went down? I had a feeling it would be the latter, which would create a storm in another port: the heart of Martha Todd.

A three-ring circus of scenarios was scrambling through my mind when Sheriff Holmberg walked out the front door and stood on the top step. The group came to attention like a squad of military recruits and even answered in unison when the sheriff said, "Good morning."

"Did you arrest her?" someone yelled from behind me. The sheriff held up his hands in a plea for silence.

He let that silence sink in for a moment before speaking. "What we have here is a very touchy situation," he said. "Depending on how you folks report it, it can be a very embarrassing situation for at least three people, two of whom have done nothing wrong. I know the TV cameras are running and you're ready to report, as you call it, live, but I wish you would turn them off for a couple of minutes and let me give you some background. After that, it's up to you what you put it on the news Do I have your cooperation?"

"What if we don't?" asked Trish.

"Then we will have a very quick minimal briefing with only the most general information provided, and you will all go away wondering what in the hell really happened."

That was slick. Holmberg was playing on our inborn curiosity, hoping the TV reporters would be willing to trade a live spectacular for the full story. There was chatter among the TV crews and then agreement not to go live until Holmberg had finished his background statement. I had my mini-recorder going in my shirt pocket as a backup to my written notes.

"As I said, what we have here is a very touchy situation," Holmberg said. "Here's what I believe occurred last Thursday night and early last Friday morning. The female person who was seen walking toward the marina with the victim had gone to the victim's cabin with him after the Thursday night party ended at something like two o'clock Friday morning. She spent the night there, or what was left of the night, and when the victim got up at quarter to five to go fishing, she walked with him to the dock, which was what the witness observed. There the victim and the woman separated, with him going to the boat and her going to her cabin, which was a few steps beyond the marina.

"So, ladies and gentlemen, you can see the problem. Do you choose to publicly humiliate the woman, her innocent husband and the victim's innocent widowed wife by having me repeat this story on live TV, or do you wish to spare them from further suffering by having me give a very much watered-down explanation that embarrasses nobody? And if the TV reporters accept the watered-down version, will the newspaper reporters follow their example? Maybe you'd like to talk it over amongst yourselves."

There was a chorus of "we will," and we all started talking at once. Eventually a semblance of order was created and people took turns expressing their opinions. Knowing I would soon be creating havoc and humiliation in the life of one cheated-upon wife, I favored sparing the other one by accepting the expurgated version. I think it was the sheriff's reference to humiliating the victim's "innocent widowed wife" that swung the rest of the crowd in the direction of mercy. Mari Gordon had lost a husband in the most awful way imaginable, and those of us who had interviewed her liked and felt sorry for her.

And so it came about that Trish Valentine and all her rivals reported live with this statement from Sheriff Val Holmberg: "After further investigation, it is clear that the person we interrogated yesterday was in no way connected with or responsible for the death of Alex Gordon. Our investigation of this sad tragedy is continuing." All the newspapers printed this statement without any embellishment. Even the most blood-hungry reporters occasionally have hearts.

I wrote and e-mailed my story while Al drove us back to Gull Lake. "Looks like you're back to square one. Come on home," was Don's reply. With Al in agonized agreement, I sent back a note telling Don what we had learned about Aaron Ross and volunteered to stay until dark if necessary to get a picture and a statement.

"Go get the bastard," Don replied. "But don't leave your bride standing at the altar."

I promised him I wouldn't. After all, what could possibly go wrong?

......*

WE RETURNED TO CRABTREE'S and re-established our little hunting blind under the handy pine tree. This time we brought blankets to cover the pine needles and we were as comfortable as possible under the circumstances while we waited for our targets to appear. We had agreed to wait as long as there was daylight, if necessary. If nothing happened before dark, we would skedaddle for home and hope for a later chance to expose Aaron Ross and his mysterious blonde.

If there had been a lunch delivery to the cabin, as Roxie and Angie had described, we had missed seeing it. As for our own lunch, we had candy bars and bottled water from a machine in the lobby of Crabtree's main lounge. The candy bars obviously were leftovers from the previous season.

Apparently Ross and his companion were deeply absorbed in some indoor activity because the hours dragged by without the cabin door opening.

"Why don't they come out?" Al whispered. "They can't be doing it all this time. They're missing a beautiful day." They were, indeed, missing a beautiful day—the best we'd seen all week. The sun was producing tiny sparkles of light that danced on the gentle ripples of the lake and the temperature had risen into the lower seventies, according to the readout on my cell phone.

At a few minutes after three, that cell phone vibrated. With my sore ribs complaining, I crawled on my hands and knees to a more distant tree to take a call from Martha Todd. "Where the heck are you?" she asked without even her usual "hi, sweetie."

"We've encountered another complication," I said. "But I guarantee you that we'll be on the road by sundown. I'll tell you all about this one when we get home. You'll love it."

"I'd love having you on the road right now even more."

"Sorry, sweetheart, but a great new story has been dropped into our laps. Such is the life of a reporter."

"Right now I'm asking myself: why am I marrying a reporter?"

"Because he's cute and cuddly and loves you like crazy?"

"I can't see his cuteness and he's been too far away to cuddle for a whole darn week. How do I know he still loves me?"

"He will show you in the most demonstrative manner you can imagine tonight," I said.

"Mmm," she said. "Maybe I should spend the rest of the day imagining."

"Maybe I should, too. Maybe one of us will imagine something new."

"And if we don't, there's nothing wrong with the old somethings. Bye, sweetie." We made kissy sounds and hung up.

Aaron Ross and a fabulous-looking woman with waves of long golden hair were standing on the cabin deck when I crept back to our tree. The blonde was a large woman, almost as tall as the lieutenant governor, who was a couple of inches over six feet. She wore a sleeveless pink blouse that left bare her broad, square shoulders, and a pair of form-fitting khaki shorts that emphasized the width of her hips. Roxie's description of her as a big-ass blonde had been right on the money.

Al's face was glued to the camera and he was taking shot after shot of the couple as they stood facing the lake with their arms around each other's waist. I almost let out a triumphant shout when they turned toward each other, embraced and kissed. Then they sat down together on a loveseat and, incredibly, Aaron Ross pulled a cigar out of his shirt pocket, bit off the tip and lit the damn thing. Even more incredibly, the woman stayed seated beside him as the blue smoke swirled around his head. Either she believed Ross's cigar smoking made him devastatingly macho and attractive or her olfactory nerves were paralyzed.

Al turned his face toward me and gave a thumbs-up. I returned the gesture and we quietly gathered our gear and broke camp. When we were out of Ross's possible sightline, we stood up and broke into a trot. Before getting into the car we did a high-five accompanied by whoops of triumph.

Now we needed a printer. Our plan was to make some damning prints and return to Crabtree's to confront Aaron Ross and get his reaction. Our expectation was for a verbal explosion, possibly followed by a plea for mercy. Having expended our day's supply of mercy on Mari Gordon, poor Ross would be, as they say, SOL.

We had seen a couple of printers in the office at Madrigal's during our sessions with the sheriff. If either of them had a port for a camera memory card, we were in business. As it turned out, both of them did and we returned to our cabin with a set of prints showing four poses—the arms around the waist, the hug, the kiss and the loveseat. They weren't on glossy photo paper but were more than adequate for our purpose.

"This is going to be fun," Al said.

"I can't wait to see Aaron Ross's face," I said.

"He's going to swallow his damn cigar."

"I hope you get a shot of that."

We decided to pack up our stuff and put it in the car so we could leave for home immediately after our visit with Aaron

Ross. When Al had only his laptop left to pack, he remembered that he hadn't downloaded the new pix from his camera to the computer. When he finished the download, he said, "Give me a few minutes to cull these things while I've got the computer open."

I really wanted to get to the lieutenant governor and then get on the road immediately, but I agreed to a brief delay. I picked up my novel and was starting to read when he said, "While I'm at it, I'm going to zip through the whole week and delete the useless crap like I always do at the end of an assignment."

"You sure this is the end?" I said.

"We're going home in about an hour, aren't we?"

"We are unless Ross and his bimbo tie us up and torture us until we agree to destroy all of those pix."

I went back to my novel. A few minutes later Al said, "Hey, come here a minute."

He was looking at an image of the inside of Alex Gordon's boat, taken a few minutes after the boat had been tied up at the dock last Friday morning. "What do you think that thing laying in the bottom up near the bow is?" he asked.

It was a dark-colored cylindrical shape about the size of something seen all too often on city sidewalks.

"Looks to me like a dog turd," I said.

"Why would there be dog crap in a fishing boat?"

"Did Alex have a dog with him?"

"Nobody mentioned a dog. And a dog probably would have swam to shore and been under everybody's feet."

"Can you zoom in on it?" I asked.

"I can try," Al said. He moved the cursor and clicked on the image. The dark brown object in the bottom of the boat grew larger and the details became more defined.

We looked at the screen and then at each other.

"Holy shit," Al said. "That's no dog turd."

"It sure as hell isn't," I said.

We were looking at a half-smoked cigar.

Chapter Thirty-Four

Bearding the Lion

"Alex Rogers probably never smoked a cigar in his life," I said.

"Only one person up here for the weekend smokes cigars," Al said.

"We should make a print of this," I said.

"Then we should call the sheriff," Al said.

"And then we should go have our visit with Lieutenant Governor Aaron Ross," I said. "This is way better than your pix of him kissing the blonde."

"Let's get started." Al was out the door with the laptop in his hands, trotting toward the lodge. He made three prints each of an overall shot of the cigar in the boat and a close-up of the cigar. One set was for Ross, one was for the sheriff and one was for us to keep as a souvenir of our week at Gull Lake.

My next move was to call the sheriff's office and ask for Sheriff Holmberg. "He ain't here just now," Shirley said. "Him and most of the crew are workin' a crash that's got Highway 10 blocked just south of town. Three cars and a semi. Traffic's backed up for miles. I figured you guys would all be there with your cameras."

"We've got a different walleye to fry," I said. "I need to talk to the sheriff. I need to have him come to the farthest north cabin at Crabtree's Resort as soon as he can get there. Tell him we've got the person who killed Alex Gordon."

"You bet," Shirley said. "Soon as he calls in I'll tell him."

"Maybe you could call out and tell him," I said.

"Oh, yeah. Maybe I could."

"As soon as pos-si-ble," I said, enunciating each syllable with the utmost precision.

"Right. Have a good day," Shirley said.

The bottom of the sun was touching the western horizon when we arrived at Crabtree's Resort and parked as close to Aaron Ross's cabin as we could get. Al started to get out, but stopped and said, "Do you think this is a good idea, going after Ross with these pictures without being sure when we'll get backup from the sheriff?"

"The sheriff will be on his way at top speed the second he hears we have the killer," I said. "Besides, what's Ross going to do, tie us up and drown us? There's two of us to one of him if it comes down anything physical."

"Okay. Let's go beard the lion in his den."

With a fresh tape in my mini-recorder, Al's camera slung around his neck and the pictures of the boat and cigar clutched in my left hand, we walked up the steps to Ross's front door and knocked.

"Who is it?" Ross yelled. I gave him our names and place of employment.

"Just a minute," he said.

"Bet you anything he's hiding the bimbo," Al said.

"He's crazy if he isn't," I said.

There was no bimbo in sight when the door opened and Aaron Ross beckoned us in. This cabin was much larger than the one Al and I were occupying at Madrigal's, and the smell of cigar smoke filled every cubic foot. We were in a spacious sitting room furnished with a sofa, a coffee table and two overstuffed armchairs flanked by end tables and lamps. Through one opening I could see into a kitchen and through another I could see down a hallway lined with the doors of multiple bedrooms. To my right was a fireplace and to my left was a closed door that I assumed was a bathroom. I wondered which door the lady was behind.

"Nice to see my favorite reporter and photographer team," he said. "Have a seat. What can I do for you boys?"

Neither of us sat down. "You could start by telling us what you're doing here at Crabtree's after telling everybody you were going on a pre-campaign swing through northern Minnesota," I said.

"Simple. I needed to get away by myself for a few days, so I made up the story about a campaign trip," he said. "First of all, I was shook up by Alex Gordon's murder. He and I worked together for the same governor for almost seven years, so his death was a real shock to me. Second, I wanted to think about my campaign strategy without a bunch of would-be experts giving me advice I didn't need."

"So the person we saw you with this afternoon isn't an adviser?" I said.

A tinge of red rose in Ross's face. "Who did you see me with this afternoon?"

"Tall blonde. Female, from the looks of her. Very pretty hair."

"You were spying on me?"

"Just doing our job covering all the events of the fishing opener."

"You were sneaking around . . . how did you know I was here?"

"A reporter never reveals his sources," I said.

"I'll be a son of a bitch," he said.

"You might be," I said. "We have something to show you." I stretched out my hand with the photos and he took them.

Ross looked first at the overall interior boat shot and then at the cigar. His face was turning a brighter crimson. He looked at both photos again. "What the hell are these?" he said.

"They show the interior of Alex Gordon's boat a few minutes after the deputies brought it in last Friday morning," Al said. "We thought you might want to see what happened to the stogie you dropped."

"What are you saying?" Ross said. "Do you think that's my cigar?"

"Do you know anybody else who was here last weekend who smokes cigars?" I said. "Alex Gordon sure as hell didn't."

"Lots of people smoke cigars. That cigar could have been dropped by the guy who used the boat before Alex."

"Friday morning was the first time that boat was out of storage since last fall," I said. "You think Madrigal's left a cigar butt in their boat all winter?"

"They could have," Ross said. "For god's sake, are you thinking I had something to do with Alex Gordon's murder?"

"That's what we're going to tell the sheriff when he gets here," I said.

"No. You can't. You cannot do that," Ross said. The decibels increased with each word.

"You can listen in while we show him the pictures and tell him what we think." Al said. "I'm sure he'll ask you for a statement."

Ross's face was glowing like a cast-iron stove on a below-zero night in January. "No," he shouted "This can't go any further. Sheila!"

I heard a noise behind me and was starting to turn in that direction when I felt a sharp pain in my head and everything went black.

Chapter Thirty-Five

Hows and the Whys

SOMEONE WAS POUNDING ON a drum inside my head and something tough but slightly pliable was holding my wrists together behind my back. I tried to open my mouth but something immovable was keeping it shut. I opened my eyes and saw Al in one of the armchairs. His hands were behind his back and his mouth was covered with a slash of silver duct tape. I was in the other armchair and I assumed I was a mirror image of Al. I had no idea whether I had been unconscious for minutes or for hours.

Standing in front of us were Aaron Ross and the blonde. In his right hand, Ross held a revolver with a barrel that looked as big as a cannon from my perspective. I was glad he was pointing it toward the floor and not at me. A child's wooden stepstool dangled from the woman's right hand. They were both looking at me.

"About time you woke up," Ross said. "I was beginning to think Sheila made the same mistake I did with Alex and hit you too hard."

I stared at him and wanted to speak. All I could do was go, "Mmmm."

"If you promise not to go nuts and start yelling I'll take the tape off your mouths," Ross said. Both Al and I nodded vigorously. An additional shot of pain through my head made me wish I had been less vigorous. Sheila ripped the tape from my mouth, giving me a new area of pain as dozens of hairs from my moustache went with it. Al suffered a similar jolt when Ross tore the tape off his face, costing him portions of both moustache and beard.

I looked at Sheila and nodded toward the stepstool in her hand. "You clobbered me with that?" I said.

Sheila smiled and nodded. "It was the only thing I could find in the bathroom."

"Old Smokey here pulled the gun out of somewhere before I could move," Al said.

"I always keep it handy," Ross said. "You never know when you might have to do away with some varmint."

"I hope you've got a permit," I said. "Or you'll have one more crime on your record."

"Always the comedian, aren't you?" Ross said. "Well you're not going to joke your ass out of this one."

I had started the mini-recorder in my shirt pocket when we'd walked in the front door. It only had a thirty-minute capacity so I decided to get down to business before it ran out. "You said you hit Alex too hard. Tell us about that. The whole story."

"Sure, why not?" Ross said. "You won't be around to write about it. And Mr. Paparazzi's camera with these pictures in it will be long gone." What he didn't know was that they would still be around in Al's laptop, which was locked in the car outside.

Ross put the gun down on the coffee table before starting his story. "Anyhow, you want to hear about how we took care of Alex. Well, you know, him and I have been coming along on this fishing opener thing for two terms—this was the eighth one—and right from the start Alex has been going out after walleyes at five o'clock Friday morning. It was some kind of ritual with him to get out on the lake before sunrise. So this year on Friday morning I was waiting by his boat, all decked out with fishing gear, when he got there, and I asked if I could go along. He wasn't real pleased to see me but I mentioned that I'd just seen him say goodbye to somebody who looked a lot like Ann Rogers at the other end of the dock so he said sure, come on along.

"I got in the middle seat and he was in the stern running the motor. He turned his back to me to fiddle with the throttle on the motor when we got out in the middle of the bay, so it was easy for me to pull an oar out of its lock and whack him across the back of the head. I just wanted to knock him out so I could take his lifejacket off to make it look like he hadn't worn one before I dumped him in the drink and let him drown. But like I said, I hit him a little too hard and he was too far gone to inhale any water.

"Anyhow, after I dumped Alex overboard, Sheila pulled alongside the boat with a boat she'd checked out here at Crabtree's. I moved over to her boat, put the rudder to one side on the empty boat so it would go in circles, and we went around to the other side of the island and buried the lifejacket. Which reminds me, why the hell were you guys on the island when you found that lifejacket?"

"Piss call for me," Al said. "When you gotta go, you gotta go."

"You goddamn weenie, if you'd pissed over the side like a man the lifejacket wouldn't ever have been found. All the sheriff would have had was the bump on the head and eventually the whole thing would have gone away for lack of evidence. It's all your damn fault that everything went viral like a freak show on YouTube."

"Best laid schemes o' mice and men, et cetera," Al said.

"Yeah, well, I got a scheme for you two that's not going to go a-gley," Ross said.

"Hey, our killer is a Bobby Burns fan," I said.

Sheila was shifting her weight from side to side, looking like she wanted to move. "We can't stand here bullshitting forever, Aaron honey," she said. "They said the sheriff is coming."

"Okay, okay," Ross said. "I'm just waiting for the sun to go all the way down so it's good and dark. We don't want anybody to see us dragging these weenies down to the boat."

Boat? That didn't sound like a cruise I wanted to take. And I had more questions. "Okay, you've told us how you killed Alex. Now how about you tell us why?"

"Politics and blackmail, Mitch old boy," Ross said. "Politics and blackmail. Alex didn't want me to run for governor and he knew I'd been having a little fun on the side with Sheila for quite a while. He'd had a photographer trailing us, like you guys, so he had pictures of us together. He told me if I entered the primary he would spill the beans to my wife and the press. I couldn't let that happen."

"Why didn't he want you to run?" I said. Then the light bulb came on in my brain. "Oh, I get it. Alex was planning to run."

"Wrong again, dummy," Ross said. "Alex's *wife* was going to run."

"His wife? Would she have had a chance to win the primary over you?"

"She'd have had Governor Anderson's endorsement."

"Why would she get his endorsement instead of you?"

"Jeez, don't you know anything about what's going on in state politics? Mari Gordon is the governor's niece."

The light bulb in my brain burned brighter. The whole screwy thing made sense in a perverse and evil way.

"Okay, boys, it's dark out. Time to go for a little one-way boat ride," Ross said.

"They'll nail you for this," I said. "The sheriff is coming to this cabin. You'll be his prime suspect if we disappear."

"I'll tell him I must have been out when you boys arrived. I don't remember seeing you."

"How about their car?" Sheila said. "Where's your car parked?"

"Gee, I forgot," I said.

"Me, too," Al said.

"Get their keys and look for a car marked *Daily Dispatch*," Ross said to Sheila. "I'll get these boys ready for the ride."

"Okay, boys, which one's got the keys?" Sheila asked. Neither of us answered.

"You look like a driver," she said to Al. She reached into his right front pants pocket and moved her hand around.

"Hey!" Al said. "That isn't keys you're grabbing."

Sheila laughed. "Not a bad package for a weenie who can't hang it over the side of a boat," she said. She pulled her hand out of Al's pocket with the key to the Ford dangling between her fingers. "See you later," she said on her way out the door.

"Park it way down by the main office so it looks like they were waiting for the sheriff there," Ross said. "Then come back here and help me move these clowns."

"Now I'm going to give you boys a choice," Ross said when Sheila was gone. "You can either cooperate and walk along with us or I can duct tape your ankles together and we can drag you by the feet down the hill to where the boat is tied up. Which will it be?"

"Walk," Al said without hesitation.

"Being in drag sounds kind of kinky," I said. "But I'll walk."

"Always the comedian," Ross said. "Well, this will keep that smart trap shut." He picked up the roll of duct tape and tore off a strip.

The drummer was still banging away inside my skull and I was looking for every possible way to stall. "Wait, I've got one more question."

"Make it a quick one."

"Your wife told me you've been sending her pictures from different campaign stops. How did you do that?"

"You talked to my wife?"

"I did. Don't worry, she still doesn't know what a cheating asshole you are." She would, though, when the sheriff found the pictures in our car after . . . after what? Just how was this evil bastard planning to dispose of us?

"You little shit, I wish Sheila had broken your skull in a hundred pieces."

Maybe I could keep him going. "She's going to find out about Sheila, though. I've got a fail-safe plan."

"What you've got is a smart-ass mouth," Ross said. He swung his hand way back, slapped me hard across that mouth and pressed the strip of duct tape across my lips with far more force than necessary to make it stick. Now I had the taste of blood to go along with the hammering in my head.

"Mmmm!" I said.

"Anyhow, to answer your stupid question, I had the pictures still in my camera from the last four or five fishing openers. Bemidji, Alexandria, Waconia, like that."

"Waconia's not up north," Al said.

"Franny's from Maryland, she don't know the difference," Ross said. "Now we'll take care of your big mouth, too." He tore off a strip of tape and stuck it in place across Al's mouth. *That's not fair,* I thought. *Al didn't get slapped first.*

Chapter Thirty-Six

Splashdown

WHILE WE WAITED FOR SHEILA, Aaron Ross took a sheet off the bed, cut through the binding in several places with a pair of scissors from the bathroom and tore the sheet into strips. He rolled the strips up into balls and stuffed them into his pants pockets.

"Car's down by the main office," Sheila said when she returned. "I threw the key way back into the woods."

"You should have waited and dropped the key into the lake," Ross said. "But there's no way anybody will find it in the woods. We can get started now. The boys have elected to be cooperative and walk down instead of having us drag them."

"Too bad," Sheila said. "I was looking forward to dragging the short one by the nuts." She could have done it, too; she was three inches taller and probably fifteen pounds heavier than Al, with biceps that looked like her hobby was lifting weights. She looked so strong that I was thinking I was lucky she hadn't killed me with that clout from the stepstool. Then again, maybe not so lucky. That might have been an easier death than what Aaron Ross was planning for me. Where the hell was the sheriff?

"Okay, on your feet," Ross said. He grabbed my shoulders and hoisted me out of the chair, sending a red-hot rocket through my throbbing head and a stab of pain through my tender ribs. Sheila grabbed Al by front of his shirt and hauled him up out of the chair with one hand. If I survived this night I promised myself that I would never challenge that woman to an arm wrestling contest.

Gripping us tightly, with their right arms around our shoulders and their left hands clamped on our left arms, they guided us through the trees and down the steep hill to a small strip of sandy beach. The moon that had shone so brightly on Ann Rogers and Alex Gordon the previous Friday had been reduced to less than gibbous and provided minimal light, making each step on the uneven ground an adventure. Every jolt reverberated through my head and ripped through my rib cage. I nearly fell several times and Al did take a tumble despite Sheila's grip on him. This earned him a kick in the belly before he was hauled back onto his feet.

Bobbing in the water at the end of a line fastened to an anchor dug into the beach was a Crabtree's boat. I wondered if it was the boat used in the Gordon murder, which could be traced back to Sheila.

As if reading my mind, Ross said, "This ain't the same boat we had last week. I bribed the marina guy to give us this without signing for it, just like I bribed the kitchen crew to make us meals and deliver them. You see, contrary to that old saying, money can buy happiness."

"Okay, now we do the feet," Ross said, throwing me to the ground without warning. My poor throbbing head hit the sand hard enough to produce a shower of visible stars and my ribs felt like they'd been separated with knives. Ross immediately sat on my knees and wrapped my ankles with duct tape before I could gather my scattered wits and start kicking.

He left me lying there and turned his attention to Al, who had tried to run and was in a no-arms wrestling match with Sheila. Sheila, who had arms, won the battle, using her weight to bear Al to the sand. She sat down hard on his chest, knocking the air out of his lungs and making it easy for Ross to grab Al's feet and tape the ankles together.

The demonic duo pulled the bow of the boat onto the sand and then came back to me. Ross grabbed my feet and Sheila picked up my shoulders. They carried me the boat and dumped me in, sending another volley of pain through my head and ribs. I almost blacked out again, and for a moment I wished I could black out. Next thing I knew, they dumped Al in on top of me and we lay like two immobile dummies in the bottom of the boat.

"Be right back," Ross said. I couldn't see anything but a patch of sky peeking between Al's shoulder and neck but I heard Ross trot away. When he came back he leaned over the boat, holding a cement block in each hand. "I spotted these yesterday in the construction site where they're building a new cottage," Ross said. "I thought they'd make cute necklaces for you two nosy little weenies."

Now I knew what the torn strips of sheet were for.

Aaron Ross stepped on our feet as he clambered into the stern and Sheila put her wet feet on our shoulders after she plopped the anchor on Al's right foot, pushed us off from the beach and jumped aboard with a splash that soaked us both. Ross got the motor going and backed us a little farther from the beach before spinning us around and heading off into the empty darkness of the lake. My range of vision was still limited to a patch of sky with a few stars beginning to shine and I began to wonder if the last thing I would see on this earth would be a black, star-studded sky.

Another thought struck me as we roared across the slightly bumpy water. Would Ross pull the tape off our mouths before sending us to swim with the walleyes? If he did, should we try to stave off the final plunge by telling him that he would be convicted by evidence still in our car? This was risky. He would be sure to go after that evidence. Would he kill us first or would he stash us somewhere—somewhere where we would have a chance to escape—while he broke into the car?

By the time the boat stopped and Sheila dropped anchor, I had decided not to mention the evidence. I was sure he would go through with this execution and then head straight for our car. My hope was that the sheriff would get here first and find the car where Sheila had left it. Where was that damn sheriff, anyway?

The boat was rocking gently at anchor with the motor idling as Ross rose from his perch in the stern and stood over us. "Here's the deal," he said. "We're out over a really deep hole, so deep that nobody fishes it. We're going to make you boys very stylish necklaces out of sheets and cement blocks and assist you in diving over the side. Maybe you'll see some walleyes on the way to the bottom, but it's awful dark out so probably you won't. When we're done, I'm going to turn this boat in to the guy I paid off and give him another nice tip to encourage him to keep his mouth shut if anybody asks any questions. You two will have mysteriously disappeared, never to float up and be seen again, and there will be no trace of you having been in our cabin. Now, let's get you ready for your swim."

They dragged us into a side-by-side sitting position in the middle of the boat, leaning against the center seat. Ross sat down on the bow seat facing us, pulled a strip of sheet through one of the holes in a cement block and tied the ends with a square knot. He did the same with a second sheet, telling us this was for extra strength. "Wouldn't want a knot to slip and leave you floating way out here all by yourself."

He rigged a second block-and-sheet combination and hung it around Al's neck. The block dropped onto Al's lap and the weight pulled his head down until his chin rested on the block. Then Ross reached over Al's bowed head, pulled both sheets tight and tied them together behind Al's neck so that his chin was permanently wedged against the cement block.

They were rigging me the same way when I thought I heard a noise in the distance. *Couldn't be,* I thought. *We're way the hell out in the middle of Gull Lake in the dark of the night. There could be no passing boat traffic.*

When Ross was satisfied with his work, he ripped the duct tape and some more of our facial hair off and asked if we had any last words.

"I hope you rot in hell when they catch you," Al said. "And I hope that happens very, very soon so you have more of eternity to rot in."

"I hope lightning strikes the boat on your way to shore and burns the skin off you both," I said. "Then may the walleyes pick the roasted meat off your bones at the bottom of the lake."

Aaron Ross clapped his hands. "Bravo! Very eloquent," he said. "Spoken like a true writer. Just because of that, you can go first, Mr. Bigmouth."

Ross and Sheila stood up, rocking the boat, and picked me up—Ross at my feet and Sheila at my head. As they hoisted me, sending more knives ripping into my ribcage, I was sure I heard a boat motor. As they turned me face down with the cement block dangling a few inches below my chin, the sound of the motor grew louder. As they swung me to the side, I took a deep breath and then wondered why. Why was I was trying to preserve another thirty or forty seconds of life—and life underwater, at that? As I hung suspended with my lungs full, a bright light illuminated us and a voice shouted, "Hold it right there."

At long last, the sheriff had arrived.

At the sound of Sheriff Val Holmgren's voice, Ross and Sheila let go and dropped me. The cement block attached to my neck landed on the gunnel, which is what sailors call the top edge of the side of a boat. When the cement block hit the gunnel, it bounced up, rapping me in the chin. When the cement block went down for the second time, the chances were an even 50/50 that it would tilt toward the boat and fall inside or that it would tilt away from the boat and go into the water.

The cement block tipped outward and splashed into the water. My head was inches behind it.

It's amazing how fast a cement block sinks. It goes down much faster than a human body, even an anti-buoyant body like mine. I felt like I was on an express train zooming downward headfirst through a bottomless tunnel of cold water. I was surprised to find that I was still holding my breath when the super carnival ride stopped and my chin again was jammed against the cement block. I knew I couldn't hang on much longer without taking a breath. A few seconds later my lights went out for the second time that day.

Chapter Thirty-Seven

Lights On

WHEN THE LIGHTS CAME back on this time I was on my knees in the bottom of a boat with my chest resting on the middle seat and my head hanging face down. I was creating a pond in the bottom of the boat beneath my head by alternately coughing and vomiting up lake water. I heard Al say, "Hey look, Mitch, I think you swallowed a perch." I tried to laugh and threw up more water from deep within my gut.

After another throat-searing coughing spell I was able to rasp out a question. "How'd I get here?"

"Deputy LeBlanc dove in after you," said Sheriff Val Holmgren. "Lucky for you, he carries a hunting knife in his belt and was able to cut you loose from that cement necklace you were wearing and bring you up. I think in another minute you'd have been a goner."

"Where is he? I should thank him."

"He's busy settling your boat driver and his lovely assistant into another boat for transportation to some waiting squad cars. That woman is strong as an ox and ornery as a mule, by the way."

"I'm well aware of that," I said. "She cold-cocked me with a kiddies' stepstool."

With the help of Al and the sheriff I was able to get myself upright on the seat. During this struggle I regained my awareness of the pain in my ribcage. "Thank God you got here," I said to Holmgren.

"You can thank somebody closer to the ground than God that we found you," he said. "We pulled into Crabtree's and saw your car in front of the office so we stopped there, thinking you'd be waiting for us inside. Then we got a call from the Brainerd 911 operator that a woman had called and said she'd seen two people take you guys down to the lake and put you in a boat. She even gave 911 your first names. So we grabbed a couple of boats and went looking. We headed for the deep hole because we figured that's where anybody dumping bodies would dump them and we saw the silhouette of your boat in what little moonlight there was. It was nip and tuck timing all the way around, let me tell you."

"You say a woman who knew our names called 911 and said she saw us being hauled down to the boat by those two bastards?"

"That's what the operator said."

"But you didn't get the woman's name?"

"That I did not. Must have been a guest at Crabtree's but I don't know how she knew your names. You may never know who saved your butts tonight."

At the Crabtree's dock we were met by two sets of EMTs bearing gurneys. We both protested that we didn't need an ambulance ride but they insisted because of my head injury and the pain and swelling in Al's right foot from the dropped anchor.

Before I was loaded into the ambulance I called the sheriff over to my side. I pulled the wet mini-recorder out of my shirt pocket and handed it to him. "Play this tape and copy it if you want to, but I need it back before we leave Brainerd," I said. "This makes me glad I spent the extra money and bought a waterproof unit."

Holmgren took the recorder and said he would return it to me in the morning in the hospital. I said no way would I still be in the hospital in the morning. "We are heading for home tonight as soon as they say we're clear. We'll stop at your office and pick up the tape. Meanwhile, if you want to see some interesting pictures, take a look in the back seat of our car. We made a set of prints just for you."

"We tried to look into your car when we got here but it's locked," Holmberg said. "Want to give me your key for a minute?"

"Oh, my god!" I said. "The key."

* * *

THE DRUMMER IN MY HEAD was still banging out a rhythm on a set of bongos when we arrived at the emergency room door. My exploring fingers had found a lump that felt at least as big as an ostrich egg on the back of my head, and they came away with small sample of my blood as well.

The sheriff had promised to call a locksmith to open the Ford so he could obtain the photos. Getting the car started so we could go home would require assistance of another sort. "We can cross that river when you come to the bridge," he'd said.

I was wheeled into a cubicle surrounded by white curtains and Al was wheeled into another. I was lying on my left side in deference to the ostrich egg, contemplating the bland whiteness of the curtain, when a blonde, blue-eyed nurse about thirty years old with substantial boobs and a name tag that said "AMY" came in. She took my pulse and blood pressure, both of which surged upward just from having my arm pressed snug against her warm, soft body.

"How'd you get all wet?" Amy asked.

"Fell out of a boat," I said. "With some assistance."

"Somebody pushed you overboard?"

"'Threw' would be a more accurate verb than 'pushed.' It's a long story."

"Nasty lump on your head," she said, pressing two fingers against it. I nearly rolled off the bed at the touch and she said, "Sorry. I guess it's kind of tender, huh?"

"That would be an understatement," I said.

"You got a headache?"

"Like a three-armed man pounding on a bass drum."

"Yeah, you probably got a concussion. Dr. Hammersley will be in shortly to take a look at it." Just hearing the word "hammer" gave my head an extra jolt. "Let me clean the blood off that bump." She produced a soft cloth, wetted it with some sort of liquid fire and applied it to the ostrich egg. I could have used a bullet to bite on.

When she'd finished torturing me, Amy left the cubicle, assuring me again that Dr. Hammersley would be in shortly. I wondered what this hospital's definition of 'shortly' was. In some hospitals that could be as long as half an hour if a wound wasn't spurting blood directly from a severed artery. I wanted us both to be out of that hospital quickly so we could get back to our car and work on getting it started.

Shortly turned out to be about ten minutes. Dr. Hammersley, a tall, thin, forty-something man with a long nose and a moustache, appeared beside the bed. He introduced himself, pulled on a pair of blue rubber gloves and looked closely at the ostrich egg. "Got a lump there as big around as a quarter," he said. Immediately I knew I couldn't trust him. I was absolutely certain my lump was a hell of a lot bigger than a quarter.

The doctor bent down and peered into my eyes with the intensity of a lover about to propose. Next he pressed his first two fingers against the lump and I pulled away like a cat pouncing on a mouse. "A little tender, are we?" he asked.

"More than a little," I said. "I was blind-sided with a kiddies' stepstool."

"Real good chance of a concussion," he said. "I'll have you sent down for a brain scan."

"I don't have time for that. My partner and I have to be on the road for St. Paul tonight."

"Don't set your heart on it. If the scan shows a concussion we'll have to hold you overnight. I'll see you after they've done the scan."

Dr. Hammersley left me fuming, but before I could express myself to Al I heard a woman's voice in the adjoining cubicle say, "We'll have to send you to x-ray to make sure your foot isn't broken."

I desperately wanted to call Martha Todd but I'd left my cell phone in the car when we went to visit Aaron Ross. This had a positive side in that if the phone had been in my pocket it would have been dunked in the lake, but it left me without a means of communication.

From the next cubicle I heard, "I'll get you scheduled for an x-ray shortly."

When the nurse's footsteps had faded away I said, "Hey, Al, do you have your cell phone on you?"

"Yeah, you want me to toss it over the curtain?" he said.

"You'd have to hit me square in the chest for me to catch it. I'm not what you'd call agile right now. Maybe we can get a nurse to bring it to me. I need to call Martha."

"That could take forever. I'll hobble over to you." I was still lying on my side when he limped into my field of vision with his cell phone in his hand. "Jeez, that's a nasty bump on the back of your noggin," he said. "It's almost as a big as a quarter."

"Your sore foot must have affected your eyesight," I said. "It's at least as big as an egg."

"Well, maybe a pigeon egg. Here's the phone. I hope Martha doesn't burn it up when she hears where you are."

Just as I took the phone it rang. Caller ID said it was Martha Todd calling so I answered. "Why are you answering Al's phone but not your own?" she asked.

I explained the phone switch and told her where we were without telling her why were there. Naturally she asked for an explanation. I gave her a quick rundown, skipping the part about my express trip to the bottom of the lake, and told her that we'd be on the road as soon as the hospital completed its tests.

"What are they testing you for?" Martha asked.

"They're checking to make sure I don't have a concussion and that Al doesn't have a broken foot. We'll be starting for home right after the tests, however long they take. But don't wait up for me; you know hospitals."

"I also know you. I'm betting they keep you overnight."

"Never happen. I'll walk out."

"Don't you dare walk out of there with a concussion. I'd rather have you late for the wedding than coming home with brain damage. God knows you're goofy enough as it is."

"Hey, that's verbal abuse," I said. "Calling a guy names when he's lying prostrate on a bed of pain."

"I just want to see you standing beside me tomorrow with your brain in one piece. Did you say Al is hurt, too?"

"He has a boo-boo on his foot where a careless person dropped an . . . uh . . . something heavy." I almost said "an anchor" but changed my mind because that might have provoked an unwanted question. This was not the time for details.

"Your mother and grandmother arrived a couple of hours ago," Martha said. "They're staying next door in Zhoumaya's guest bedroom. She hasn't turned hers into an office like we have, and she actually has a bed in there. What should I tell them about why you're not on the way home?"

"Tell them we were covering breaking news: the arrest of the two people involved in the murder of Alex Gordon. That's the truth."

"Mitch Mitchell and Alan Jeffrey reporting live?"

"You got it. Now all I have to do is get hold of my laptop so I can write the story. We need to cut this chatter so I can call the city desk and let them know we've got a blockbuster coming."

"All right, sweetie," Martha said. "Please let them find nothing in your head."

"That's a given," I said. We made kissy sounds and hung up.

Al took his phone back for a quick call to Carol. Then he shuttled the phone back to me and I called the *Daily Dispatch* to give Fred Donlin a rundown on what we had for a story and pix.

"That's incredible. I'll leave a note for Eddy Gambrell to save a large hole on page one," Fred said. Eddy was the assistant city editor who took over for Don O'Rourke on Saturday. "Did you say you're both in the hospital?" Fred asked.

"Just for tests," I said. "We'll be in St. Paul before midnight. The story will be waiting in Eddy's inbox when he gets in."

My brain scan was conducted fifteen minutes later. A young man in blue scrubs wheeled my bed to an elevator, took me down a floor and deposited me beside the machine. The constant pain in my head had eased somewhat, but moving from the bed to lie on the narrow slab of the machine brought back all the intra-cranial drums and sent fresh knife blades into my ribs. They ran my head in and out of a tunnel a couple of times and put me back on the bed so the young man could take me back to my little white tent. As I rolled past Al's cubby hole I saw that it was empty. Good. Soon we'd both be in a cab on the way to Crabtree's, where we'd face the problem of starting the Ford without a key.

I was almost dozing despite the bongos in my brain when Sheriff Val Holmberg appeared beside the bed. "The locksmith got your car open and we might be able to get it started if we connect with the right computer," he said after inquiring about the state of my head. "We also found the woman who told 911 that you were being taken to the lake."

"Who was it?" I said. "Do I know her?"

."I believe you do. Would you like to see her?"

"I'd like to hug her and kiss her if my head didn't hurt so much. Is she here?"

"She is. Come on in, miss. He's ready to see you."

"Hi, Mitch," said Roxie Robideaux. "How are you feeling? You look like you got hit by a truck."

Chapter Thirty-Eight

Saved by the Belle

I DID HUG ROXIE. I sat up so abruptly that the lights faded and almost went black, but as they slowly returned to normal I opened my arms and said, "Come here, you gorgeous creature." We had a long, long hug before I asked her how in hell she happened to see Al and me being led to the slaughter.

"It was all because I forgot my hairspray," Roxie said. "Remember we told you we spent a couple of nights in the cabin next door to the cigar smoker and the blonde? Well, I took a shower just before dinner tonight and when I went to fix my hair I couldn't find my hairspray. I looked all over everywhere and finally decided I'd left it in that cabin at Crabtree's, so I went back to look. I had turned in my key but I talked the desk clerk into giving me another one so I could get in just for a few minutes. Sure enough, my hairspray was still there in the bathroom. When I opened the door to come out, I saw you guys with your hands behind your back being pushed along by the stinky cigar guy and his blonde.

"You went past me close enough that I saw that you had tape over your mouths. Anyhow, I followed you down the hill as quiet as a mouse long enough to see that they were going to put you in a boat. Then I ran back up the hill to where those two couldn't hear me and called 911 on my cell phone."

"My god, saved by a whore with a can of hairspray," I said.

"You could make that the headline for your story," Roxie said. "It's like those books you read where the good guy gets saved by the bad woman with a heart of gold."

"You're not a bad woman, but you surely do have a heart of gold. And guts of platinum to follow us down the hill with those two killers. If they'd heard you they could have grabbed you, too."

"I thought about that. In fact I started to run back down and make a fuss so they knew they'd been seen but then I thought, what if they come after me? There wouldn't be anybody to show the cops which way the boat went."

Al came hobbling into the cubicle. "Do I hear the voice of Roxie?" he asked.

"You heard the voice of the woman who saved our asses tonight," I said.

"Roxie made the call to 911?"

"I did," she said. This got her another long, grateful hug.

Next to join the crowd surrounding my bed was Dr. Hammersley. He shooed everybody out and stationed himself in front of me with his arms folded as I remained sitting on the edge of the bed. "Sorry to tell you this, Mr. Mitchell, but you do have a concussion, just as I suspected," he said. "I know you're in a hurry to get on the road but I'm sorry to say we'll have to keep you overnight for observation."

This was like being hit with the stepstool again. "You can't keep me," I said. "I have to get married tomorrow."

"We'd be guilty of malpractice if we didn't keep you," he said. "And you'd be guilty of stupidity if you didn't stay. You could have any number of unpleasant complications on the way home. I'm sure your bride-to-be would rather have you arrive alive and conscious rather than any of the possible alternatives. Hopefully you'll be well enough to ride home in time for the wedding. And notice that I said *ride*—you are not to try driving a car until your doctor in St. Paul clears you. Now, I've ordered a room for you and your friend. I'll have them take you up immediately and your friend will be joining you as soon as they put a cast on his foot."

Another blow. "They're putting a cast on his foot?"

"It's broken in three places—three separate bones. He'll be in a cast for six weeks."

After Dr. Hammersley shook my hand, said he'd see me in the morning and departed, I ran our situation through my mind. We had one man not able to drive because of a concussion. We had one man not able to drive because his right foot would be in a cast. We had one car with zero ignition keys. Adding one and one and one and zero, I came up with a negative three. I tried to imagine what I was going to say to Martha. Nothing coherent came to mind.

The sheriff returned to say good night and brightened my night a wee bit by handing me my laptop. "I grabbed this out of your car when we opened it," he said. "Thought you might could use it while you're in here." At least I could write my story and communicate with the *Daily Dispatch*. I almost gave him a hug.

Next in to say good night was Roxie. I did give her another hug. "You're the best," I said. "Al and I will be grateful forever."

"You guys are the best, too," Roxie said. "Nobody was as nice to Angie and me as you two were."

"So do us a favor and try to find another, safer line of work, okay?"

"We will as soon as we make enough money to pay for grad school. There's no decent paying jobs out there right now and we can make a hell of a lot more money flipping dicks than flipping hamburgers, if you know what I mean."

I laughed, pulled my soggy wallet out of my back pocket, tugged out a wet business card and handed it to Roxie. "Call me in about a week and maybe I can help you gals find something in the city."

She thanked me and with some effort slid the card into the back pocket of those unbelievable jeans. I could see the outline of the card against her butt as she walked away.

Roxie's derriere was barely out of sight when the young man in scrubs came in, unlocked the wheels of my bed and wheeled me through a series of twists and turns until we found an elevator that took us to the top floor. Since I was the first arrival in the double room, I chose the bed by the window. I had traded my wet clothes for a dry Johnny and was sitting up pecking away at my story when Al was brought in via wheelchair with his right foot encased in a gleaming white plaster cast. Complaining loudly about the size and weight of the cast, he was helped out of the chair and into the bed by a nurse.

"Looks like you got a club foot," I said.

"I'll club you if you think this is funny," he said.

"I've already been clubbed once tonight. And I expect a verbal clubbing from Martha when she hears I'm stuck here until morning. How about loaning me your phone again?"

"I'm not delivering it this time."

"So toss it. If you hit me in the numbers I can catch it." I put the laptop on my bed table and turned toward Al. The phone arced across the space between us and hit me in the belly button. I managed to trap it with my hands and hang on.

"Where are you?" Martha said by way of a greeting.

"I'm in bed," I said. "They've imprisoned me for the night because I have a concussion." I prepared myself for an explosion.

She surprised me. "Oh, no. You really are hurt that bad? Oh, you poor darling. What happened? Who hit you? What did he hit you with?"

I really appreciated the "poor darling" bit so I gave her a condensed version of our encounter in the cabin, again stopping short of our journey onto and into the lake. I ended with, "They're just keeping me for observation. The doctor is sure that I'll be well enough to travel in the morning."

"Will you be able to stand up and say your vows?" she asked. "Should I be looking for a wheelchair or something?"

"I will stand up and say my vows even if I have to lean on Al's arm. On second thought, make that somebody else's arm; Al has a broken foot."

"It really is broken? What did they drop on it?"

I decided it was time for true confessions and said it was an anchor. This of course brought forth a stream of questions and I was in the process of telling almost the entire story when Al interrupted. "Hey, save me some battery," he said. "I've got to call Carol and my charger is in my bag back in the car."

This was the perfect excuse to wrap up my story before reaching the part about being chucked overboard wearing a cement block around my neck. Martha and I exchanged loving goodnights, made kissy sounds and hung up. "Catch," I said, underhand flipping the phone across the room. Weighted down by his plaster bootie, Al almost let it sail over his head. I was holding my breath when he speared it with his left hand, arm fully extended. "Good thing I played shortstop in high school," he said.

* * *

THANKS TO SOME POTENT pain pills I was able to sleep off and on between assorted wakeups for the taking of vital signs and the shining of lights into my eyes for observation of my pupils. Any moment of rest a patient gets during the night in a hospital is purely by chance.

At 6:00 a.m., both Al and I were awake and ready to depart. I buzzed for a nurse. A woman with a name tag that said "NATALIE" answered the call and told us that I could not be discharged until I'd been examined by a doctor. "So please get a doctor in here," I said. "I have to be in St. Paul in time to get into some decent clothes and get married at one o'clock."

Nurse Natalie hustled off to see if she could find a doctor. I thought about getting dressed while I waited for the doctor but

I had no idea what had happened to my clothing. I had entered the hospital wearing a T-shirt, jeans and undershorts that were all dripping wet. I doubted they would be completely dry, but it was either go home soggy or go home exposing my butt out the back of my Johnny. No-brainer; it had to be soggy.

To Al, I said, "Did you rinse out your undershorts last night?"

"No, I just had the nurse stand them up in the closet," he said. "But at least mine are dry."

Twenty minutes passed before Nurse Natalie returned. "Doctor Hammersley has ordered another brain scan and he should be in at about eight thirty to examine you," she said.

I sat up quickly, which torched my ribs and sent a wave of pain blasting through my skull, waking up the drummer inside. "Eight thirty! Do I have to wait for Doctor Hammersley?" I said. "Can't someone else check me out? We've got to get a taxi out to Gull Lake and we've got a two-and-a-half-hour drive from there."

"Who's driving you?" said Nurse Natalie.

Al and I looked at each other. "Who is?" Al asked.

"I guess I'm stuck with it," I said.

"No way. I'm not riding with a guy with a concussion. Once again, we're up the creek without a canoe."

"Guess you're not in such a big hurry after all," said the nurse. She turned and left the room before I could throw my half-empty water glass at her.

"Okay, chicken, I'll go alone and leave you here," I said. "I can't miss my own wedding."

"You can't do that. You might pass out and kill yourself, or even worse, you might kill somebody else," Al said. "I should have asked Carol to drive up to get us."

Angry and frustrated, I slammed myself down onto my back and paid a painful price when the lump on my head hit the pillow. Every expletive I could think of poured out of my mouth at high volume. A nurse passing in the hallway turned into our room and asked if we were okay. We lied and said we were just fine.

"You don't sound fine," she said "Please be more careful with your language."

Somehow I swallowed an obscene response and uttered a meek, "Sorry."

Several minutes later another young man in blue scrubs arrived with a wheelchair and took me for my morning brain scan. When I got back to my room an aide came in to check my vitals. "Whooie," she said when my blood pressure nearly blew away the cuff. For some reason it was at an all-time high.

"That's the highest blood pressure number I've ever heard," Al said when she was gone.

"Me, too," I said. "Hey, speaking of high, I wonder if there's a flight from Brainerd to the Twin Cities this morning."

"I'd Google it but my cell phone battery is dead," Al said.

"So are my chances of getting married today. And maybe forever. Why would Martha marry an idiot like me?"

"I've never understood that," Al said. "She seems extremely intelligent otherwise."

"This is no longer a joking matter," I said. "I'm going to have to work up the guts to pick up that phone," I nodded toward the bedside phone, "and call Martha with the news that the car won't start and even if it did, neither one of us could drive it. If I was still drinking I'd kill a quart of vodka right now."

It was twenty minutes after eight when Doctor Hammersley walked in. "Good news," he said. "The scan looks good. If your eyes are focusing you'll be good to go. How are you getting home?"

"We're not," I said. "We have no car and we have no driver."

"Oh, yes you do," said a familiar voice from behind the doctor.

Chapter Thirty-Nine

Victoria's Messenger

IN THE FINAL MOMENTS of Bertolt Brecht's marvelous *Threepenny Opera* there is no hope for the loveable villain MacHeath, better known as Mack the Knife, who is about to be hanged as a thief, a murderer and a whoremonger. Macky is just a few steps away from the noose when the music flairs, a man bearing a scroll comes trotting down the center aisle and the chorus sings, "Victoria's messenger riding comes, riding comes, riding comes . . ." Sure enough, the scroll is a letter of pardon for Mack the Knife, signed by Queen Victoria.

I felt very much like MacHeath when I saw Sheriff Val Holmberg standing behind the doctor, dangling a set of car keys in his right hand. "Here's the keys," he said. "And I'm going to drive."

Al almost slid off the side of the bed. "Where'd you get those keys?" he asked.

"We recruited a bunch of volunteers—guests of the lodge and some of the people who work there—and sent them out hunting through the woods, starting at sunrise this morning," Holmberg said. "A little girl about ten years old found them hanging on a wild blackberry bush about forty minutes ago."

"Did I hear you say you were driving us to St. Paul?" I asked.

"You did. Deputy LeBlanc will lead us in a squad car with all lights flashing and give me a ride back to Brainerd after the wedding. I am invited, aren't I?"

"Invited, hell, you can be my best man if you want to," I said. "You can also be the first one to kiss the bride. In fact, the bride will probably kiss you when you deliver me to the church."

Doctor Hammersley stepped forward, shook my hand and said he would send in a nurse with the paperwork for my release. Al was already getting out of his Johnny and clumping his way to the closet to retrieve his clothes. Nurse Natalie walked in, saw a naked man, spun a quick one-eighty and ran out. "Come on back," Al yelled. "I'm not bashful."

"I'll come back when you're decent," the nurse said. "You could at least pull the curtain so everybody in the hall doesn't see you."

"What about me?" I said. "What happened to my wet clothes?"

"They're hanging in the closet with your name on it," Nurse Natalie said. "We ran them through the hospital laundry last night. Your shoes are still wet, though. We were afraid they'd shrink if we ran them through the industrial strength dryer."

My canvas tennis shoes were still damp and chilly but nothing could throw cold water on my mood at that moment. Victoria's messenger, in the form of a north country sheriff, had riding come. He would get me to the church on time, a line which, come to think of it, is from another great musical called *My Fair Lady*.

"What time's the wedding?" Holmberg asked when we had settled into the Ford with me in the front passenger seat and Al in the back.

"One o'clock," I said. "But I need time to look for something to wear and change into it." The digital clock on the dashboard read 9:18, and we had 130 miles to go.

"Piece of cake," Holmberg said. "We've even got time to grab ourselves some breakfast along the way."

We picked up breakfast sandwiches and coffee at a drive-through, and I dug my cell phone out of the door pocket where I'd left it the night before. "Guess what, we're actually on the road," I said when Martha Todd answered.

"You mean I don't have to grab some guy off the street to take your place as the groom?" she said.

"Nope, no surrogates needed. The real groom will be there with bells on. Actually, I should say with sirens on. We have a uniformed chauffeur and we're getting a real live police escort all the way from Brainerd to St. Paul."

"In that case, I'll start getting dressed for a wedding. If it was just you and Al coming on your own I'd wait until I saw the whites of your eyes."

We'd barely finished making kissy sounds and ending the call when my cell phone, which was still in my hand, chimed. To my surprise, the caller was Don O'Rourke.

"How are you?" Don asked. "I heard you got a pretty nasty whack on your funny bone. Are you going to be okay for the wedding?"

"My skull, to which you refer in such a flippant manner, is bloody but unbroken," I said. "I do have a concussion but I'll be fine for the wedding. Thanks for asking."

"That's not the only reason I called," Don said. "I've got an assignment for you."

"An assignment? I'm on a week's vacation as of today," I said. "I'm getting married and going off to Niagara Falls for my honeymoon, remember?"

"I do remember. In fact, that's what my assignment is about. Before you go home or to the church or anywhere else you might go, I want you to stop at Artie's All-American Rental Shop at University and Avon."

"Why should we stop there?"

"We heard that your wedding suit burned up the other night, so because you couldn't get home to get fitted for a new one we rented you a tux at Artie's. He's promised to do a fitting and an instant tailoring job while you wait."

"Who is the wonderful 'we' who ordered this?" I asked.

"The *Daily Dispatch*, who do you think? We're also paying for it," Don said.

"You're kidding. I can't believe you're doing this."

"Well, believe it. Some of us are coming to the wedding and we didn't want to see you looking like a slob beside your beautiful bride."

* * *

THANKS TO DEPUTY LEBLANC'S flashing lights, we reached Artie's All-American Rental Shop before 11:30 a.m. Artie, the owner, greeted me and steered me into a changing room, where I found a white shirt with ruffles, a black bow tie and a dark gray tuxedo on hangers. I emerged wearing these items, mounted a small wooden platform and watched Artie make everything fit with a few folds and a handful of safety pins.

From Artie's it was only a few minutes to the Unitarian-Universalist Church, where the minister had agreed to unite us two non-churchgoers. The sheriff dropped me off in front of the church and drove Al home to renew acquaintances with his family and change into wedding attire. I wondered if he would split the leg of his suit pants to fit over the cast on his foot, as a nurse at the hospital had done with the khakis he'd come home in.

I actually had an hour to kill before the music would start and I would take my place in front of the Reverend Sarah Jefferson-Schneider to await the entrance of my bride. I used that hour to pace in circles around a small back room, growing more nervous and sweaty by the minute. The pain killer administered at the hospital began to wear off and the drummer inside my skull started to pound again.

Al joined me ten minutes before the hour, and I observed that he, or probably Carol, had indeed split the lower part of his right pants leg and fastened the edges together with safety pins. He had acquired a pair of crutches that made it possible for him to walk without clunking the cast on the floor.

"Sorry you had to sacrifice a good pair of pants to be my best man," I said.

"Carol says she can sew it back together when the cast comes off," he said.

Neither of us spoke further as the minutes ticked by and the tension grew.

The door opened a crack and I jumped six inches off the floor. Sheriff Val Holmberg stuck his head in and said, "Five minutes." I thanked him and said, "What is this, opening night at the theater?"

"The bride asked me to check on you," the sheriff said and closed the door.

"You'd think we'd given Martha some reason to doubt our prompt presence," Al said.

"I'll never understand women," I said.

At two minutes to one, the cell phone in my pocket rang. "Damn, I should have turned that off," I said. "Think I should answer it?"

Al shrugged, so I answered.

"This is Grace Wong," said my caller. "Is this a good time to talk?"

"I'm due in front of the minister in less than two minutes," I said.

"Then I'll make it quick. Ms. Todd's grandmother can stay in St. Paul. Ms. Todd can call me later to get the details. Have a long and happy marriage." I barely had time thank her before she broke the connection.

The door opened and the sheriff popped his head in again and said, "Time to go, boys."

"Yes, sir," Al and I said in unison. With Al on his crutches and me keeping my head straight and level to avoid any jolts, we marched out of the little room, down the hall and into the main sanctuary. I was stunned to see how many people were seated there. We'd invited our immediate families and half a dozen close friends. At least two dozen more co-workers and friends had come to view the proceedings. Among them, seated beside Crow Wing County Sheriff Val Holmberg, was St. Paul Homicide Detective Lieutenant Curtis Brown.

Al and I took our places at the Rev. Jefferson-Schneider's left side and turned to face the people in the pews. My mother and Grandma Goodie were in the front row on the center aisle and Grandma was dabbing her eyes with a white cloth hanky. Zhoumaya Jones sat smiling like Alice in Wonderland's Cheshire cat in her motorized wheelchair at the end of the first row.

The unexpected size of the crowd brought a practical problem to mind. I leaned close to Al and whispered, "How are we going to feed all these people?"

Al leaned close to me and whispered, "Carol told me that some of the extra guests were bringing food."

I leaned close to Al and whispered, "You mean we're having a potluck reception?"

Al just grinned and nodded.

My legs began to feel like they were about to fold like a sheet of origami paper. However, I managed to remain upright thanks to the Navy, where I was taught never to lock my knees during an inspection, and this was certainly the ultimate inspection. My armpits were soaked and a bead of sweat was starting to trickle slowly down my forehead toward the bridge of my nose. I was fighting the urge to brush my hand across my brow when the most gorgeous, smartest and funniest woman I have ever known appeared at the rear of the church on the arm of her father, Arthur Todd.

My physical discomfort was forgotten as my soon-to-be father-in-law escorted my soon-to-be bride down the aisle at a pace that seemed slower than the proverbial snail. When at last he passed Martha to me and we joined hands to face the minister, it took every bit of strength I possessed to refrain from wrapping her in my arms and kissing her like a castaway who'd seen his first woman after six years alone on a desert island.

I remember nothing of the next few minutes except that Martha was wearing a lavender dress that set off her coffee-with-cream complexion and dark brown eyes to the utmost bedazzlement. Befogged as I was, I must have given the correct answers to Rev. Jefferson-Schneider's questions because eventually I heard her pronounce us man and wife and tell me I could kiss the bride.

As we embraced, I whispered, "Wong says Grandma Mendes can stay." Martha tightened her grip and we kissed for a long, long time—much longer than any just married kiss I've ever witnessed. When finally we disconnected and turned to walk down the aisle my eyes were wet with tears, but I could see that every person in the room was applauding our performance.

THE END

Acknowledgments

My sincere thanks to the management and employees of Madden's Resort, who unlocked the door and allowed me to tour their lodge in their off-season so I could visualize a model for the fictitious Madrigal's Lodge, where this story takes place.

Thanks also to the St. Paul field office of the U.S. Citizenship and Immigration Services for information about the process of obtaining citizenship.